DUST TO DUST

DUST TO DUST

Margaret Duffy

This first world edition published 2016
in Great Britain and the USA by
SEVERN HOUSE PUBLISHERS LTD of
19 Cedar Road, Sutton, Surrey, England, SM2 5DA.
Trade paperback edition first published
in Great Britain and the USA 2016 by
SEVERN HOUSE PUBLISHERS LTD

British Library Cataloguing in Publication Data
A CIP catalogue record for this title is available from the British Library.

ISBN-13: 978-0-7278-8613-2 (cased)
ISBN-13: 978-1-84751-714-2 (trade paper)
ISBN-13: 978-1-78010-775-2 (e-book)

Typeset by Palimpsest Book Production Ltd.,
Falkirk, Stirlingshire, Scotland.

ONE

When Richard George Rowallen, 14th Earl of Hartwood, one-time army colonel, ex-MI5, a senior official of the National Crime Agency, was murdered the repercussions were enormous. The killing sent shudders through the latter organization, MI5, MI6, his old regiment, the Metropolitan Police and other forces, not to mention his many friends. His professional name, a pseudonym, had been Richard Daws.

'But he lived in a castle with any number of security devices and a bodyguard!' my husband Patrick burst out with, furious, grieving, tears in his eyes.

Privately, I was more upset about the bodyguard, whom we had only ever known as Jordon, a charming and highly educated young man who had also acted as butler. It was a relief to know that Daws' wife Pamela had not been harmed in the attack, which had happened at night. A bad sleeper, she had her own rooms.

And as Patrick had said, how had the killer penetrated the security?

Patrick is an 'adviser' to the NCA and I work as a part-time 'consultant', mostly to him, the quotation marks important as, so far, the job has been very much hands on. The rest of the time I am an author. Prior to Daws' murder, we had been told, by him, that if proposals he had been working on were accepted we would be offered different, less hazardous positions due to what he had described as restructuring. At the time these new roles were unspecified. I knew Patrick would possibly find this new direction in his career tedious – more time spent in an office perhaps and possible stints of giving training lectures – after a very active life also spent in the army and MI5. I was welcoming the change as we were responsible for five children, three of our own and two adopted after Patrick's brother, Larry, was killed. Not only that, we were getting older.

The media had described Daws as a senior adviser to the

National Crime Command, which is a branch of the NCA, but he had been far more than that and the position was too important to leave unfilled for any length of time. Not long afterwards a new person was appointed, temporarily or not, no one seemed to know – a woman by the name of Marcia Lindersland. She immediately tossed out the proposed restructuring arrangements and announced that she would shortly publish her own. The seismographs continued to tremble as although it appeared that she was being given free rein there were mutterings that she did not really have that kind of authority. We decided to keep our heads down and Patrick carried on working on routine matters at HQ in London during the week, and came home to Hinton Littlemore, Somerset, for the weekends.

Meanwhile, Sussex Police were investigating the murder while suffering from a dire shortage of evidence. Everything was being made more complicated by the fact that for the first time in its history certain parts of the castle were now open to the public. Worse, the security system in the private apartments had failed to detect the intruders, which apparently baffled the installers who were brought in to check and advise.

As far as any further security was concerned there were two gun dogs and Pamela's dachshund on the premises, but they were kept in what was described as a boot room at the rear overnight and if they had barked no one had heard them. This was understandable as castles are large and Daws and his wife's accommodation, an extensive apartment, was situated on what he had always referred to as the top floor of a wing added in his great-grandfather's time – not quite correct as above that there were equally extensive attics. On the ground floor there were additional private rooms, although the general public was allowed to look into them from the doorways, that were used for large-scale entertaining at Christmas and when Pamela hosted meetings and receptions for the various charities with which she was involved.

Eventually, when the police had released Daws' body a few weeks later, no further in their investigation, the funeral, which we attended, took place, followed by internment in the family vault in the pretty parish church. It was a surprisingly small and muted affair in the village of Hartwood that had, over the centuries, grown up around the castle. This was situated on what had obviously been regarded as a strategic spot on the South Downs. We were told that, in several months' time, there would be memorial service in London.

All this was in the public eye. It had been made known that the NCA was liaising with Sussex Police but nothing had been said about the fact that the security services had been immediately involved, a fact revealed to me by Patrick. This insider knowledge had come from Commander Michael Greenway, Patrick's immediate boss. Greenway then hinted to me in a conversation when I had rung him about a routine matter that there were also other undercurrents that ran dark and deep. He had given no details.

Patrick had been asked if he would act as one of the pall bearers, a great honour and proof that one person at least was aware that he had been Daws' protégé. I had an idea that Pamela, Lady Rowallen, whom we had met on several occasions, might have been behind this as she was fully aware that the apprenticeship had been an extremely tough one. But no mention of this was made when we were invited by her to go to the castle after the funeral, although I noticed that she had given my husband a very warm smile when she first caught sight of him.

A simple service, then, in a country church. Daws had served his country well during a long career. He had been older when he died than I had thought – sixty-nine – and it had been brought to an end in a vicious and calculated manner. But I still wept a few tears for Jordon, who had died with him. His funeral had taken place a week earlier, somewhere in the north of England.

Ashes to ashes, dust to dust.

Later, I rather felt that Marcia Lindersland – why was she present when the rest of the mourners gave every impression of being mostly friends and family? – whom I had not met before, was behaving as though she was some kind of guest of honour. With the benefit of height she was around six feet tall, wore a large hat more suited to Ascot Ladies' Day and towered over just about everyone present. Dressed all in black for the occasion and seemingly prone to utilizing dramatic body language, here was someone who expected to be the centre of attention.

'Just your sort of female,' Patrick whispered to me wryly.

Why is it that one sometimes dislikes a person on sight?

But the moment passed. We stayed for as long as politeness demanded, chatting to people we didn't know, and then made a move to depart.

'You will come and see me, won't you?' Pamela said quietly as we took our leave of her. 'I really mean it; I'm not just making polite noises. I'd like to talk to you about what happened.'

We promised her that we would.

The gathering was being held in the large beamed sitting room in the private apartment and people had spilled out into an area that was almost as big at the head of a wide staircase. Marcia Lindersland, to whom so far we had not spoken, appeared to be holding court there, unwittingly perhaps standing right in front of a shield on the wall bearing the family's arms.

Fixing us with her sharp gaze across the heads of others, she called, 'Monday, my office, ten thirty. All right?'

'No, sorry,' Patrick answered. 'I'm having Monday off.'

Well, he was now.

'That's not convenient,' she snapped back.

'I'll give you a ring when I get in on Tuesday morning,' he replied, squeezed my arm and we left.

'Not your sort of female?' I queried gently when we were in the car.

'Am I getting old and cranky or was she damned rude?'

Oh, yes, terribly, terribly rude.

I fully intended to turn up as well in response to this summons and reckoned I had every right to as Patrick and I do, for most of the time, work together. My intuition, however – what my father used to call my cat's whiskers – was telling me, loud and clear, that there would be trouble.

There was, instantly.

'I don't think we need Mrs Gillard,' Marcia Lindersland said with not so much as a 'good morning' as soon as we walked through her office door on the following Wednesday.

'Ingrid is my working partner,' Patrick answered, looking astounded. 'She's on the payroll. It's official. You must know that.'

'She is *not* part of the restructuring,' the woman countered.

'In that case I resign.'

She rose to her feet, her pale face flushed with anger. 'Daws always said that you were difficult.'

'Then I'm absolutely delighted to be able to live up to his opinion of me,' Patrick retorted.

There were a few moments' silence during which I pondered the 'always'. Daws had never once mentioned the woman to us. And then she reseated herself and gestured wordlessly to the two chairs facing her desk. Patrick immediately moved them a little farther away, near the wall and out of venom spitting distance, perhaps, and we sat down.

This had been Daws' office, I had to remind myself, and she obviously wasn't superstitious either as it was Room 13. It was a slight shock not to see the cabinets containing his jade collection and the room seemed soulless without the steady tick of his grandfather clock and the various small paintings on the walls that had been in his previous office. There was nothing here that gave even a hint of the personality of the woman in front of us. She looked less imposing without the large black hat she had been wearing when we had last seen her but, nevertheless, here was someone with attitude. Her hair, also black, was cut in a bob with the ends flicked under, just touching the shoulders of the jacket of her very expensive grey suit, which she wore with a white blouse. No jewellery except for tiny gold stud earrings, no wedding ring, her hands tiny – I reluctantly deleted the bitchy 'useless looking' from my mind – like those of a child.

'You're aware of the National Crime Command's Four Pillars of Strategy, I hope,' Lindersland began, making a point of addressing Patrick only.

'Pursue, protect, prevent and prepare,' he obediently recited.

Was it my imagination or was she disappointed that he had remembered or, come to think of it, actually bothered to read it up?

'That's right. And I'm sure you also know that since the NCA was set up it has been decided that each Regional Organised Crime Unit shall have a senior officer from the NCA embedded in it.'

'I am aware of that.'

'It was what Richard Daws had planned for you, within the Avon and Somerset Police Force. Which is the area where you live, I understand.'

Patrick said, 'I do, but Daws hadn't actually gone into details of what he had in mind when we last saw him.'

'No. I'm of the opinion that your "talents" will be wasted in a region that has such low crime rates.'

Yes, she really had said it like that, a finely plucked, or perhaps threaded, eyebrow quirked for good measure.

'A city posting would be preferable for all concerned, don't you think?' she continued.

'Have you ever been to Bath or Bristol?' Patrick asked her.

'No.'

'They're cities.'

There was another silence broken by Patrick saying, 'In view of various assignments in the past that have taken a physical and mental toll on the pair of us and the fact that we have five children—'

'Oh, I know all about that,' she broke in with. 'My predecessor had a mind to give you an easier job. He was entitled to, of course. I think he pandered to the pair of you over the years as he was fond of you. I can't afford to be like that – it's dreadfully unprofessional.'

I found myself coming up to the boil.

'I'll do you a deal,' Patrick said. 'In order to get the local posting that I would prefer – and don't entertain for one second that there's anything easy in crime prevention and catching criminals in that area – I will undertake to arrest whoever killed Richard Daws and/or find out who was behind it.'

'No,' was the immediate reply.

'You're not thinking.'

'The NCA's already involved with that, liaising with Sussex Police.'

'Liaising's no bloody good.' He left it at that, sat back and stared at her.

'No,' she said again.

'You're still not thinking.'

'I have thought, at length. I want you to stay right here, in

London, and carry on as you were before but without your wife.'

Patrick gave her a broad smile. 'So who said to you something along the lines of "batter down Patrick Gillard and get him eating out of your hand to prove that you're the man – sorry, woman – for the job"?'

She bridled. 'No one!'

'OK,' he said, getting to his feet. 'Suppose I just go and find Daws' killer anyway?'

'If you do that I *will* expect your resignation.'

'In that case, ma'am, I shall be happy to hand it to you.'

Outside, in the corridor, I could not contain myself. 'She strung you along! Made you start to think that she was going to give you the West Country job!'

'Coffee,' was all my husband said just then. 'Strong coffee.'

Daws had revealed, on the last occasion we had seen him, that he was proposing to put Michael Greenway's name forward to take over from him when he retired in roughly twelve months' time. He had added that the commander was aware of this. But if Greenway was chewing the landscape about the recommendation coming to nought he gave no sign of it, greeting us cheerfully when we ran him to earth around a quarter of an hour later as he was leaving a meeting. We had not seen him for a while as he had been abroad when Daws' funeral had taken place.

'I can see by your faces that something's wrong,' he said, and set off in a direction that would lead us out of the main entrance of the building. 'Decent coffee, then. Somewhere else. Follow me.'

It was still just as hot and humid as when we had first arrived and as we crossed the road there was a distant rumble of thunder audible above the traffic. However, we did not have far to go, our destination a new restaurant that clearly the commander had patronized before. We were all subdued, and except for Patrick remarking that it would really make his morning to be struck by lightning, nothing else was said until we were seated in a quiet corner and were placing our order. The place was practically empty.

'Kids OK?' Greenway asked laconically.

'Thank you, you've just reminded me that five young people are far more important than my job,' Patrick said quietly. 'Yes, fine.'

'Still got to feed 'em, though,' the commander said with a chuckle.

They went on talking.

Feeling as though I might as well be Patrick's fluffy toy mascot with about as much to say, my contribution to the day having so far been sweet zilch, I miserably stirred my coffee. Patrick related what had happened and Greenway had commiserated, telling him that Lindersland had upset quite a few people since her arrival but not to worry, there was a job to be done so best get on with it.

'I'm not going to knuckle down and carry on working the way I have been,' Patrick said. 'And if she's writing Ingrid out of it I don't want to work for the NCA at all.'

The spoon Greenway was wielding to put three lumps of sugar in his coffee looked like a toy in his large hand. Everything about him is large. He is at least two inches taller than Patrick, who is six foot two, and good looking in a slightly battered way, indicating time once spent playing sports of various kinds. His mane of ash-blond hair, as usual, like Boris Johnson's, needed a refit. Right now his green eyes fixed on me.

'The lady author's despondent,' he observed gently.

I actually felt like crying but swallowed hard and said instead, 'In just a few words she destroyed everything Patrick and I have achieved.'

'Oh, she's a bitch all right,' Greenway responded briskly. 'You'll have to have her come to a sticky end in one of your books.'

This was him all over, at times somewhat without understanding, although I would not wish to describe him as shallow. I gave him a wan smile then went on drinking my coffee.

'I'm going after who killed Daws,' Patrick said into the silence.

'You really meant it!' I exclaimed, shocked out of my gloom.

'I wasn't just winding her up.'

'I thought you might have been fishing for information about the inquiry, that's all.'

'I didn't get any, did I?'

'I understand we're closely liaising with Sussex Police,' Greenway murmured.

'We understand that too but it's hardly unexpected,' Patrick replied sharply. 'And who's "we"?'

The commander shrugged. 'Pass. But you mustn't get the impression that nothing's being done by us.'

'Pass!' Patrick exploded. 'You don't know?'

'Everything's a bit chaotic right now. I'll find out, though.'

'What about the undercurrents you hinted at around a week after the murder occurred?'

'Well, apparently MI5 and MI6 are involved.'

'I already knew that too. And it's understandable as he worked for one and his cases sometimes touched on the other. What about this deeper and darker involvement of someone or something?'

The other man smiled without humour. 'I think those must be words from an inventive imagination.' Again, he looked at me.

'Yes, you dropped a hint,' I agreed. 'When I contacted you about a report I'd recently sent you.'

'Oh, it's nothing dramatic.'

'And you can't tell us?' I persisted.

'I was told the information must go no further.'

'Instructions from Lindersland?'

He seemed to find my interrogation of him amusing. 'Hell, no. OK, I'll tell you. I know you're both very discreet. Someone suggested recruiting a one-time operative of MI5 – no name mentioned – who brought to justice a bent civil servant by the name of Nicholas Haldane. Apparently Haldane succeeded, some years ago and for a short while, in taking over Richard Daws' job when he was head of one of their departments, and then actually tried to kill him. He's in prison, or was until very recently. God knows who got hold of Haldane – getting that kind of information out of MI5 is beyond difficult.'

Patrick and I exchanged amazed glances.

'You two know about it then?' the commander hazarded.

Patrick cleared his throat. 'It was me.'

'You!'

'Haldane was in the pay of a top international bank official who was trying to prevent Daws arraigning him for organizing the death of a young officer in his early army days. The man had accused him of misappropriating mess funds. It involved someone tampering with the brakes of a car but at the time Daws was junior to this character, had no real evidence and couldn't touch him. Then, years later, he popped up on MI5's radar in connection with something else.'

Unusually for him, Greenway appeared to be lost for words.

Patrick continued, 'In a nutshell, Daws slipped on ice in a car park near the office and damaged some ribs. When he was taken to hospital he developed pneumonia and they found he had a slight heart problem. He recovered slowly and spent time in a nursing home as he lived on his own and hadn't then met Pamela, who was actually married to someone else at the time. Haldane was brought in to cover for him and proceeded to wreck the department, D12, and bring it into disrepute.'

The commander got his voice back. 'And you were brought in to sort it out.'

'Not in the way you're thinking. I'd been forced to resign as I'd allowed a subordinate to shoot and kill a fairly serious criminal who'd pasted all hell out of him. I was still in the army then and it was a bad mistake. Haldane, knowing my loyalty to Daws, pulled some strings and had me posted abroad, to a war zone, hoping I'd be killed and somehow or other doctored my records to make it look as though I was in disgrace. But I was brought home. Someone who had an idea there were seriously dodgy things taking place, partly because I had previously mentioned my worries to him at some bash or other, had also pulled strings. I was ordered, unofficially, to find out what was going on.'

'Whoever it was must have been pretty senior.'

'He was the then Chief of the Defence Staff.'

'Bloody hell.'

'Daws was still a serving officer too, a colonel in his MI5 days and intended for very high office. He made me his protégé, although I didn't really realize it at the time. He was like gold dust to Number 10 because he had contacts inside the Kremlin and China as well as in various organizations in the UK.'

'Go on.'

'There's not a lot more to tell. Haldane had thought that in getting Daws to a nursing home as far away as possible, to Scotland, no one would be able to find him. It can't have been a very efficient establishment as they failed to notice that their patient was being drugged to keep him quiet by his so-called minder. I arranged for him to be spirited away to somewhere safe, but low-life working for Haldane still managed to find him and he was taken home, to his castle in Sussex, where Haldane and this banker johnny – they both, frankly, had screws loose – had rigged up a showdown where they planned to kill him. They failed.'

'Thanks to you.'

'I played a small part.'

This was a massive understatement. I said to Greenway, 'I'll give you the full story when you have an hour or so to spare.'

On reflection, I rather hoped he remained busy, as if I had to recollect everything that had happened I would probably get upset. Haldane's hired thugs had set fire to our Devon cottage, where we had lived before moving to Somerset. The damage had been extensive and I had lost a lot of treasured family possessions, including my late father's watch. The house had been rebuilt but it had never felt the same. Violated.

'Who suggested recruiting this one-time operative to investigate Daws' murder?' I asked the commander.

'I'm told he had friends in very high places,' he replied vaguely after a short pause.

'You usually do when you're a member of the aristocracy,' Patrick pointed out dryly.

Probably driven by our continuing to gaze at him encouragingly, Greenway then added, 'It might have emanated from Number 10 but that's only a guess. Whether the PM's been reading up about it, it was something that occurred before he was in power . . . I presume it's all in secret reports?'

'Written by me, tidied up and printed by my trusty assistant,' Patrick answered. 'Yes.'

Greenway carried on where he had broken off. 'Or someone else has been doing a bit of research – I have no idea.'
Someone else? I mused. Who?

There had been an unspoken understanding at that juncture that there was no point in discussing the subject further. Patrick carried on with everyday matters that did not concern me, tying up the loose ends of a couple of cases where his responsibilities ended. Greenway had promised to inform him of any developments but whether this would be more routine work or what Lindersland had insisted she wanted him for, the highly dangerous assignments for which he is regarded as a specialist, was anyone's guess. As far as the latter went the answer would be no, as he had already intimated. For as Daws had rather cold-bloodedly put it, his exact words at our final meeting were that we 'should no longer be squandered going after violent low-life', and, referring to our most recent case, 'having to arrest insane trash'.

As Patrick had pointed out, the West Country job would not mean an absolute end to this kind of thing. It would not be straightforward or easy. But he would be on home ground, with good connections in the form of Detective Chief Inspector James Carrick of Bath CID, and others. He would be near our home, the old rectory where we live with our children and Patrick's parents, John and Elspeth. John is the local rector.

But first, I knew, he would go after Daws' killer.

Having been away since the previous day and a lack of reasons for my staying in London, I went home, catching up with the stormy weather in the late afternoon when I arrived. I got rather wet just running indoors from the Range Rover and even wetter fetching my overnight bag, having forgotten it. I then found James Carrick sitting in the kitchen with Elspeth, drinking tea.

'I knew you wouldn't mind,' said Elspeth after we'd hugged. They have their own accommodation in an annexe. 'A man's trying to fix the fridge and there's stuff all over the place in there.'

'You can put the food in the one in the utility room,' I offered. 'I think there's only a few bottles of wine in there at the moment.'

'I'll help you,' Carrick said.

She thanked us both, saying that John could give her a hand, took her mug of tea with her and went.

'I was just passing,' James said.

'You're always welcome,' I told him. 'No need for any reasons.'

A huge crash of thunder rattled the windows.

'I was also wondering if you were around and could tell me if there were any developments with regard to Richard Daws' murder. It's a very bad business.'

Omitting the bit about the possibility of an ex-employee of MI5 being recruited to look for his killer, officially or otherwise, I told the DCI what had taken place.

'Despite what I've said in the past it would be good if Patrick got the job in our Regional Crime Unit.'

'It's unlikely he'd be based in Bath so wouldn't get under your feet,' I said with a laugh, remembering exactly the kind of things this policeman had very forcefully said on more than one occasion when they had both become involved in the same cases.

'God alone knows *who's* going to be based in Bath. They've sold the nick to the university to save money.'

'*What?*'

'It's true. I shall probably be working out of a stationery cupboard in the council offices in the Lower Bristol Road.'

I somehow could not imagine this.

'Oh, and some good news,' Carrick continued. 'I've got rid of David Campbell.'

This was the DI, another Scot. For some reason – nothing to do with clan connections – they had never got on.

'He was homesick and his mother's poorly so he applied and succeeded in getting a job in Police Scotland, in Glasgow,' Carrick went on. 'And I've practically gone down on my knees to get Lynn Outhwaite promoted. She's wasted as a DS. Meanwhile, I don't have a DI so Lynn's sort of acting.'

I was pleased for him, but good news did not come Patrick's way. The following morning, and as I had feared, the news came through that someone else was going to be given the West Country job.

TWO

'**G**ot my orders, hot off the presses from Lindersland, or rather in an email just before I left,' Patrick announced, having arrived at home for the weekend that Friday evening, gone to say hello to everyone else, found that no one was around and had a shower. He then fixed himself a tot of whisky and dropped into an armchair.

'What?' I asked. His tone had been light but I could see that he was still angry about it.

'I'm to go undercover, keep watch on a suspect in Paddington and find out what he's all about, starting Monday.'

'I see,' I commented, also lightly. Something about his manner suggested that he had no intention of doing any of this.

'She did warn me that the last man on the job disappeared without trace.'

'Better and better.'

'I emailed her straight back, reminding her that I was promoted a few months ago and no longer had to work at the coalface on that kind of assignment. Besides, I happen to know the Met already has someone on the job.'

'But Greenway usually gives you your orders. She appears to have sidelined him.'

He thoughtfully took a sip of whisky. 'Umm.'

'Perhaps you'd fetch me a glass of wine,' I said.

'Oh, sorry.' He got up to remedy the omission. 'I'm going off to Sussex tomorrow to see Pamela and find out how far the police have got with the investigation. I take it you want to come too?'

'Definitely.'

At that point we were inundated with children. They had been with Carrie, our nanny, and their grandparents to a fete at the local primary school. It was an inrush of balloons, candyfloss, a huge blue fluffy teddy bear, sticky fingers, plus a small but very noisy ongoing war. I think Matthew, the eldest at thirteen, and Patrick's late brother Larry's child, along with his sister, Katie, was embarrassed at being part of this fracas. He had won the teddy bear at some stall or other and promptly given it to Justin, who had just had his seventh birthday. Racing cars are Justin's thing and he had turned up his nose at the bear, whereupon little Vicky had joyfully grabbed it. Needless to say, our son had then wanted it back, stamped feet, a royal tantrum, the lot. But Vicky refused to let go even though it was bigger than she was, and it took the pair of us – the others having bolted with baby Mark, their patience clearly at an end – to calm everything down.

Vicky got to keep the bear.

Hartwood Castle, which is not far from the small town of Steyning in West Sussex, looks massive but its size is exaggerated by its position, which is, like just about every castle, on high ground. It is nowhere as large as Arundel Castle, which is some fifteen miles to the west. The effect is emphasized by the intimidating height of the curtain walls of the keep on a mound at one end which adjoin the more recent addition to provide domestic accommodation. But even this is constructed of uncompromising granite with knapped flint decoration, the effect of a grim fortification only a little mitigated by the rambler roses and creepers trained up the walls and around the windows.

We had been instructed to enter a drive marked Private and not try to go through the main gates, which were closed on police advice while the investigation was ongoing, the place temporarily not open to the public. These gates, I already knew, allowed access to the original entrance of the castle that lay beyond on the other side of a substantial archway guarded by a pair of cannon. Our instructions had come from Pamela herself and I gathered she preferred not to use her full title.

We came to a security gate with a numbered keypad on a post to one side, this, Pamela had told Patrick, a comparatively recent development. He had been given the entry code and we were soon progressing slowly along a narrow lane bordered by beech trees, the leaves just beginning to turn an autumn gold. There were paddocks beyond these on either side in which some kind of rare-breed horned sheep grazed. The lane joined the main drive but a short distance further on we left it and branched off into a gravelled road that led around to the rear and into a courtyard which was actually the inner area of the keep, an ancient stone cross in its centre.

I noticed Patrick gazing grimly at this. 'Haldane had you tied to that, didn't he?'

'I almost froze to death,' he muttered, parking next to a small pale blue hatchback. 'But that wasn't the worst. Our house was the worst.'

'No, it wasn't. They kidnapped Justin from Sark where some friends of your parents had taken him for safety.'

'I hadn't forgotten that, but it's had no lasting effect on him. He just enjoyed a trip to a castle with someone who gave him plenty of sweets and crisps to keep him quiet. What was actually going on went right over his head because he was so young.'

Mothers tend to look at things differently. But I kept these thoughts to myself and said, 'And now, according to Greenway, Haldane's out of prison. I wouldn't be surprised if he was connected with Daws' murder.'

'He won't live to see the inside of jail again if he was.'

Patrick is not prone to making empty statements.

Where we were was, in effect, the back way, although even this entrance was represented by a very substantial oak door garnished with large iron studs. Spookily it swung open soundlessly at our approach to reveal an empty wide passageway which could only mean that our arrival had been noted. A smooth-coated dachshund dashed out, barking excitedly.

I made a point of not chattering to Patrick as we went in as he had switched to professional mode – that is, the man who used to work for MI5 rather than his more recent role of policeman. He eyed the door carefully, both inside and out – not looking for clues, of course, the police had done that – to try to work out if the killer had entered this way. Unconsciously, perhaps, he shook his head slightly – there were enough historic bolts on the inside of it to withstand a siege never mind a modern intruder.

'I saw you coming and you can have no idea how pleased I am to see you,' called the countess, having shushed the dog as she approached us down the rather dim passageway, two black

Labradors plodding at the rear. 'And my apologies for asking you to come in the back. I always use this way. Richard fixed it so one can just press a button and not have to lug it open. The main entrance is even more bothersome with its heavy doors.' She gazed at us both. 'It seems ages since you were here and it was all rather formal then. I don't mean the funeral. I hardly had a chance to speak to you that day.'

She was referring to another case. A political scandal. A press conference.

'Is it still lieutenant colonel?' she was enquiring, grasping Patrick by the hand after giving me a hug.

'No, just Patrick,' he answered, kissing her cheek. 'I resigned my commission a while back.'

'That must have been a real wrench.'

'It was,' he replied.

'And do just call me Pamela. I try to meet the visitors – I sometimes help with the teas and some of the Americans seem to know who I am and practically bow and curtsy. It's so dreadfully embarrassing.'

Yes, but she and her husband's photographs had been on the front pages of several national newspapers, never mind the rest of the media, in connection with their other interests, charity work and, more recently, his death.

'Richard never really talked about what he did,' she continued. 'And all I know about you is that you now work for the National Crime Agency, as did he, and have five children. You only had four when he last mentioned things like that. But come upstairs, we can't stand talking here.'

It was quite a long walk, first of all along the corridor in which we were standing, no doubt originally part of below stairs – the kitchens, store rooms and so forth – and then, after passing various other doorways, we found ourselves in part of the old castle, the armoury, scene of the press conference and before that the showdown with Haldane. There were no lights on in here and the windows, high up, were small but it was easy to make out the array of weapons on the walls together with shields, spears, lances, knives and daggers arranged in patterns, and also banners, some of the latter tattered with age. Several cannon stood around the sides of the room, including, I knew, a rare and valuable sixteenth-century falconet. I shivered in the gloom and not just because of the chill emanating from the stone walls. It brought back bad memories, for I too had been present and thanked God that Justin had been too young to remember the violence that had taken place here. It was a relief to leave by one of the doors that led off and, crossing an imposing and much lighter hallway, the walls lined with paintings of the late earl's forebears where cleaners were busy at work, we went through yet another door and then up the wide staircase with which we were familiar. Pamela shepherded us into her sitting room and, at her bidding, Patrick and I settled ourselves on a long sofa.

'I hope you're staying for lunch,' she went on. And, without giving us time to reply, added, 'But before that, coffee.' She went to another door and disappeared for a few moments, the dogs following her, and I heard her ordering them into their baskets. Returning, she continued, 'One of the girls who lives in the village, Amanda, is giving me a hand before she goes back to university. She's wildly clever but, bless her, doesn't mind cooking for a silly woman who's hopeless at it. Oh, you probably don't know that the cook left, saying she didn't feel safe anymore. I can understand that in a way.'

There is nothing silly about Pamela – she is a highly intelligent woman. She is also modest and I knew from a previous conversation with her on a less troubled occasion that she fears her problem with pots and pans makes her some kind of failure. Now, looking at her, immaculately dressed in cream slacks and black silk blouse with a pink scarf at the neck, I could see that her loss had taken its toll. She looked ill.

'It's not just Richard. I miss Jordon terribly, you know,' she continued. 'But you mustn't take that amiss just because he organized nearly everything that can be described as domestic for us. I don't mean it like that. If he had been horribly wounded instead of being killed and couldn't work anymore I would always have looked after him. He was almost like a son to us.' And with that she burst into tears but quickly pulled herself together, apologizing, when the phone rang.

It was a routine call, a reminder about some appointment or other.

'Naturally, I went to his funeral,' Pamela resumed, wiping her eyes. 'His family were disappointed after he got his degree when he took a job as merely a butler but of course they didn't know the half of it as he had to sign the Official Secrets Act. His father got a bit sniffy with me about it so I told him the truth. There was no reason to keep quiet now and I wanted them to know how excellent he'd been, how he'd been specially trained by some agency or other that had ex-military people on the staff to be a bodyguard as well as having to know all the society ins and outs of entertaining and things like that. And then . . .' Tears again threatened.

Fortunately our coffee then arrived, together with a plate of biscuits; Amanda, pretty and petite, giving us a big smile. I offered to take charge of the pot but Pamela said it always dribbled, which I would feel bad about so she would do it. It did.

'The police have been very good,' Pamela continued after taking a sip of coffee. She frowned, then put in a lump of sugar and stirred thoughtfully. 'And very thorough, although I won't pretend that I'm a judge of such things, as well as being good to me personally, not barging about like a pack of hounds indoors. But can rural police forces investigate crimes like this – effectively, I mean?'

'Most certainly,' Patrick replied as she obviously expected an answer from him. 'And now all forces either have, or will have, an officer from the NCA embedded in them.'

'I wish you were involved.'

'I am.'

She almost knocked the plate of biscuits over. 'That's wonderful!'

'Unofficially,' Patrick added.

'Ah. I happen to know that you've done things unofficially before. Will you get into trouble?'

'Probably.'

'And this woman . . . Marcia Lindersland. I can't make her out at all.'

'I don't think anyone can. Don't worry about her.'

'I was rather put out when she turned up at the funeral, especially when she behaved as though she was the Queen.

Although I'm quite sure Her Majesty wouldn't have conducted herself like that.'

'Do you feel up to telling us what you know?'

'About the night Richard and Jordon died?'

'If you wouldn't mind.'

'We ought to go to where it happened. But first I should tell you that the alarm people can't find anything wrong with the security systems and could only say that someone had either forgotten to activate them that night or they'd been switched off.'

'No damage? No wires cut?'

'No.'

'No cameras?'

'Not indoors. Richard said they would make him feel like an intruder in his own home and for that reason wouldn't have any infra-red movement detectors upstairs here either, although they're everywhere else and on the staircase. But there are a few cameras outside. Apparently one of the recordings shows a shadowy figure but the others were covered up by someone who managed to do it without actually appearing on camera.'

'Where's the control centre for all this?'

'In a room downstairs that used to be the butler's pantry.'

'I take it you don't have a security officer.'

'No.'

'So who monitors the screens in there?'

'Jordon kept an eye on them in between his other duties when the place was open to the public. But that's all really. I have to say that Richard was very relaxed about the whole thing.'

'Can you remember if you keyed in the security code when you went downstairs to admit the police?'

'No, but I would have done it automatically.'

'So you don't really know if it had been set in the first place.'

'No, I suppose not.'

'And the place is now open to the public. Not difficult then for a bogus visitor to note where everything like that was situated.'

'It was a mistake, wasn't it? I'll be frank – we didn't really need the money. Richard just thought that the admission fees would help pay the gardeners and endless maintenance costs. I think he also felt that it would be good to share what we have with other people. But we actually ended up spending quite a lot in smartening everything up, putting in loos and converting the carriage house and harness room into a café. You simply have to have those or people won't come. Patrick . . .'

'Yes?' he encouraged when she stopped speaking.

'You don't think there could be any connection between what happened and the ghastly episode with that Haldane character?'

'Anything's possible,' Patrick responded urbanely, wisely not telling her that the man had been released from prison.

Pamela smiled. 'You sound just like a policeman.'

'I'm not allowed to go around with a knife between my teeth these days.'

She laughed, which was good as Patrick had told me that he would try to make our visit as easy as possible for her.

I said, 'Do you mind my asking who inherits the title?'

'Oh, the rules of primogeniture are so complicated and I don't pretend to understand it all. Until very recently there was a male-descended relation in the States – New York – the descendant of a younger son who didn't get the title back in historic times. His name was Samuel Zettinger – he was in his eighties and in a care home, ga-ga apparently. He died. I understand he has – had – an illegitimate son who my solicitor tells me is keen to inherit but hasn't a chance under English law. Apparently he's made contact to say he's very angry, that he's going to fly over and tackle someone about it, which bothers me a bit as I don't want him here. He's Irving someone or the other, my solicitor did say. The title will die out – has died out, in fact.'

'And you?'

'As Richard's wife – and naturally he'd made a will – I've been left the estate. I haven't yet decided what I'm going to do with it. I can't see myself living here on my own, though, not even in this lovely flat.' She rose. 'Shall I show you where it happened?'

All signs of a police investigation had gone from the room into which we were shown. It was tidy and impersonal, as though the usual inhabitant had gone away for a while but was expected to return shortly as there were fresh flowers – garden flowers – in a vase on the wide window ledge. At least twenty-five feet square and with windows that looked over a large walled garden at the rear, the room was quite sparsely furnished. No ancient four-poster bed as one might expect, just a modern double with drawers underneath it, the headboard painted in a pleasant shade of pale green, as were two wardrobes. The only other items of furniture were a bookcase, a bedside table with a portable radio and lamp on it, an antique and heavily carved chest of drawers, the wood black with age, an oak blanket chest at the foot of the bed and two armchairs, one with a reading lamp behind it. A few framed prints, or more likely, original drawings, were on the walls. The carpet, however, had been taken up to expose the floorboards beneath, because of bloodstains, no doubt.

'Richard kept all his gardening, dog walking and shooting clothes in one of those wardrobes,' his widow said. 'The other one's empty except for a few pairs of shoes and some odds and ends. His best clothes are all in the dressing room next door.'

'Are the police working on the theory that it was a burglary that ended in violence because whoever broke in was disturbed?' Patrick asked.

'Detective Inspector Barton did mention that but he was only discussing the possibilities with me.'

'Is there anything that is very valuable kept up here?'

'No, not *really* valuable, nothing that would be a real draw, even to someone who knew about art. Richard's jade collection has been kept in the bank since he brought it here from London and had it valued just before he died. He was going to have more secure showcases built. Any other bits and pieces are downstairs.'

Such as the Chinese porcelain covered jars and vases, bronze figures of animals and dozens of paintings including a couple of racehorses by John Skeaping? I thought.

Patrick asked, 'Do you think it's likely that you were asleep and mightn't have heard people talking before the shots were fired?'

'It's possible as I was woken by the shots. And my dressing room's between my bedroom and this one.'

'What time was this?'

'Well, as you might imagine I didn't look at the clock just then but it was the very early hours, probably around two a.m.'

'Whoever it was could have been after something in particular and didn't necessarily have murder as a top priority. Where was Jordon's accommodation?'

'In the room beyond the en suite and Richard's dressing room. It's a small flat actually with a sitting room, bedroom, bathroom and small kitchen. All the rooms interconnect for security reasons and it looks as though Jordon, on hearing the shots, ran in here, armed, and was also gunned down. His body was in the dressing-room doorway over there.' She sank into one of the chairs, fumbling for the tissue in her pocket.

Patrick sighed, no doubt deeply regretting the fact that he himself had not had a hand in the training. Even I know that you don't run pell-mell into rooms where shots have just been fired. Jordon would surely have been taught that by whoever from the military had trained him but had obviously forgotten. If Patrick had undertaken to do the instruction he wouldn't have forgotten – fact. Without asking for permission he went from us and out of sight through the doorway.

Pamela wiped her eyes. 'I'm a very restless sleeper. I actually suffer from insomnia, so sometimes I get up and make myself a warm drink and then sit up in bed to listen to the radio for a while. You can't inflict that on your husband.'

'The shots must have been very loud,' I ventured.

'Oh, yes, terribly loud. Two shots. I was terrified. For a few moments I actually thought that one of the shotguns must have gone off all on its own but that's impossible and, anyway, they're all kept in locked cabinets downstairs. Then I thought that Richard must have taken leave of his senses and was firing at someone or something out of the window, but of course that was nonsense too. Then I heard another shot followed by people running in—'

'People?' I interrupted. 'More than one?'

'Yes, now I come to think of it. I told the police I thought it was one but perhaps not . . .'

Patrick came back. 'I heard what you just said. There was more than one intruder then?'

'Yes, two, probably. They ran along the corridor past my room. Heavy footsteps as though they were wearing boots.'

'Is there another way to access this area?'

'There is but not normally now. If you carry on along that corridor in the same direction you come to another staircase. It used to be a backstairs one for servants. It leads down to the original kitchens, the ones Richard's great-grandfather put in, that is. We had them done up with old pots and pans for visitors to see and put a door at the bottom marked private.'

'Is it usually kept locked?'

'Yes, always. Nobody uses it now as the steps are stone, very worn and it's rather twisty and narrow, but the lock's on this side so it can be used as one of our fire escapes. You can't open it from the other way.'

'May I go and look?'

'Yes, but do be careful. There's a light switch at the top.'

When he had gone, she murmured, 'Richard was still alive when I got to him. He was lying on the floor not far from Jordon who I could see was quite dead. He said . . .'

Again she abandoned herself to tears and I bent to put an arm around her.

'He said,' she resumed in a choked voice, '"I was so looking forward to our holiday." And then he . . . died.'

'He didn't say anything about who had attacked them?'

'No, but I expect they were wearing hoods or something, don't you?'

Patrick returned, shaking his head. 'All's exactly as you described with no signs of disturbance, which means that they either came up the stairs as we did or through one of the windows. Are the windows alarmed?'

'I *think* so,' Pamela replied. 'The local police will know as Inspector Barton was here when the security man came and he was talking to him.'

'Who normally set the alarms?'

'Either Jordon or Richard.'

I said, 'But what happens when you make yourself a drink in the night?'

'Oh, I've a little corner in my dressing room where I can do that. Richard had it put in for me. There's a pretty little floor-standing cupboard with an electric kettle on it and a tiny fridge for milk.'

'So someone has to cancel the alarms from up here before anyone can go down in the morning?'

'That's right.' She smiled. 'You only forget the once.'

'Do any of the staff know the security code?'

'No, it was just the three of us.'

Patrick said, 'Have you any theories how these people managed to get in without setting off the alarms?'

'I can only think there was insider knowledge. You'll probably say perhaps we forgot to set them that night, but how could anyone else have known that?'

'Insider knowledge?' Patrick repeated.

'The alarm company. Who else?'

'Don't you trust them?'

'It's not that. It's just that . . .'

'Anyone in particular?' Patrick persevered when she stopped speaking.

'Look, I might get someone into trouble.'

'What happens to information you give me is my responsibility. The police will probably have interviewed them all anyway, or at least the man in charge.'

'Yes, him. He gave me the creeps. I thought him revolting actually.'

THREE

'I read the post-mortem report and the shots were fired by a Glock 17, the same as mine,' Patrick said later when we had had lunch – cold chicken and ham pie and salad followed by chunks of homemade fruit cake – and, at Pamela's suggestion, were taking a stroll in the grounds. She had eaten very little.

'Ye gods! I hope someone's not going to try to hang these murders on you!' I exclaimed. It wouldn't be the first time.

He smiled at me. 'Relax, kid. We were abroad, remember?'

'And this American . . . I don't like the sound of him at all.'

'Perhaps not, but you know what they're like when it comes to English titles. And we must be careful, not call him a bastard – yet.'

We were not just drifting around aimlessly but had decided to assess the castle's weak points, these likely to be a result of work that had been done in comparatively recent times with the view of bringing the private accommodation up to modern living standards and communications. All we had noted so far was a Victorian extension that had been converted into an office.

'This will take longer than I thought and I'm not dressed for it,' Patrick said after three-quarters of an hour or so.

I said, 'We should have asked Pamela if Jordon had friends who visited him here. Or would tight security have prevented that?'

'It might have done. And his parents don't seem to have been here or they would have realized there was more to his job than they'd imagined.'

'You don't think he was gay and they – or perhaps just his father – couldn't stomach that either?'

'He was and no, his father couldn't.'

'How do you know?'

'I'd guessed and Daws confirmed it some time ago.'

'You didn't tell me.'

'There was no point – he was never mentioned at home.'

'Did he have a boyfriend?'

'We ought to ask.'

Returning from our patrol, Patrick with a view to making a proper job of it at the earliest opportunity, we questioned Pamela about it, tactfully, and she told us that her husband had said nothing about it to her. She knew that Jordon had several friends of both sexes – no one special that she was aware of, but his contract had forbidden him from inviting them or his parents to the castle. He had had generous leave, though. They had never enquired what he had done or where he had gone when he was on holiday. She went on to say that he had once shown them a photograph of himself with a group of young people somewhere on a beach in Spain. Pamela finished by saying that Jordon had been the sort of person who would feel he would bore people by recounting his own activities. This fitted our impression of him.

As Patrick wanted to talk to Sussex Police in the shape of DI Barton first thing on Monday morning, we had booked into a hotel for the rest of the weekend. Pamela had been waiting for her daughter by her first marriage to arrive to spend a couple of nights with her so we had, again tactfully, refused her kind offer to put us up.

The following day, Sunday, we hoped to try to discover how the killers had gained access. Pamela suggested we do it in the afternoon. But the opportunity came before that when she rang Patrick mid-morning.

'Lindersland's turned up without warning,' Patrick reported. 'With a bloke who's a bit threatening. She's asking about any work-related documents or files on a computer that might be in Daws' study. They were asked to leave but ignored the request. As you can imagine, Pamela's not at all happy about it and would like us there.'

We quickly finished the coffee that we had been drinking on the hotel terrace and drove the five or so miles to Hartwood.

This time we went to the front entrance of the modern accommodation extension, as that was where a top-of-the-range black BMW was parked. The door was opened by a good-looking

woman who appeared very worried. She was holding the dachshund under one arm.

'Hello, I'm Judy. Mummy said it was probably you. Please
come in. They're being rather horrible to her and the man's
frightening me a bit.'

Patrick strode in purposefully and, given our surroundings,
I could almost hear spurs clinking and a sword clattering at his
side, his pace forcing Judy to walk a bit faster. After crossing
the hallway where we had seen the cleaners working and
mounting the wide staircase, we arrived in the large area at the
top. The three of them were standing there, Pamela holding the
collars of both gun dogs, whose hackles were raised. They
began to growl as the man approached them.

'What do *you* want?' Marcia Lindersland demanded to know
of us.

'Good morning, ma'am,' Patrick responded. 'We are old
friends of Lady Rowallen and have come to chuck you out.'
He eyed her associate, cropped-haired and beefy. 'Starting with
him.'

'This is one of your superiors, Superintendent Matherson,'
the woman retorted loftily. 'He's liaising with Sussex Police in
this matter, not you.'

'Balls,' Patrick said crisply. 'He looks too much like a bone-
headed nightclub bouncer to be a senior cop.'

Not surprisingly, this individual came swiftly in Patrick's
direction.

'Warrant card?' my husband asked sweetly.

'You'll have this instead,' the man said and raised a chunky
fist, possibly, on reflection, not to strike but as a warning.

Patrick took no chances and, moments later, Matherson had
rolled down the stairs and landed heavily on the marble floor
of the hall.

'Out!' Patrick said to Lindersland.

'You seem to have forgotten who I am!' she raged.

'No, *you* have.'

'And you'd attack a woman.'

'No. But Ingrid's quite good at this kind of thing.'

'You haven't heard the last of this.'

'Now you're getting really boring.'

She went, ignoring the untidy state of affairs at the bottom of the stairs who was just picking himself up. The outer door slammed behind them.

'Have you any idea what they wanted?' Patrick asked.

'That's the trouble – I don't know,' Lady Rowallen replied. 'But why come here like this, unannounced, in an almost menacing way? Why not just pleasantly phone and ask if she can look for the papers or whatever it is?' Pamela threw up her arms in despair. 'Come and have some coffee. I almost think I could do with a drop of brandy.'

'Thanks for that,' I muttered to Patrick as we followed the other two into the sitting room, the two dogs protectively at their heels.

'I *was* bluffing.'

Judy did indeed give her mother a little brandy and then went away to make the coffee. Amanda, we were told, did not work on Sundays but prepared food for Pamela in advance that she could reheat.

When we were having our coffee – so strong I thought I'd be dancing on the ceiling any time now with all that caffeine – Patrick said, 'She must have explained her behaviour somehow.'

'She just said that she wanted to look in Richard's study as she thought important information was in there.'

'A paper file that could be here instead of at work?'

'Heaven only knows. I never asked Richard about things like that. It wasn't any of my business really.'

'Do you know if he'd been working on anything here at home? Had you got the impression he was investigating something unofficially?'

Pamela frowned. 'Richard didn't normally work at home at all. I *think*. But he did disappear into his study for hours at a time. He was a great reader and there are hundreds of books in there and he was always ordering more. But I have to say that he had been a bit preoccupied at times lately, not that men don't sometimes go a bit deaf when their wives are talking, especially if they're expected to do something.'

'Would it be impertinent of me to ask if I could have a look in there?'

'Not at all. You need to so we can find out what this is all
about. But I haven't a clue what the passwords are on the
computer.'

The study was a short walk away, past the kitchen and doors
to what I guessed were further bedrooms. I noticed that Pamela
and Judy were tense: of course this was difficult for them.
Patrick, too, looked very grim. Never mind the assumption that
he had not worked at home, in my view this had been the real
seat of power of the man who had shaped Patrick's career, his
life really.

'Silly, I suppose, but I feel that Richard's still in here,' said
his wife quietly as she unlocked the door and we went in.

The room was not large and three walls were lined with
shelves – most, as his widow had intimated, filled with books.
Various other mementoes including silver trophies and framed
photographs were on the rest. A small window that overlooked
the garden was in the fourth wall with a wooden shield carrying
the family coat of arms above it. Each side of the window were
filing cabinets and at right angles to it a short distance away
was an antique kneehole desk upon which was an Apple
computer, a pen tray and a leather-framed blotter.

'I've left it just as it was,' Pamela whispered and then sobbed
quietly.

Judy mimed to us that she would take her mother away and
they went out.

'The dragon's den,' I said quietly. Yes, Daws was here. Every
second I expected to see him standing by my shoulder.

Seemingly not so affected, Patrick sat in the black leather
swivel chair behind the desk. 'It must have crossed his mind
that something like this might happen,' he observed. 'A man
like that would have made some kind of preparation and I'm
talking work here, not home. Are those filing cabinets locked?'

They weren't.

'So there's nothing highly confidential in them then. Unless,
of course, it's supposed to look like that.'

I had a look. He had been a keen rose-grower – the garden
was full of them. True enough, the first cabinet I looked in
contained catalogues from rose-growers, correspondence with
the same, pamphlets on the growing of them and not much else.

The second was stuffed full of files of research, going back years, of his family history, records of shoots, treatises on breeding gun dogs, copies of letters he had sent to newspapers on various subjects, including refuting criticism of SOCA and the NCA. Correspondence he had had with the local council was there also, mostly of the daggers drawn variety. Obviously he had not wanted to trust everything, or even anything, to computers.

'You have a Mac,' Patrick said a while later when this idea had been exhausted. 'See if you can get into this one.'

True enough, it asked me for a password.

'Try his wife's name and the date of her birthday,' he suggested.

I had to go and ask about the latter.

No.

'What was his?' Patrick went on to ask me.

For some reason I knew this one, but that too was rejected.

After quite a few tries with several combinations of these details I was host to a strange impulse and typed in Patrick's first name and surname and the numbers of the day, month and last two numbers of the year of his birth. That didn't work, so I added the first two numbers of the year.

Eureka.

'It's you,' I told him.

'*What?*'

'Something here has to be for your eyes only,' I said as I vacated the seat.

Patrick came and sat down, speechless for a few moments. 'But why not Mike Greenway?' he finally managed to get out.

'I agree they were quite close but this might be a military thing, going right back to when you were serving with the Devon and Dorsets. Daws had known you for years and years. He got you the job in MI5 when you were injured. Later on he recruited you for SOCA and then made sure you stayed on when it became part of the NCA.'

'If that's true I don't understand how Lindersland knew there was something here of interest to her. It was probably why she turned up at the funeral – to case the joint, as the saying goes.'

'She's had plenty of time to find out what he was working on. One can only surmise that, somewhere or other, there's a gap.'

Patrick was clicking through all the files listed. 'And I still don't have a clue as to what's here. It'll take me ages to go through this lot. I know one thing, though: this computer's not leaving here and I'm not forwarding any of the information it contains either to our home or to HQ. If it's not safe in a castle it's not safe anywhere.'

'People have got in already,' I pointed out.

'I should imagine that all the security numbers have now been changed. We must check with Pamela about that.'

'Perhaps that's why he was killed – because he wouldn't reveal the password.'

Patrick breathed out gustily. 'Imaginative, like quite a few of your theories, but—'

I interrupted with, 'Or the intruders were questioning him, Jordon heard voices and burst in.'

'No, Pamela heard two shots and then one other. If you remember the forensic report said Jordon was hit once and Daws twice, so he must have been killed first.'

'I still don't understand why Lindersland's behaving the way she is.'

Patrick gazed up at me. 'She would only behave that way if whatever it is she wants, or thinks she wants, is of vital importance.'

'But can she be trusted?'

'She could be on the line and doesn't trust anyone else.'

'With a yob like that in tow?'

'I happen to know that he *is* a super by the name of Matherson. She's probably taken him on as her minder.'

I think I gaped at him. 'But he might arrest you for assault!'

Patrick was busy with computer keys. 'He wouldn't dare. Besides, she wouldn't let him.'

This left *me* speechless until I really thought about it. Yes, of course. She wouldn't want to draw attention to her activities.

It was arranged, in view of what we had found, that we would stay at the castle that night. Patrick and I would work as late as we could and continue with it on Monday after we had spoken to DI Barton during the morning at the police station at Horsham, assuming that this would be possible. Meanwhile,

I drove to the hotel to collect our belongings and pay the bill. They did not mind the change of plan as they were booked solid and were still receiving enquiries due to an important equestrian event taking place in the area.

'This isn't going to be too complicated,' Patrick said a little later that day when we were in Daws' study. 'For as we know, he didn't have a flair for IT – hated it, in fact.' He sighed. 'I'm starving.'

'We are invited to dinner.'

'Are you sure that's OK?'

'Yes. I said we'd planned to eat out but they wouldn't hear of it. Judy's doing the cooking.'

'I'd better put on a tie then.'

It was that kind of place and those kind of people and I fully intended to change out of what I had been wearing all day into the dress I had brought with me just in case. As it was the decision was the right one, Pamela celebrating having visitors by getting out some of her damask and cut glass, and we ate by candlelight. Some of the colour came back into her pale cheeks.

Afterwards, at one thirty in the morning, having gone back to work at ten thirty, we were a third of the way through reading the files. Some, Patrick knew, were copies of those at HQ and could immediately be discounted; others dealt with unsolved criminal cases in the early days of SOCA. We made short notes of the contents of these in case they were relevant to anything we found later and carried on. At two a.m. we had both had enough and went to bed.

DI Adrian Barton was of medium height, slim, dark-haired and had just arrived for work on his motorbike. Apparently he lived in Findon. I got the impression that the journey had been a fast one as he was still fizzing with adrenaline when we were shown into his office. Or perhaps he fizzed normally.

'Just get rid of this lot,' he said and took himself, his helmet and leathers into an adjoining room. When he emerged he was in jeans and sweatshirt. 'I do have a suit for attending cases,' he explained in businesslike fashion. 'What can I do for you?'

'Is DI Jessica Sturrock still here?' Patrick enquired.

'No, she bailed out. Went back home to Leicestershire and is finding herself organizing the policing of anti-hunt demos. Got involved with the NCA on a serious case – you may know what it was – and found it all a bit too much.'

'It was us,' Patrick told him. 'The Keys Estate farm case.'

Barton laughed. 'I'll try to have a bit more bottle.'

I warmed to him while feeling a little sorry for his predecessor. She had, after all, had to dive to the ground when a hail of bullets were fired at us.

'The 14th Earl of Hartwood,' Patrick murmured.

'Ah, it would figure. My problem with it is that there's no real evidence. No prints except of those who lived or worked there, no DNA, as yet, but we're still working on that, no sightings of strange vehicles or people hanging around. All I know is that it wasn't a run-of-the-mill burglary.'

'Pros then.'

'Too right.'

'May we look at the case file?'

'Sorry, but first I shall have to ask to see your IDs.'

We duly produced them.

'And it's not the kind of case where one can usefully undertake house-to-house enquiries,' Barton went on, handing them back. 'The team working on it have knocked on the doors of a few cottages nearest the castle entrance but with no results. We've searched the garden, grounds and surrounding country lanes and found absolutely nothing. I can only think that the intruder, or intruders, knew the security system codes.'

'Lady Rowallen now thinks there were two of them.'

The DI made a note of it.

'But they still had to get *in*,' Patrick said. 'Where was the entry point?'

'No sign of forced entry or broken windows. We've interviewed the staff and they seem OK.'

'The cook left in a bit of a hurry,' I told him.

'She lives locally,' Barton said. 'We've spoken to her. She's in her seventies and nervous, which is understandable in the circumstances.'

Patrick asked, 'What were your first impressions when you arrived at the castle?'

'Lady Rowallen let us in and as you must realize was in a state of shock. I asked Jill Hanson, my sergeant, to stay with her while a doctor was called to check her over and then went upstairs with another couple of members of my team. Obviously we touched nothing until scenes-of-crime people arrived. But first impressions? The complete lack of signs of a break-in made me wonder initially if one man had fired at the other and then turned the gun on himself. All wrong, of course. And until I was given the full picture I had no idea of the position the earl had held.'

'What about the security company?' Patrick mused. 'Did they test the system at the castle in your presence?'

'No, but I was assured there was nothing wrong with it.'

'Lady Rowallen doesn't like the man in charge; said he gives her the creeps. She's not a particularly nervous lady.'

'They came round at my request. But I don't think the guy I spoke to was the boss and I wouldn't describe him as creepy. I'll send someone to see if he's around if you like.'

'Mind if we do it?'

'Not at all.'

'Where do they operate from?'

'Brighton.' He rose, or rather bounced up. 'I'll get you a paper copy of the file. The company's name and address is in it.'

'It's not for lack of trying then,' I commented when we had arrived at the security company's headquarters not far from Brighton railway station and were waiting to see the managing director, George Harding. No one seemed to be around. 'Barton's team, I mean,' I added.

Patrick came out of his reverie, having had a quick look through the case notes. 'This seems OK but crimes like this don't crop up very often. He might find Special Branch breathing down his neck next.'

Fifteen minutes later, when my husband was getting a little restless and looking at his watch, a nearby door opened and we were called into a large office. The man who had done the calling, who introduced himself as Harding, was dressed in a slightly too-tight suit worn with a lavender shirt and matching tie, both of which clashed horribly with his red face. He gestured

extravagantly in the direction of a group of brown leather chairs
and invited us to seat ourselves.

'Always delighted to help the police,' he said. 'Although I
can't say I've heard of the National Crime Agency.' He was a
little out of breath after crossing the room.

'Perhaps you don't read the papers,' Patrick replied, clearly
put out at being kept waiting so long.

'Oh, too busy to bother with that kind of thing. All boobs
and rock stars.'

'Are you the owner of this company?'

'No, it's part of a consortium.'

'How long have you been in charge?'

'Six months. Not that that's any business of the police. I take
it you're here in connection with the murders at the castle?'

'We are. What went wrong with the security system there?'

'Nothing went wrong!'

'Someone got in and shot two people. I call that a complete
cock-up on your part.'

Harding's rather florid face went a deeper shade of red. 'Look,
they got in because someone had cancelled the alarm system.'

'Are you suggesting the murder victims let them in? That's
absolute rubbish!'

'I'll have you know that—'

'It may well have been installed correctly but now your
system, Mr Harding, is crap. How tight is your own security
here with regard to the secrecy of customers' code numbers?'

'Very tight,' Harding said a little hoarsely. 'Very tight indeed.
We really do everything to please our clients, you know.' An
oily smile. 'Someone *must* have let them in. Perhaps they knew
whoever it was.'

Patrick rightly ignored these theories. 'Who regularly services
and tests the system at the castle?'

'I'd . . . er . . . have to look it up.'

'Then please do so. I want to talk to whoever it is.'

This entailed Harding leaving the room, even though there
was a computer on his desk. He was gone for several minutes.
When he returned he was as out of breath as if he had had to
negotiate several flights of stairs.

'He's left,' he panted. Sweat sheened his forehead.

'Left!' Patrick exclaimed.

'Walked out three days ago apparently.'

'And you didn't know he had? Or why he had?'

'No. I – I don't have much to do with the day-to-day running of the company.'

'How long had he been working here?'

This entailed Harding having to go off again. 'Not all that long actually,' he said, or rather gasped, when he came back, mopping his face with a none-too-clean handkerchief.

'So who does know what goes on round here?'

'My assistant. But he's not here at the moment.'

'Where is he?'

'In Turkey on holiday.'

Highly unprofessionally, but still grieving and faced with a total incompetent, Patrick told him exactly what he thought of him. It wasn't pretty.

FOUR

'I simply can't understand why Daws employed such an outfit in the first place,' I said when we were walking back to the car.

'The company probably wasn't like that until Harding got his hands on it,' Patrick muttered. 'I intend to run a check on it and him.' By threatening to arrest him for withholding information from a police officer if he refused, he had wrung from Harding, who had protested that their staff details were confidential, the name and address of the employee who had suddenly left.

We had a light lunch and then went back to Hartwood to carry on looking through the files. At a little after three Pamela brought us tea and cakes.

'I'd like to undertake an experiment tonight,' Patrick said after we had thanked her, the refreshments very welcome. 'I want to attempt to break in – without doing any damage, I hasten to add – and try not to set off the alarms. They probably will go off but the exercise will serve to prove their efficiency, or not, and give us an idea whether they were set that night. When was the system last serviced?'

Lady Rowallen shook her head in perplexity. 'Sorry, I've absolutely no idea. Richard always dealt with that kind of thing.'

'But he was in town quite a lot of the time. Can you remember any occasions when you noticed a van outside and the alarms were going off several times as someone tested them?'

'No, I can't. But I'm out quite a bit too.'

'When Jordon would have seen to it. Never mind. We'll see what happens.'

'You must stay another night. You can't sleep in the woods just because you're testing the alarm system. And what about Ingrid?'

'Ingrid will be trying to break in too,' I told her with a smile, then felt Patrick's gaze on me. 'You rang?' I enquired.

'This time—' he began.

'You'd rather I stayed out of the way,' I butted in with.

'Be honest. I don't necessarily want to have to climb anything or crawl over roofs but you're not very good at things like that.'

'True.'

'You must have dinner first, though,' Pamela said to him. 'Judy's staying until the morning but Amanda's made a meat pie for me to heat up so it's absolutely no bother and there's plenty for us all.'

'A sandwich will be fine for me, thanks. It'll take me a while to do a proper surveillance before it gets dark. That's something the intruders must have done beforehand. Is your alarm system connected to the police station?'

'No. They discontinued that service a while ago as people's alarms were going off all the time when there was nothing amiss.'

'It might be a good idea to warn the people in the cottages closest to the main gates.'

'I'll phone them. I know them all.'

We carried on working and finally were left with the remaining nine files. All the way through I had been making notes of points that Patrick had dictated to me. Not many people can read shorthand these days and we were taking the added precaution of locking the notepad when it wasn't in use in the cubby box between the front seats in the Range Rover. This also houses Patrick's Glock 17 when he isn't carrying it in the shoulder harness – he was now – plus my short-barrelled Smith and Wesson and ammunition for both weapons. This little safe can only be accessed by using a password, changed each month, using a concealed key pad in the lid.

'These last files seem to be part of the same group,' Patrick said. 'But my eyes are crossed from reading from a screen. Tomorrow.'

A while later he got changed into his dark-blue night-time surveillance tracksuit and black trainers – all kinds of gear like this is kept in an old kit bag in the car – and went out. I could fully understand his reluctance to have me along as I'm an added responsibility for him when carrying out this kind of exercise and also have the bad habit of getting the giggles during particularly tense moments.

*   *   *

The ladies had a convivial evening and we enjoyed the 'all girls together' atmosphere. This was helped along by Pamela producing a couple of bottles of her late husband's best Chablis on the grounds that there was no point in condemning a good wine to dust and cobwebs while it was at its prime.

No, quite.

'Oh, I forgot to give Patrick his sandwiches!' Judy cried at some stage, I'm not sure in hindsight exactly when. Then to me, 'Where is he likely to be, do you know?'

'Sorry, not a clue,' I answered truthfully.

She hurried off, only to reappear quickly. 'I was sure I'd left them on the kitchen worktop, all ready to give to him. But they're not there.'

'He might have found them himself,' I said.

'But the outside door's locked.'

As the man can move so silently it's downright spooky, I amused myself with the thought that he might have been standing right behind her while she made them. The moment passed and we carried on chattering and laughing while enjoying a thoroughly good meal. This, of course, was doing Pamela the world of good. No doubt with this in mind, Judy suggested a brandy nightcap.

Patrick had asked Pamela to make sure she set the alarm system as normal when we all went to bed. As there was no reason for Judy or me to wander around at night as every guest room had an en-suite bathroom, this was perfectly practical.

The nightcap did its stuff and I went to sleep as though hit over the head with a brick. I awoke with a huge jolt when someone got into bed with me who then leaned over to kiss me goodnight and then settled down to sleep. Having to make absolutely sure about the important matter of identity, I switched on the bedside lamp.

'You should have known it was me,' Patrick protested, blinking into my scrutiny in the sudden bright light.

'A whispered word would have been nice,' I scolded. Actually, there were two of him.

'I thought you'd be asleep.'

'I was. Very. And then a bloke smelling of dungeons invaded my space.'

'That was the weak spot – the dungeons, now the wine cellar. Do I really smell?'

It has to be said that this man of mine is very fastidious about that kind of thing. Unless he's working undercover and has disguised himself as a drop-out, that is, when he's happy to stink to high heaven.

I switched off the lamp. 'Oh, just a bit cobwebby. Go to sleep. I'll find a vacuum cleaner and give you a going over in the morning.'

'You reek of booze.'

I woke up for a moment. 'Did you find the sandwiches?'

'No, the dogs had found them first and scoffed them in a corner. All that was left were a few crumbs and the remains of the plastic bag.'

'You must be starving!'

'Nope. I went down to the village pub and had steak and kidney pie and chips.'

In the morning Patrick's amusement was boundless when he discovered that we all had hangovers. He dished out strong headache pills from the first-aid kit in the car and then waited patiently for them to take effect.

'Oh, dear,' Pamela lamented. 'But didn't we have fun.' She laughed tiredly and then, looking at Patrick afresh, exclaimed, 'But I didn't hear the alarms go off!'

'They didn't,' he informed her. 'The system must have been tampered with – electronically, that is – some time ago. I really want to ask your alarm people why they failed to discover the fault. I think the circuits for the exterior cameras are all right and the intruders knew that so covered up the one that would have registered their presence, but with regards to indoors all your little sensors flash on and off downstairs but nothing seems to be reaching the central control console. On second thoughts, I suggest you contact an independent security company as I have absolutely no faith in the present lot.'

'Terry Meadows,' I suggested.

Terry used to be Patrick's assistant when he worked for D12 and now has his own very successful business.

'Yes, but he's not involved with domestic stuff, is he? I thought he mostly provided security staff and armed personnel to protect oil tankers in the Middle East.'

'He does install security systems but only on a largish scale,' I told him. 'Country houses, stately homes, exhibition centres, that kind of thing.'

'OK, I'll give him a ring.'

'I know him, don't I?' Pamela said. 'He was here with you during the Haldane episode. Patrick, how did you get in last night?'

'It was easy. But first I must tell you something. I take it your wine cellar was originally part of the deepest regions of the keep. Possibly even dungeons.'

'That's right, and it's horrible in there,' she answered. 'I have to brace myself before I go in and down those steep steps. Somehow you just know that people have died horribly down there.'

'At some time or other a doorway was made to give access to it, and it must have taken them a while as the walls there are a good five feet thick. When you go through and make your way beyond the passageways with rooms off them you come to a space with what I'm guessing is a well cover in the floor, perhaps at one time the castle's water supply in times of emergency. And in the wall is another doorway, more like a cross between a window and a hatch, a large strong-looking affair that opens about twenty feet up over the dried-up moat. I guess it provided access for provisions when the moat was full. It would have been a serious weak point in the defences. It still is.'

'The river used to flood in the olden days and swamp the moat,' Pamela said. 'The place used to be completely cut off for days or even weeks. And I don't think the castle ever got involved in sieges as the earls always sided with whoever trotted past with an army. I understand they always studiously kept abreast with the politics of the time. Is that how you got in? You climbed up from the bottom of the moat?'

'No, having had a look round earlier I got in through one of the utility room windows off the kitchen – the catch isn't very good and the magnolia growing against the wall was most helpful. I'd seen a lad with the dogs a little earlier and assumed he was taking them for a walk before they were put in the boot room for the night.'

'I've hired Tommy, a boy in the village, to walk them twice a day until I feel up to it,' Pamela explained.

'Before it got dark, I explored and apologise as you must be aware of all, or most of what I'm about to say,' Patrick continued. 'Although there's a high stone wall around the private garden on three sides, the front aspect is bounded by a ha-ha – a deep ditch with a wall hidden from the house side to prevent stock in the fields beyond from escaping but giving those in the house an uninterrupted view of the countryside. The rest of the property's boundary is represented by farm fences, which, although they seem to be in good order are completely porous to human intruders. There's not a lot that can be done about that, but don't worry about it as you want your ring of security around the house itself.'

'Highgrove doesn't seem to be surrounded by razor wire,' I pointed out.

'Prince Charles has made such a wonderful job of that garden,' Pamela enthused.

'There are signs of forced entry on the hatch-cum-doorway that the police didn't notice,' Patrick went on. 'Although the whole thing looks sound it's pretty rotten. I had a look at it from the outside through binoculars and you can see that someone has cut the lock out with a specialist saw and forced it back in afterwards. That's how they got in, having climbed up the wall. The stone is rough enough for someone with the ability and there's plenty of ivy growing on it, some of which looks as though it's been pulled loose.'

'But the inner door from the wine cellars is always kept locked,' Pamela said.

'It's old and very easy to pick. I managed it, from both directions.'

'You're very clever,' Pamela told him admiringly. 'But your findings don't make me feel at all safe.'

'Easily remedied.' He beamed at her. 'May I make myself some breakfast?'

'Oh, you poor man!'

*　*　*

It looked as though we would be staying for a couple more days at least as Patrick wanted to check up on the man, Jason Whitley, who had serviced the castle's alarm system. According to his ex-employer's records he lived in Tongdean, to the north of Brighton. There was no postcode listed. Rather than drive all the way over there and find that no one was at home, Patrick rang directory enquiries to get the phone number. There was no record of the name.

'Perhaps they don't have a landline,' he murmured. 'Did you bring your iPad?'

I Googled in the address. After a little delving it became obvious that it didn't exist.

'Right, I've changed my mind about this and shall inform Barton,' Patrick said. 'It's not my job to do his job and I'll suggest he checks up on George Harding too. With a bit of luck he'll keep me posted with any progress. Let's get back to the files. Right now, they're more important.'

'What did Terry say?' I asked.

'Oh, sorry, I forgot to tell you. He's coming along this afternoon.'

'Where does he live now?'

'Petworth.'

Petworth being very upmarket, he had clearly done well for himself.

A little later Pamela entered, flustered. 'Sorry to disturb you but please come. That American's arrived – just pushed his way in – and he's walking around as though he owns the place!'

That American, Irvine Baumgarten, had brought with him a man who was introduced as Clancy Elferdink, his attorney. Both wore smiles like toothpaste adverts and were large and colourfully dressed, the later in an amazing yellow and orange tartan suit.

'These are my old friends Patrick and Ingrid Gillard,' said Pamela a trifle nervously, and I was grateful to her for using my formal title as the fact that I write books is sometimes a distraction. She glanced at the business card the lawyer had just given her and then dropped it on a low table as though it carried contagious diseases.

The two eyed Patrick. Men do. If he wants to he can look bloody dangerous. He was now.

'In the circumstances of the earl's recent and tragic demise I'm acting as ejector of unwanted and uninvited visitors,' he informed them calmly.

The smiles vanished.

'But I'm a relation of his,' protested Baumgarten. 'I intend to contest the will.'

'The earl left everything to his wife.'

'But not the title!'

'It's ceased to exist. I'm sure you've been informed of that.'

'Under American law . . .' the attorney began.

'It doesn't apply in this country, as well you know. Your client is not the son of the marriage of his father. He's illegitimate so can't inherit the title. Period.'

'He should still get a share of this place.'

'Look, I don't mind if she wants to stay on for a while,' Baumgarten exclaimed.

Patrick took a deep breath. 'This is Lady Rowallen's home. Leave.'

'I insist on speaking to her attorney.'

A bell rang.

'Oh, dear, someone else,' Pamela agonized. 'Are there any more of you?' she demanded to know of the two men.

'No, ma'am, just us,' Baumgarten replied. Smiling, he seated himself on a sofa. Elferdink followed suit and they sat there like a couple of fat and horrible cats in something by Disney.

'I'll go,' I offered.

'Thank you, Ingrid,' Pamela said. 'Please get rid of whoever it is.'

This was a good idea as we didn't necessarily want witnesses to the two Americans being forcibly ejected.

It was Terry.

'I decided to drop everything and come this morning,' he said after kissing my cheek. 'I can always tell when the boss is a bit anxious about something by the tone of his voice.'

My cat's whiskers crashed in with a big one.

'There are two Yanks upstairs, one claiming to be a relation of Daws,' I whispered. 'They've just arrived and hoping to get their hands on this place. I think they're extremely dodgy.'

'Is Patrick up there?'

'Yes, and about to lose his temper.'

He knew his way and went up the stairs two at a time, which meant that I had to run.

'Terry! How lovely!' Pamela cried.

He gave her a charming, courtly bow and then turned to the Americans. 'Hi, folks. I'm the new butler-cum-bodyguard and I'm starting right this minute.' And to Patrick, 'Great to see you again, Chief. One each?'

The two Americans were heaved out of their chairs and frogmarched off the premises, protesting. Patrick and Terry watched from the front door until the car – obviously hired as Elferdink couldn't drive it – had disappeared, gears crashing, from sight.

'Patrick gave me the gist of what's been happening and I'll find someone for you, today if possible,' Terry promised Pamela on his return. 'I have all kinds of contacts and supplying discreet staff with the highest references is the speciality of a lady I know. But until someone arrives, and obviously you can interview them before they're employed, I'll stay if that's all right.'

It was all right to the extent that the lady of the house gave him a big hug.

His youthful good looks hadn't changed: thick, wavy brown hair, brown eyes, mobile features. Not quite as tall as Patrick but with broader shoulders, he was clearly still very fit as he had effortlessly hefted the portly Baumgarten from his seat. The only thing that was different about him was a certain gravitas of manner.

However, the kiss on the cheek I had received on the threshold and the twinkle in his eyes had been all about the fact that, some years previously and for reasons that I have never been able to explain, we hadn't *quite* gone to bed together.

The three of us went to Daws' study, Patrick and I back to work and Terry to organize the vital helper-cum-minder after he had been fully briefed as to what had occurred. Contacting two agencies, he came up with three possibilities, one of whom was free to be interviewed the following day and the others the day after that. Terry then left us, saying he would get some kit from his car to check the security system.

Patrick had been working in silence. This meant that I had nothing to do but look out of the window. A thick early autumn mist swirled around the trees in the garden, the sun, a bright red orb, gradually burning through it. It would be a hot afternoon.

'This is unreal,' Patrick suddenly whispered, shaking his head in disbelief. He did not speak again for a full half a minute and then said, 'And as hot as hell. The first three files of the nine left are in connection with the restructuring he was planning to do and it's obvious he intended to do more work on it and go into more detail. Some of it's quite radical but doesn't really concern us now. I'm on the last one of these final files and its pretty sensitive stuff. In short, he's been carrying out a lot of investigations into various police forces – remember the Rotherham child abuse scandal? – and those involved in that and other cases. I've had a quick scan through them and they're devoted to six individuals who are either not directly connected with the police or were and no longer are. Again, there are gaps where he probably intended to do more work or was awaiting information. One of those listed is dead, a chief constable in the Midlands, so that file's closed although Daws has made a note that other individuals mentioned should be included in any subsequent investigation. Of the other five and, as I've just said, I haven't looked closely at them yet, just read the conclusions: three are the chairmen of county councils, one in the north of England, one in Wales, and the third in East Anglia – all of those have ongoing criminal connections, apparently – another an MP and the last, a woman, late of the Metropolitan Police and now working for the NCA, is Marcia Lindersland.'

'What on earth did he have on her?' I asked.

'Nothing concrete but he suspects the same ongoing criminal connections. He's noted that he's only instigated his inquiry because she's now working for the NCA as he's known about her for a while.'

'But she would have been closely vetted until the pips squeaked!'

'According to what he describes as a reliable source, her extra-mural activities are well buried. If true it's hardly surprising that she wants to get her hands on this stuff.'

'But how did she know that he was investigating her?'

'Pass.'

'I take it we're not mentioning the content of this to either Pamela or Terry.'

'Definitely not. I'm reluctant even to print this and take it off the premises.'

'I think you ought to get Mike Greenway here.'

It immediately became obvious that in order to apprise Commander Greenway of the findings we would have to give Lady Rowallen an idea of what was going on as we could hardly invite someone else to her home without doing so. Therefore, Patrick told her that we had discovered something important that he needed to report to higher authority without compromising the information's present security. She was perfectly content with this and said she would be pleased to meet him. Not to mention, I realized, pleased to have the added security of the presence of another friendly man in the house, if only for a short while. I knew I would have the horrors if I was rattling around in a castle all on my own at night after my husband had been murdered.

I must have shot a worried glance at Patrick as these thoughts went through my mind for he looked at me and asked, 'What's up?'

But I shook my head and said, 'Nothing.'

We worked through the rest of the files and I made notes on everything pertinent except the contents of the one on Lindersland, finishing at a little after four thirty. We both read it right through. The only evidence appeared to be in the possession of a retired assistant commissioner in the Metropolitan Police – the reliable source who Daws intimated he had known for a long time.

'It's all rather cloak-and-dagger,' I commented.

Greenway had said he would take the following day off, Wednesday, and be with us mid-morning. He had added that he hoped it was going to be worth his time as he was desperately busy. The commander is always desperately busy.

'I take it you're not going to sleuth off again and will have a glass of wine with us tonight,' Pamela said to Patrick when we reported to her with the key to Daws' study. She preferred it to be kept locked.

'It would appear to be my turn,' he replied, straight-faced, and she mimed gently smacking his face.

While we were having drinks before dinner, Marcia Lindersland phoned.

'She apologised for what happened and actually sounded as though she meant it but wants to come here again and take Richard's computer away for examination,' Pamela hissed, having told the woman that she would have to put the phone down in order to find her engagements' diary. 'She says there's information on it she needs in order to do her job properly.'

'Say yes,' Patrick whispered. 'But tell her you're committed to other things for several days. Your charity work, that kind of thing.'

'I do have meetings actually. Are you sure?'

He nodded.

After arrangements had been made for Lindersland to visit the following Monday, Pamela's workload and the weekend preventing anything earlier, Patrick's mobile rang.

'That was Greenway,' Patrick said, having had a short conversation with whoever it was. 'He can't make it tomorrow as he'd forgotten a vital appointment and is otherwise madly busy so will drop by on Saturday morning. Lindersland's asking him why I'm not at work or reporting from the job she gave me,' he finished saying with a chuckle.

I felt the commander wasn't giving it the priority it deserved but said nothing.

'Terry, old son, do you have an IT wizard chum who would remove a file from the computer and fix it so it doesn't look as though it ever existed?' Patrick continued. 'I don't trust myself to do it and neither does Ingrid. You must appreciate we don't want any record of this so they'd have to be absolutely trustworthy.'

Terry stirred in his armchair where he was, like Patrick, enjoying Sussex real ale, Harveys Armada, a few bottles of which Pamela had unearthed from somewhere. 'Y-e-s,' he said slowly. 'But we haven't been in touch for ages. I'll try and get hold of him.'

'D'you reckon this place is being watched?' I wondered aloud, off on a tangent.

'As we all know, telephoto lenses enable a snooper to be a long way off,' Terry answered. 'But the actual driveway is fairly well screened by large trees. Having said that, anyone can hang around on the public road and note down the numbers of cars going in and out.'

'What did you make of the security system?' Patrick asked him.

'I haven't yet covered every room that's supposed to be protected but the main control panel has either been tampered with or was installed by an idiot. My money's all on the former.'

FIVE

To avoid any unnecessary trouble and allay suspicion, Patrick went back to work the next morning. I decided not to go with him. Bloody-mindedly, I told myself that although I remained a part-time employee of the NCA, whatever the woman was saying her plans were, there was no point, right now, in my rocking the boat. Terry had to stay on in Sussex as he had interviews to conduct and a computer boffin to find – both a matter of urgency – and, aptly, he promised to help hold the fort while Patrick was away.

I had no intention of sitting around doing nothing, however, or going for long walks in the admittedly wonderful countryside. Having dropped Patrick off at the railway station I then doubled back and headed for Horsham. It was a trifle early to call in to see DI Barton so I whiled away an hour in a small hotel that was open to non-residents and had a Continental breakfast. Neither of us had had time for anything except a quickly downed mug of tea.

Barton was in his office but showed no signs of fizzing and seemed quite glad to be interrupted. An untidy heap of files was on the desk in front of him.

'Crime statistics, reports, juvenile outreach programmes, training timetables . . .' He sighed. 'I hate this side of it.'

'We have a DCI friend in Bath with exactly the same problem,' I told him.

'You want to know if we've discovered anything about Harding, I take it.'

'Yes, but look, I'm not chasing you up. First of all I want to tell you about some iffy Americans who turned up.' I had written down their names and descriptions and added my own conclusions about the pair of them.

'You reckon this Irvine Baumgarten character is basically stupid and his lawyer a real shyster,' Barton said, looking up from reading.

'In a nutshell, yes. And I don't think Lady Rowallen's heard the last of them.'

The DI laid the sheet of paper on his desk as though it was a wreath. 'I shall make enquiries. Now, Harding. He's on the sex offenders' register and has six points on his licence for speeding but that's all we can find on him.'

I felt that was quite enough to be going on with but we were talking about murder here. 'Blackmail?' I suggested. 'Someone found out about his past so he's lying about what's going on?'

He shrugged. 'Could be. I'll send someone to talk to him. Grill him a bit. What did you make of him?'

'Yuck.'

'I get your drift.' He picked up a couple of the files that had slid on the pile and were crowding him and slammed them into a tray on one corner of his desk. 'The other one, the technician who suddenly left . . . remind me what the hell his name is.'

'Jason Whitley,' I prompted.

'That's it. We can't trace him. The address doesn't exist, as you and your colleague found out, and we reckon it's a false identity. We're looking for him but don't have a lot to go on. Harding's saying he knows absolutely nothing about him and that his assistant deals with that side of things. The assistant's in Turkey.'

'He might be lying and there isn't one.'

Barton looked me straight in the eye. 'Lady, I know you normally work on really big cases but that doesn't necessarily translate to rural Sussex.'

I eyeballed him back. 'Detective Inspector, although it wasn't for public consumption, the fourteenth earl was one of the most powerful and influential people in British policing. The NCA is working on the theory that he's been removed to make way for what I'll call elements with criminal connections.'

I wasn't at all sure about this but, hey, we were now.

'Evidence?' he asked stolidly.

'I can't tell you yet. But think of the implications, the access to intelligence.'

'Sold to the highest mobster bidder,' he mused gloomily.

'Suppose you and I go and talk to Harding.'

'But you didn't really get anywhere with him, did you?'

'He said he'd never heard of the NCA.'

'No, but he's damned-well heard of me!' the DI said, shooting to his feet, appearing to take it personally.

'Patrick was very rude to him,' I said as we descended the stairs, at speed, to the ground floor.

'Is he permitted to do things like that?'

'No.'

He guffawed with laughter.

I was half hoping that I would make the journey to Brighton as a pillion passenger on his motorbike but was ushered instead into an unmarked car. The DI had first checked that Harding was at work and, having satisfied himself about that, had then spent five minutes or so with his team. I was asked to wait in the reception area while this happened, presumably checking on general progress on this and other cases. As he left the room I had heard him say over his shoulder, 'Details, that's what I want. And I do not want to hear anyone say I think, I assume, I'm of a mind or anything like that. Details and facts, not opinions or intuition.'

That kind of thing does have its uses, though.

When we arrived we were told, by someone who appeared to be just wandering through, that Harding was with a prospective client and had taken him/her to a nearby café. My opinion of Barton rose several notches when he demanded to know exactly where this particular establishment was situated and, having been told, marched back out of the front door, this author hurrying after him.

The pair were seated at a small table in a corner behind one of the sad-looking potted plants that were dotted around. It was I who first spotted Harding's infused features through the foliage, and I touched the DI's arm and pointed him out without saying anything.

'Sod off,' Superintendent Matherson said when he saw me.

Had I imagined the twinge of alarm that had crossed his face?

Matherson gave Barton a dark glower. 'Who's he?'

Barton told him.

Matherson found his ID and, getting to his feet, shoved it under the DI's nose. 'Sod off.'

'I have an appointment to interview this . . . gentleman, sir,' Barton told him, his jaw jutting.

'That's what I'm doing. Sod off.'

'I have to point out that I'm investigating two murders.'

The other man stared him down and there was nothing we could do but leave.

'He appears to work for the NCA too,' I explained when we were back in the car. 'Patrick chucked him out of Hartwood Castle and I'm sorry if that made it difficult for you.' I had noticed a small bruise on the side of the superintendent's face.

'Difficult is that man's middle name,' Barton said under his breath. 'I shall have to report this, of course, as he's prevented me from interviewing a potential suspect. These people are supposed to liaise with the local forces, for God's sake.'

'You really regard Harding as a suspect?' I asked. He appeared to have forgotten for a moment that I too work for the NCA.

'I don't like the cut of his jib, as my grandad used to say. I don't like blokes who abuse young girls either. No, I'll talk to him all right. Tomorrow. Meanwhile, I'll make a priority of finding this Whitley character.'

I phoned Patrick and related what had happened that morning. He told me he had seen no sign of Lindersland so had carried on dealing with routine matters. He still had absolutely no intention of carrying out her orders regarding the Paddington job.

'I've done a little quiet digging on Matherson,' Patrick went on to say. 'He's late of a couple of departments in the Met dealing with anti-terrorism and seems to have been temporarily seconded to the NCA. Nothing iffy or of interest about him at all. And I suppose he's perfectly entitled to tell you and Barton to sod off if he's carrying out what he regards as a legitimate investigation. But as Barton said, he is supposed to be liaising with the force investigating Daws' murder.'

'Are you staying up there until the end of the week?' I asked.

'Yes, I can usefully work on things here. See you on Friday evening unless something crops up.'

Something did.

Barton rang me at eight thirty the following morning. 'We've found Whitley,' he reported. 'Trouble is he's dead – murdered. I'm on my way there now. Do you and your colleague want to come over?'

'Patrick's in London,' I told him. 'He's only investigating this unofficially. But I'll tell him straight away.'

Patrick said he would get a train directly to Horsham and asked me to pick him up at the station.

'A clumsy attempt has been made to make it look as though he had committed suicide,' Barton said. 'A dog walker came upon the body, or rather her dog led her to it hanging from a tree in a small patch of woodland near Devil's Dyke. If you're not familiar with it, it's a beauty spot north of Brighton on the Sussex Downs. I'm being careful with identification as although there's a driving licence in a wallet in his pocket with a different address – incidentally among other things including credit and debit cards – it could be a scam and the body's that of someone else entirely.'

The DI had returned to the nick mid-morning, leaving a team from Brighton CID at the crime scene, by which time Patrick and I had arrived and were drinking coffee in the canteen.

'What sort of clumsy attempt?' Patrick enquired.

'It wasn't the hanging that killed him, although you must realize that this is only the pathologist's first impression and the PM will tell all. He'd suffered several heavy blows to the head which would have rendered him deeply unconscious if not resulted in death. The skull's actually dented. I asked myself if the man had been living rough, having done a runner after the castle murders if he felt he might be indirectly involved, but the body gives no impression of that. It's clean, even the hands and fingernails, although the face has a couple of days' growth of stubble, not that that means a lot now it seems to be the fashion.'

I said, 'I shouldn't imagine there's a lot of use in getting George Harding to make an identification. He told us he didn't deal with staff.'

'I've every intention of getting him to the mortuary, though,' Barton said succinctly. 'But before that, and while the body's moved, he's overdue for questioning.' He stood up in his jack-in-the-box fashion. 'I'd be glad if you'd both accompany me.' When the DI was halfway towards the exit, Patrick gave me a little smile. He was quite content to be a witness to the investigation until events demanded otherwise.

'I've been instructed to answer no more questions,' Harding said when we found him in a back room, a kitchen of a sort, making himself a hot drink. As usual, the place seemed to be deserted. The manager's hands were shaking and he quickly put down the kettle before he spilt the boiling water and scalded himself.

'By whom?' Barton enquired, knowing, I was sure, full well.

'That senior cop who came here yesterday. He said it was restricted information on account of the identity of the man who was murdered. He said the security services are involved.'

'They are,' Patrick said. 'But the local police are still the prime investigators. You have a duty to answer questions, whichever law agency asks them.'

'I don't care what you say; I won't be bullied any more, so leave. It's not on to have three of you turn up.'

I was of a mind that we had cornered him, which was wonderful, so gave him a big smile as I took charge of the kettle, poured water on to the instant coffee already in a mug and, after conferring with Harding, added a little milk from the carton also on the worktop.

'Suppose I talk to Mr Harding,' I said to the other two.

Barton glanced at Patrick, who nodded and they left the room, closing the door.

I handed over the coffee, seated myself on a plastic chair and patted the one a few feet from me. 'Better?' I asked.

'I still refuse to be grilled,' Harding told me truculently.

I leave grilling to Patrick, but Harding had wasted far too much police time already.

'What did you tell the senior cop?'

'The same as I've done all along – the truth. That someone had cancelled the alarm system and it was nothing to do with us.'

'Did he believe you?'

'Yes.'

'I don't.'

'That's your privilege.'

'A man who appears to be your ex-employee, Jason Whitley, has been found murdered near Devil's Dyke.'

A near impossibility perhaps, but he went pale. Then, 'Appears to be? What d'you mean, *appears* to be?'

'A driving licence and credit and debit cards found on the body have his name on them. But until he's formally identified . . .'

I left the rest unsaid.

'Don't expect me to do it. As I've said all along, my assistant deals with staff.'

'So what exactly do *you* do?'

'I talk to the clients, arrange visits to their properties . . . that kind of thing.'

'How long has this consortium you mentioned owned the company?'

'Six or seven months.'

'So you were taken on shortly afterwards.'

'That's right.'

'What was the firm called before?'

'The same. It was a highly regarded and quite long-established family business. I have no doubt that's why His Lordship chose it in the first place.'

Well, at least that answered one question.

'What is the name of this assistant of yours?' I went on.

'Er . . .'

'I suggest to you that there isn't a formal assistant and because you're utterly incompetent a girl in an office runs almost everything. Was it Whitley who spoke to the police when your company was first called in to investigate what had gone wrong with the alarm system?'

'I think so. Before he went away.'

'You mean he bolted to save his own skin, don't you?'

His mouth clamped shut.

'Did someone pay him to do a bad job or to sabotage the equipment?'

'No!'

'Perhaps you were the one handed a wad of cash.'

'Of course not!'

'Or are you being blackmailed because someone's found out about your criminal record and the fact that you're on the sex offenders' register?'

'No!'

'Little children, was it? You're a disgusting fat creep, aren't you?'

Moving faster than I would have expected, he wildly hurled the contents of his mug in my direction and ran, aiming a blow at me that missed because I ducked as he went by. Judging by the resulting turmoil he ran straight into Patrick, who, as I was fully aware, would have stationed himself just outside the door.

Although I had moved quickly and some of the coffee had splashed the shoulder of my jacket, most had hit the wall behind me. I slipped it off before the hot liquid could penetrate the linen material and went in the direction of Harding's protesting shouts. As he paused for breath I related what had occurred and Barton arrested him for assault.

'That was risky,' Patrick whispered to me as we followed the pair out of the building, Harding submissive with his nemesis right behind him.

I merely gave him one of his own enigmatic smiles. How the hell else could we have got Harding inside the nick?

We left the security company manager or as Patrick said, teasing me, what was left of him at Horsham police station to be interviewed first by Barton or one of his team, and drove back to Hartwood. Patrick would question him later but I could not be present as I was the victim of the assault.

With Pamela's blessing Terry had organized people from his own company to bring the castle's alarm system up to standard, requesting that they first write a detailed report of the failings and suspected sabotage they found on the premises. But he had not been able to find a discreet computer expert, his main hope now working abroad.

Lady Rowallen had to go out and before she went suggested that we search the drawers of her late husband's desk and look carefully through the bookshelves in case there was anything else hidden away that might be important. This took most of the afternoon as there were hundreds of volumes and we felt it necessary to flip through each one in case anything was concealed between the pages. All we found of any importance, in a drawer of the desk, was a gift-wrapped present for his wife for her birthday which had fallen a week previously and a loaded Swiss SIG Sauer handgun with a box of ammunition. Patrick put the weapon back in the drawer, which could be locked, and we said nothing about it just then. The former was duly handed over and when Pamela beheld the pale lilac-coloured cashmere jumper it contained she predictably burst into tears. I shed a few as well.

The second person to be interviewed for the job of butler/minder had been deemed the most suitable – an added advantage being that he could start the following Monday – and would arrive on Sunday evening. Terry said that he himself could stay until after Lindersland had removed the computer. It was decided that Patrick and I too would remain on the premises, but out of her sight unless needed, until after she, and presumably Matherson, had gone. The uprating of the security system would also start on Monday. The more people around the place the merrier, I thought.

Which meant that we only had the problem of removing the Lindersland file from the computer.

George Harding had already admitted to Barton that he had lied and had no business partner. He had recruited staff and technicians, but offered low pay when he employed them to save money as the business was in serious decline. Jason Whitley had been one of these. Harding had an idea he might have had a criminal record but hadn't checked as at the time he was finding it impossible to keep staff. (At this point Barton had asked him if he thought his managerial skills were next to hopeless, and Harding had confessed that he had only ever been in charge of a betting shop.)

That was all the DI's interview had achieved, the man then refusing to answer any more questions and saying he did not want a solicitor as he had done nothing illegal.

On arrival at Horsham police station during the late afternoon, Patrick had a sudden rethink and told Barton that he was keen to talk to the security company manager in connection with the murder case and not about anything else outstanding. This would enable me to be present at the questioning and take a few notes for our own use. I was duly summoned – I had been hoping to look round the shops and was just locking the car – and we were shown into where Harding sat brooding in Interview Room 1.

'I'm not remotely interested in coffee being thrown over my assistant,' Patrick began by saying, chucking a thunderous frown in my direction as if it had been all my fault, thus embroidering his role of Mr Nasty. 'It's concerning the murder at Hartwood Castle. And as you're aware, this interview is being recorded.'

We were sticking to professional rules; even with friendly cops – Barton had not been told that we are man and wife – because, frankly, you just never know in cases like these. Patrick's priority has always been that I should never be targeted by criminals as a result of his own actions. Even police personnel gossip.

'How many more times do I have to say it?' Harding growled. 'The alarm wasn't set properly.'

He then realized, his eyes nervously shifting from one to another of us, that cooperating might be a good idea, as the man sitting there looking as though he enjoyed twisting people's ears round a few times might just do so, no records kept.

'We've had an independent survey done,' Patrick informed him silkily. 'Early findings suggest that the system was perfectly OK when it was installed but has subsequently been tampered with.'

Harding shrugged. 'Perhaps someone messed around with it.'

'Yes. And my money's on Whitley. Perhaps I ought to remind you that he's been murdered.'

Harding sighed as if this was all just too tedious. 'I think he had a drink problem. Used to turn up for work looking a bit spaced out. Or perhaps it was drugs. I don't know. I just wish to God now that I hadn't taken the job.'

'OK, let's move on to who recruited you.'

'It was an agency. I've never met the actual owners of the company.'

'Any idea why the previous people sold up?'

'As I've already said, it was a family-run thing. The old guy died, his brother was in a nursing home, beyond doing anything useful, and the younger members wanted something more interesting to do with their lives. I got the impression from what the woman in the agency said that the business had been going downhill for a while and some foreign company took it over. That's all I know.'

'You got really angry when my assistant suggested you'd been blackmailed because of your criminal record.'

'Who wouldn't be?'

'I've done a little investigating. You pretended to be a teenage boy on the Internet so you could lure young girls to your house. You were traced, arrested and served a prison sentence.'

'We all make mistakes.'

For some reason known only to himself, Patrick kept his temper.

I thought of Katie at that impressionable age, at home on her computer . . .

Patrick said, 'I'm wondering if the agency was asked to recruit someone who would be a caretaker manager until either the business folded or could be sold on.'

Again, Harding shrugged. But he was sweating, the moisture running down his heavy red jowls. 'No one said anything like that to me.'

'But you're so bloody inept. The only other credible scenario is that you were given the job on condition that you kept your eyes and ears shut and merely scouted for new business. You were threatened that if you interfered with anything else a woman would come forward and accuse you of sexual harassment or something along those lines.'

'Not true.'

'I suggest to you that Whitley was sabotaging alarm systems that had been installed by the previous owners of the company, no doubt quite correctly, so the properties they protected could easily be burgled.'

'I know nothing of things like that.'

'You're lying. Has this scheme just kicked off? If not we can check crime patterns in the area and see how many more of your customers have had break-ins.'

The man said nothing.

'If it is early days it's failed already,' Patrick went on cheerfully.

More silence.

'Who are these people?' Patrick persisted. 'If you don't know, if you didn't even try to find out it means you've been even more abysmally useless than everyone thought. In that case you deserve to be the one to go to prison for being an accessory to murder.'

'I am *not* an accessory to murder!' Harding shouted.

'Then talk. Convince me.' A Mr Nasty smile. 'Actually, I'm your only hope.'

Desperately, Harding said, 'But I don't know who they are! I just – I . . .' He stuttered to a stop.

'Go on. You just what? Get your orders over the phone?'

'Yes.' The man gulped.

'Names? They must call themselves something.'

After another silence, Harding said, 'He just says, "It's Nick." Just that.'

'No surname, no other names?'

'No.'

'Have you met him?'

'No.'

'What are they, or he, threatening you with?'

'As you said, that Tracy in the office will say I laid hands on her. She's part of it. I hate her – she keeps tormenting me about it.'

'There didn't seem to be anyone in the outer office when we saw you last time.'

'No, she's off sick.'

'What's her surname?'

'Finch.'

'Any other threats?'

'That I'll be done over. That would finish me. I've got high blood pressure, an iffy heart and I'm on God knows how many pills a day.'

'Why the hell do you stay?'

'He says they'll find me if I make a run for it. I'm finished already, come to think of it; they'll know I've been arrested. He said he knew everything that went on.'

'It was just as well you were arrested. I want you to make a full statement to Detective Inspector Barton. Every last detail. Will you do that?' When no reply was forthcoming Patrick added, 'If you don't I can't guarantee your safety. You might need police protection.'

'Can you do that?'

'Yes, I can.'

Harding sighed again and then nodded. Prompted for an audible reply on account of the interview being recorded, he then replied in the affirmative.

'Nick?' I queried when we were outside the interview room. 'Nicholas Haldane?'

'We mustn't jump to conclusions,' my husband predictably responded.

We reported to Barton, suggested that Tracy Finch be brought in for questioning and asked to be kept informed of what she said. Our next move now depended on Greenway's visit and his reaction to the files on Daws' computer.

After lunch the next day, Friday, and realizing that they were probably bored, Pamela asked Patrick and Terry if they fancied a little rough shooting and gave them the keys to her late husband's gun cabinet.

'Don't be shy, use the Purdeys,' she instructed as she went off to another of her charity meetings. 'If you bag anything the butcher in Steyning will buy them.'

This was a bit like handing a shooting man the crown jewels.

The men took the two Labradors with them and bagged three brace of wood pigeons plus a rabbit that they surprised as they left a copse. More interesting prey was the man who rapidly left his hiding place in an oak tree where he appeared to have been keeping watch on the castle, dropping his binoculars as he fled. This might have had something to do with Patrick having fired high over his head to ensure that he was deluged with leaves, twigs and spent shot.

'They'd have asked a few questions in the butchers if you'd turned up with that one,' Terry remarked at the time.

Joking apart, this was serious. Patrick retrieved the binoculars, which were a very good make, holding them with his handkerchief to protect any fingerprints that might be on them. Back at the castle they were put in an evidence bag – we always carry a few of these, together with gloves – and Patrick then phoned Barton and told him what had happened. The DI said he would send someone over to pick them up. This happened just under an hour later, and not for the first time I admired the DI's efficiency.

The men cleaned the shotguns and then Terry handed over the three pounds fifty pence he had received for the game to his hostess, to her great amusement. She was not told about the man watching from the tree. As far as the computer went we would have to try to handle the file ourselves as all Terry's contacts – he having spread his net a little – were either unavailable or, in one case, seriously ill. Some record, I reasoned, would have to be kept, however, as it was evidence. I forgot to ask Patrick if he had saved the file on Lindersland.

All this became irrelevant when, that evening, quite late, the police conducted a raid.

SIX

There was no warning. We were all in a room that did not overlook the front aspect of the private wing and therefore not in a position to notice approaching headlights. Pamela jumped up in alarm at the sudden pounding on the front door and then someone with a loudhailer announced that it was the police and demanded entry.

'Please stay with Pamela,' Patrick said to me and he and Terry quickly left the room.

'D'you think its genuine?' asked Pamela. 'I mean, why on earth should Detective Inspector Barton behave in such a way?'

I shook my head. It wasn't Barton.

The two men returned and in their wake came Marcia Lindersland, Superintendent Matherson and two members of one of the Met's riot squads in full gear. The pair appeared to be unarmed.

'This is outrageous!' Lady Rowallen cried. 'How dare you!'

Calmly, Lindersland said, 'I believe you are in possession of information, probably in a computer, which, if it falls into the wrong hands will compromise national security.'

'You don't work for the security services,' Patrick pointed out.

She ignored him.

'Leave my house!' Pamela shouted.

I moved closer to her to be able to offer support if it was needed.

Matherson jerked his head at the uniformed two. 'Go and find the computer. Look everywhere. Force doors if they're locked.'

'Search warrant?' Patrick rapped out, and at the tone of his voice the men paused.

'It would save time if you told us where it was,' Lindersland said to Lady Rowallen. 'And possible damage.'

'You still need a search warrant!' she retorted.

Patrick's attention was on Lindersland and he did not appear to see Matherson come up to him from the side until it was too late. He was struck hard on one shoulder and as he turned under the force of the blow Matherson followed it up with a brutal punch to the face. Patrick staggered and then fell as he cannoned into a low coffee table. In the next few seconds Terry launched himself at Matherson, only to be grabbed by the riot squad men while I headed for Patrick, who appeared to be out cold. I got there just before Matherson did, the expression on his face murderous, but could not prevent the vicious kick he aimed at Patrick that took him in the ribs. I gave Matherson a hefty shove when he drew back his foot again and he lurched backwards.

'Stop it!' Pamela shrieked. 'Stop it this minute! I'll give you the wretched thing! But stop this!'

I was prepared to go into full Husband Protection Mode here and, despite the fact that I was wearing a dress, was primed to kick Matherson where he least wanted to be, adding a chop across the neck when he folded up. I have floored men just as big as this bully.

'Matherson, no!' Lindersland shouted to him as he again advanced. But her eyes were on me.

'Here,' Pamela said, fumbling to get the key to her late husband's study from the little drawer in a bureau where it was kept. 'Turn right out of the door and it's the third door on the left. No, to hell with it, I'm coming with you to make sure you don't steal anything else!' she finished by yelling at Lindersland.

She marched off, back rigid, and Lindersland and Matherson followed, leaving behind them an edgy scenario. Lindersland then returned.

'What's the computer password? She said she doesn't know it.'

'She doesn't,' I replied.

The woman stalked out.

'You do realize,' I said to the two cops, 'that two people in this room work for the National Crime Agency. I'm one of them and the other one's on the floor having been beaten up by some shitty super.'

They exchanged worried glances.

Nothing else could be done, nothing else said and, a couple of minutes later, the foursome went.

The slam of the front door still echoing in the hallway, Patrick, who I now realized had been playing possum, sat up and waited for the world to stop going round, the pain in his chest to subside, trying to control his temper. I offered him a hand but he got to his feet unaided and walked down to the other end of the room, turning his back to us.

He was raging. Feeling a fool and second rate, a frame of mind always close to the surface since serious injury during his service days meant that he had to have the lower part of his right leg amputated. The replacement, which cost roughly the same as a medium-sized family car, is powered by lithium batteries and no one looking at him moving around can tell. But it does impose limitations on him.

'Only beastly cowards hit a man when he's not looking, never mind kick him when he's down,' Pamela declared, coming back into the room. Unsteadily, she poured rather a lot of whisky into a cut-glass tumbler, went over to Patrick, briefly put an arm around him and gave him the drink. Then she sat down suddenly in the nearest armchair and looked as though she was going to cry.

I went over and stayed by her side for a few moments, kneeling by her chair.

Terry, I think, had suddenly felt awkward, an intruder. He also knows a lot more about the man he still sometimes jokingly refers to as the boss than perhaps I had given him credit for. 'Well,' he said, 'for someone who at one time would have put that warthog in hospital that was bloody wonderful.'

Pamela seemed about to remonstrate with him for the apparent sarcasm but refrained when she saw the reaction the remark had had on Patrick who had turned, taken a sip – no, a mouthful – of whisky, swallowed it and then given his one-time lieutenant a fleeting smile. The side of his jaw was reddening.

'I was half expecting her not to stick to the arrangements,' Patrick said and then shared the rest of his whisky with the three of us.

I too had wondered if Lindersland would play dirty and had known it would only be a matter of time before Matherson would seek to even the score. What had happened though seemed like pure fiction: the police do not behave like this in modern Britain.

Or perhaps they do.

'They now have the computer,' Patrick said. 'Fact. The big question still remaining is how did she know what was on it?'

'Daws may have hinted to her that he had suspicions,' I suggested.

'It's possible. She could still be on the line but a complete control freak.' He ruefully rubbed his rapidly bruising face. 'I hate working like this.'

'I have an idea you saved that file on to disc.'

'It was the only thing I could do. It's in the cubby box in the car. And the least number of people who know about it the better.'

'She's not stupid. Surely she'll suspect that you've made a copy.'

'That's possible too. It'll be interesting to see what she does next.'

'Patrick, she doesn't want me on the job and I have an idea she'll try to get rid of you too now. Whether she's on the line or not is immaterial if she comes to the conclusion that we'll be the ones to bust her cover. Is the job getting to the point where it's just not worth carrying on with?'

'I'll try to answer that when I've had a chat with her next week.'

This was not remotely the reply I had been expecting. Me, I wanted out. Preferably right now. You can't work for someone you don't trust an inch.

'I'm going to carry on as though nothing has happened,' Patrick went on. 'With a bit of luck she'll think I've knuckled down.'

'I hope that doesn't mean you'll agree to do that Paddington job.'

'Not a chance.'

We were talking in our room, just the two of us, getting ready for bed, and planned to go home the following morning. There was little that could be achieved by staying any longer and we both felt the answer to Daws' murder lay elsewhere, not in

Sussex, even if DI Barton and his team turned up important evidence. There was also the matter of the five young people in Somerset for whom we were responsible.

Patrick had told Greenway what had happened to save him a wasted journey and the commander had been non-committal. Terry would stay on to supervise his team dealing with the alarm system and to double-check that the new bodyguard-cum-butler was as suitable as he had seemed at the interview.

'I thought you were bloody wonderful too,' I said. 'You didn't lose your temper and do Matherson real injury. That would have achieved absolutely nothing and done quite a lot of harm.'

'Come here, battleaxe,' Patrick said, grabbed me in a bear hug and then whispered, 'Ow!' because his ribs hurt.

He's bloody wonderful in bed too.

DI Barton was on the doorstep early the next morning as Patrick and I were due to leave.

'I had to come over this way anyway,' he began. 'I thought you'd be interested to know that the girl, Tracy Finch, has disappeared.'

'Disappeared?' I echoed.

'Not at the office yesterday, which is barred and bolted, nor at home. She lives with her mother in Portslade, which is just along the coast from Brighton. Mrs Finch said that Tracy arrived at home much earlier than usual the day before yesterday – it must have been shortly after Harding was arrested. She's been off sick with the flu but her mother doesn't know whether she'd gone back to work or not as she might have been staying with a friend. Anyway, she threw some possessions into a suitcase and left. Not a word of explanation. She and her mother don't get on all that well apparently, mainly on account of the company she's been keeping. Nightclubbing, drinking, possibly drugs – the usual sort of thing. The mother seems a good sort and is now very concerned. We're going to talk to her again if Tracy doesn't turn up soon to see if she knows anything about the friends the girl might have gone to stay with.'

'Do we have a description of her?' Patrick enquired.

'Yes, she's nineteen years old, five feet five inches tall, very slim, long blonde hair – her mother did mention that some of it was extensions – blue eyes and a pale complexion.'

'Did Harding have anything else to say when he made his statement?' Patrick went on to ask while I was noting down these details.

'No. He virtually repeated what he'd said to you. He's a frightened and sick man. Frankly, I didn't like to push him too hard in case he died of heart failure right there in the nick.'

'Ought I to drop the assault charge?' I said.

'No!' both men exclaimed as one, Barton going on to explain that it enabled him to keep tabs on the man, who had been escorted home to Brighton, a basement flat in the town, where he had packed a bag and then been taken to a safe house.

The DI's gaze focused on Patrick. 'Have you been assaulted?'

'Yes, I was thumped by a superintendent,' Patrick answered. When Barton became lost for words he added, 'I'll tell you about it one day.'

'I'll look forward to that,' the other responded. 'I'd better go and say good morning to Her Ladyship and keep her up to date with the investigation, not that I have a lot to tell her.'

'We haven't mentioned to her the man watching from the tree,' Patrick said as the DI turned to go.

'Just as well. They definitely weren't police-issue binoculars.'

As he had said he would, Patrick went back to work on Monday as though nothing had happened, and nothing carried on happening. Lindersland did not summon him for a carpeting, to apologise or otherwise, and when he made enquiries he was told that she was not at work. As the week progressed, the stories from different sources were that she was ill, on unpaid leave and at a conference. Whatever the reason, like Macavity, she wasn't there.

In between other jobs – and he had plenty to do now as Commander Greenway was standing in for someone who had gone sick, leaving Patrick responsible for some of his duties – he instigated a low-key investigation into the whereabouts of Nicholas Haldane. He discovered that he had been released from prison almost exactly four months previously and his home – the only address in records, a semi-detached house in

Roehampton – had been sold to an official of the Lawn Tennis Association. This last detail rather pointed to the fact that someone was still following his activities, or at least trying to. Having phoned DI Barton to see if he had any news – he hadn't – and between family matters, I carried on with my latest novel, aware that the murder inquiry had come to a standstill.

During a phone call to me early on the Wednesday morning, Patrick said that he had dropped investigating the reliable source mentioned in the file for the moment, the complication being that he had no idea of the identity of the retired assistant commissioner in question.

'Shouldn't you be giving priority to finding him rather than Haldane in case he, or she, is in danger?' I asked, doing my consultant thing. 'Talking to whoever it is might give you important clues in the murder inquiry. Besides which, the "Nick" George Harding spoke of could easily be another man altogether.'

'You think I'm fixated on Haldane?'

'Mildly,' I tactfully lied.

He made no further comment and we went on to talk about something else.

How difficult is it to find a retired assistant commissioner? I decided to start asking questions and accessed a Met website that is restricted to the use of police and other institutions connected with the law. Needless to say, there were rather a lot of possibilities and I did not even know when the person in question had left the force. I ended up with eight, thinking that the past ten years should be about the right timescale. How old was Lindersland? In her early- to mid-forties?

I dug deeper and was surprised that records were still being kept on these people when to all intents and purposes they had cut the chains on their desks and departed. Of the seven men and one woman three had died, one by his own hand, two had emigrated to live with their families, in Canada and Australia respectively, and the remaining three were still living in the UK at the time the information had last been updated, which was recently. This did not mean, of course, that we only had these three to investigate, as one of those who had left the country – both men – could be the individual we were looking for. I made a note of the names but no addresses were given.

Why had Daws been so cagey? Why had he not provided more details about his source? Not wishing to involve an old friend in a possible scandal if whoever it was was connected with Lindersland in some way? Had he been dubious about the accuracy of what he had been told?

Realizing that I should have done so before, I rang Pamela, first to ask how she was getting on with her new member of staff. She told me that the butler's name was Christopher and she liked and was impressed with him. He had spent most of his time since he arrived finding his way around the castle and the private wing, important to someone who was also a security officer. Terry's team had completed work on the alarm system and made sure Christopher had familiarized himself with it.

'Pamela, do you know anything about an old friend of your husband's who's a retired assistant commissioner in the Met?' I went on to ask.

'It could be Martin Grindley,' she replied. 'They were in 14th Intelligence together but Martin resigned his commission quite early on. Heaven knows why. I think his wife had something to do with it. She told me ages ago that she was fed up with all the travelling abroad he had to do. So Martin became a policeman.'

'Where do they live?'

'They're still in London, but the last I heard was they were thinking of moving to the South Coast as he's retired now. That was a while back, though.'

'Are you still in touch with them?' I went on to ask, having to smile. I too am married to a man who resigned his commission and became a policeman, in Patrick's case because he thought it would be less hazardous on account of his now being a family man. It hadn't quite worked out like that.

'He was at the funeral and I had a short chat with him,' Pamela said. 'But, you know, it's a Christmas card kind of thing with them. Richard used to send them one and that's all, although I think he phoned him occasionally.'

I told her that my enquiry was in connection with something that had been on a file in the computer and asked for the address and a contact number, only the latter of which she could give me as she did not know exactly where they lived. I rang it but there was no answer, not even when I tried again later. My patience, always in short supply, ran out at this point. I would check that everything was running smoothly here at home and if so go to London and talk to this man, with or without Patrick. Grindley's name had been one of those listed as still being in the UK.

Shortly afterwards the words came back to me: running smoothly. I paused in tidying my desk, feeling guilty. The three eldest children were at school right now, the two smallest somewhere in the house with Carrie. Vicky had recently started going to a toddlers' club held two mornings a week in the village hall. I had arranged it and understood baby Mark thoroughly enjoyed going along too, watching all the other children playing. The little girls thought he was really cute and gave him soft toys to hold, wave around, throw or perhaps chew on – he was teething – when Carrie wasn't looking. I felt a sudden pang of unhappiness and even more guilt that I had chosen not to be present for this innocent fun. Would these young people know who I was when I gave up working for the NCA and, eventually, stopped writing? My blithely telling myself that I was dealing with family matters had perhaps salved my conscience when all it had involved was paying bills and doing things like making sure that nothing needed to be taken to the dry cleaners.

I was a lousy mother.

I gathered up my two mobile phones – one private, the other for work only – put them in my bag, shut the door on my writing room and, having dumped my bag down in the hall, went upstairs. The huge blue teddy bear was on the landing so I moved it to one side where no one would trip over it. Vicky was in the little nursery helping Carrie get Mark, wriggling, into the pale blue denim jacket that Patrick had bought for him in Bath. It has a large, soppy-looking snail wearing a bow tie embroidered on the front pocket, is wildly impractical on a dribbly baby and had cost a small fortune.

'They're like getting eels into clothes at this age,' Carrie lamented.

'Is this the morning for the toddlers' club?' I asked, having forgotten.

'No, that's Tuesdays and Fridays. We're off to see a mum I chat with there for coffee at her house. She has a little boy Vicky's age and they get on famously. I'm a bit late actually.' She looked up at me a trifle anxiously. 'That's if it's all right, Ingrid.'

'Of course!' I replied in jolly fashion. 'Have a good time. I just wondered if you needed a hand with anything.'

Why did I want to cry?

When I got downstairs my work phone was ringing.

'Is Patrick there?' said a woman's voice very quietly, almost whispering.

'No, he's at work,' I told her.

'Only his phone's switched off.'

'He might be in a meeting.'

'Is that Ingrid?'

'Yes, it is.'

Did I know that voice?

'I need his help,' she went on. 'It . . . it's Marcia Lindersland.'

There was something about her tone that made me ask her where she was.

'I've no idea where I am.'

'What on earth's happened?'

'I've been—'

Cut off.

I was baffled. Was this some kind of trick?

Common sense prevailed. She wasn't the kind of woman to play silly tricks. Behave like the Wicked Queen and remove something by force and underhand methods from a heavily fortified castle, allowing her henchman to batter down any possible resistance when said resistance just happened to be looking the other way? Yes. Play hide-and-seek? No.

Without thinking, I tried a redial but that only got me as far as a voice telling me the call had come in as 'Unknown'.

Damn the woman to hell.

I then rang Patrick's personal mobile. No one at HQ now Daws is dead, except Greenway, knows that number, and I just got the messaging service. I did not leave one. Less than five minutes later he phoned me back.

'Lindersland's been trying to contact you,' I told him. 'She rang me here.'

'What the hell for?' He sounded preoccupied and annoyed at the interruption.

I related what she had said and how she had been cut off.

'She'll just have to find me tomorrow.'

'Patrick, I repeat, the woman said she doesn't know where she is.'

'I can't be expected to—'

'*You're still not listening!*' I bawled.

He took a deep breath and then swore quietly as his sore ribs reminded him of their presence. 'OK, the oracle has erupted with blues and twos. I'll make a few enquiries.'

I thought better of asking him if he'd seen Matherson.

Torn between several courses of action, I finally decided to stay with my original plan and seek out the one-time assistant commissioner, Martin Grindley. For, after all, if a branch of the NCA couldn't find their own boss who could? But when I tried the Grindleys' number there was still no answer.

As he does normally, Patrick had left the Range Rover at home and gone to London by train. Before setting off anywhere in it I always check the cubby box between the front seats to make sure he has left spare ammunition for his Glock. He had, together with that for the Smith and Wesson. Then, having decided not to take the latter, I changed my mind and fetched it from the wall safe in the living room. I had an idea this whole wretched episode was not going to finish by everyone singing 'The Wheels on the Bus Go Round and Round'.

Patrick always stays at the same hotel in the West End, and we have a priority booking courtesy of his job in one of a few rooms reserved for the NCA. It includes a parking space when he is there. It is not an overly ostentatious place as the impression we want to give, should anyone recognize us, is low-key – an author having a few days in town with her retired army officer husband.

Depending on the time of day and in an effort not to be

recognized by people who might regard us with malice afore-thought, the husband, when on his own, projects all kinds of personas. Perhaps he is one of the several million tourists in jeans, leather jacket and carrying a camera, or an executive dressed in a smart suit with briefcase and laptop, or someone just back from a jog in the park: tracksuit, trainers, water bottle. We are still on the hit lists of several terrorist groups.

Later, early evening, and having told him that I had arrived, I booked into his room under my professional name, unpacked, had a shower, put on a dress for a change and seated myself in the bar just off the entrance lobby. I then discovered that the husband was already there, giving the impression of a slightly shifty individual entering the illustrious portals to meet the boss who was, no doubt, a wheeler-dealer wearing far too many gold rings and chains, who the police wanted to help with their enquiries.

'You look like an Irish horse dealer,' I told him when he had come over and seated himself.

'Damn, I was trying to look like an Irish hitman,' said Patrick. He swept his hair off his forehead, back roughly where it normally lives, grinned and suddenly was himself, almost the boy I had fallen in love with at school. Well, almost – he hadn't had a shave this morning. 'Is there a special reason why you're here?' he went on to ask.

'I'll explain when you've organized a glass of wine for me.'

A waiter was already on his way, perhaps something to do with fielding the smile and thousand-yard grey stare.

'She's gone off the map,' Patrick said, coming up for air from his pint of Fuller's London Pride a couple of minutes later. 'Her mother, who lives quite close to her apparently, doesn't know where she is and a neighbour someone spoke to hasn't seen her for days. Not that that means a lot.'

'She's unofficially missing then?'

'Definitely. There's a whole coop of headless chickens running around.'

'What about Matherson?'

'Shitting himself. Actually asked me if I knew where she was.'

That suggested desperation, I thought.

'I offered to blow his head off and he went away muttering.'

'And?' I knew there was more.

'He came back a bit later and officially asked me to help find her.'

'And? Patrick, I'm having to wring this out of you word by word!'

'Sorry. I told him I was committed to finding Daws' killer. That seemed to throw him a bit, which surprised me slightly as I would have thought Medusa would have fully briefed him. I didn't mention Haldane.'

I said, 'I came up to London to look up a man by the name of Martin Grindley. He's a retired assistant commissioner with the Met and an old friend of Daws. I asked Pamela about it. He might be the source of the information about Lindersland.'

'Well done. Why didn't I think of asking her?'

Patrick finished his beer and went off to change out of the somewhat disreputable jeans and leather jacket which presumably he had worn for work, and to have a shower. I waited in the reception atrium as I knew he wouldn't be long.

One of the uniformed porters appeared at my elbow. 'Miss Langley?'

I said that it was. He proffered an envelope addressed to us both on a small silver salver. Inside it was a voucher printed smartly on expensive card which represented dinner for two at a nearby Italian restaurant that we had patronized in the past.

When he appeared I wordlessly handed the voucher to Patrick. Then I said, 'You smell *gorgeous*.'

'I've run out of aftershave so I used some of yours,' he muttered, perusing the voucher.

'I don't use aftershave!'

He chuckled. 'The stuff in the tall bottle.'

'That's L'Occitane Verbena eau de toilette.' This man of mine will slosh on anything that smells on the conservative side of the Chelsea Flower Show.

'It did sting a bit.' He tapped the voucher with a forefinger. 'Are you game for this?'

'I think it's dodgy.'

'It's twenty-four-carat dodgy.'

SEVEN

It had been raining for most of the day but had now stopped, though the pavements were still wet and shiny and slightly slippery. I held on to Patrick's arm as I was wearing higher heels than I do normally – what I refer to as my London evening shoes, Jimmy Choo – and had no desire to trip or slide over. Perhaps, I thought, bearing in mind the most recent development I should have gone back to our room and changed into a more sensible pair. A bit jittery, I held on to Patrick more tightly.

There was a taxi parked right outside the restaurant, a very smartly dressed black man just getting out. He smiled winningly at us both and then sprayed something in Patrick's face from a small aerosol can hidden in his hand. Patrick collapsed but the man caught him under the arms and heaved him into the back seat of the vehicle. He pocketed the aerosol then I caught the glint of metal in his other hand, a handgun of some sort.

'Now, be sensible,' he said, eyeing the Smith and Wesson I was now holding. 'As you can see, this is pointing at your husband's head. My friend in the driving seat, who isn't really a taxi driver, has a gun aimed at you.'

'I can't see him, or it,' I said.

'Jules, be a good chap and show yourself,' said the man.

Jules and his pistol duly came into view.

'What do you want with us?' I asked.

'Just get in and you'll soon find out.'

They weren't taking Patrick anywhere without me, and it would be madness to start shooting.

I got in the taxi, our abductor sitting in the middle.

'Put the gun back in your bag – you won't need it,' he said. We drove off.

'God,' whispered the man. 'It's Harry, by the way – Harry. I'm your friend, not your worst enemy. God, I'm sweating. Gillard on one side likely to wake up at any second and with a Glock 17 in his armpit and you on the other with a revolver

that still isn't in your bag. Can you imagine what that's *like!*'
The final word was delivered falsetto.

'Relax, Harry,' said the driver irritably.

'You think I don't know their reputation!'

I rammed the weapon back in my bag and said sarcastically,
'Happier now?'

'Look, lady, we're couriers. We don't act like this normally.
We're not used to it. I have degrees in English and Ancient
History. I like roses, puppies and stuff like that. All right?'

'No, it's not all right!'

A minute or so later Patrick stirred and peered around Harry,
perhaps to see if I too was there.

'Now if I lean on you really hard you won't be able to get
to your gun, will you?' Harry said to him hopefully. And then,
louder, 'Jules, are we nearly there?'

'No, as you can see perfectly well we're stuck in 'effin traffic
almost where we started from!' Jules yelled back.

I leaned forward and looked at Patrick. But the light was
bad, even when we passed streetlights, and it was impossible
to tell how he was.

Patrick started swearing by way of a reply, slurring his words
slightly. When he vents his feelings like this I don't know what
most of it means anyway, which is just as well. I gazed miserably out of the window. Constitution Hill, Buckingham Palace,
The Mall, Whitehall, Horse Guards Avenue . . . The situation
was completely surreal.

The taxi turned sharp left and went down an incline that
disappeared under a large building. We came to heavy security
gates and the driver leaned out and savagely punched a forefinger
on a keypad, as though it had just insulted him. The gates
opened and we entered a subterranean car park. There were
hardly any cars in it.

'Bloody hell, the perennial cliché,' Patrick groaned. 'Barrel
of lard mobster with stainless-steel dentures meets cop to warn
him off case before henchmen beat him to shreds and chuck
him in a litter bin. It's been done in movies a thousand times.
Can't you think of anything more original?'

I was wondering if Marcia Lindersland had also been grabbed
by these people, whoever they were.

We drove right to the far end and parked where Harry made shooing motions with both hands and then put his head between his knees. Patrick and I got out of the taxi.

'We were told not to touch you,' Jules explained, staying right where he was and looking at us as though we had just insulted him too.

'Knock-out sprays are illegal,' Patrick said to him with sufficient venom to poison most of London.

'But you wouldn't have come otherwise.'

There was no answer to this bit of logic.

'Here he comes,' Patrick said under his breath, the sound reaching our ears of the whine of a lift and then its doors opening somewhere just out of sight.

They hadn't taken our weapons from us.

Three men came around a pillar, one walking slightly in front of the others. He was tall, slim, looked familiar and, moments later, I was able to put a name to him. His minders appeared to have been fashioned in a factory that made nuclear reactors and, to my partly trained eye, were armed.

'I don't have to be tranquillized like a soddin' rhino,' Patrick said to the man in front when he got closer.

'My apologies. I was given advice that you are cautious enough not to believe any conventional requests to meet me.'

'A text or email quoting the code words of the time I worked for D12 would have provided authenticity.'

'Then I apologise again. Shall we go somewhere more comfortable?'

Patrick glanced at me, a reminder to those present that I was not his current lay but his wife, working partner and the mother of his children. His expression also somehow conveyed to all those present that he thought the reason given for our treatment to be beneath contempt.

'Here'll do,' I said to the head of MI5. 'Come to think of it, I used to work for your organization as well.'

But for a flicker of his eyelids the man did not register my remark, saying to Patrick, 'I understand you're hunting down Richard Daws' killer. You told Marcia Lindersland that's what you intended to do.'

'I did,' Patrick agreed.

'That was a dangerous thing to do.'

'Dangerous to who?'

'To you. And it's not your job.'

'She forbade me to.'

'With good reason.'

'I know her reasons. They don't involve MI5. Why is she reporting to you?'

'She isn't.'

'You have her office bugged then.'

This was not denied.

'She seems to have disappeared,' Patrick observed.

The man ignored that comment as well. 'I understand she removed a computer from Daws' home very recently.'

'Virtually by force.'

'Why did she want it?'

'She told us it contained information that concerned national security. She lied. Daws had been working privately, investigating various individuals. Lindersland was one of them, and in the opinion of a contact of his she has criminal connections.'

'How have you become involved?'

'We're old friends of Lady Pamela's. At one time she was married to a senior official in MI5 who called himself Westfield after the village near where they lived in Sussex. You can easily check up on that. She and her husband, who was dead when we first met her, had known Richard Daws for years. It involved two previous cases, that's all.'

'The Haldane case was one of them.'

'That's right.'

'On several occasions recently Haldane was seen in London with a man who was of interest to us. He was a trade union official by the name of Ronnie Shaddock. Shaddock had cronies who are connected with an anarchist group run by a man who calls himself Dimitri Lemotov. They have the usual blow-up-the-Establishment-and-be-damned mindset but can't be dismissed as just another bunch of cranks. Most of them are criminals: drug dealing, burglaries, money laundering.'

'You're talking about Shaddock in the past tense.'

'Yes, he was killed in a car accident last week. Almost

suicidally over the limit, went off the road, down a bank and hit a barn in Epping, no other vehicles involved.'

'Where were they seen together?'

'At a wine bar in Ilford. I understand it's opposite the main entrance to a small public park in South Street, but the name of the bar is anyone's guess as the illuminated sign over the door has been smashed, possibly deliberately. I'm a bit annoyed that no one seems to have thought of asking around.'

'Why were you monitoring Haldane?'

'We weren't and still aren't – just keeping watch on Shaddock and taking note of all his contacts. Why Shaddock was involved with Haldane is anyone's guess but from his past behaviour Haldane does seem to have what I shall politely call mental issues. Another point is that Lindersland might not have lied. Some years ago, before she was promoted, she adopted at least two false identities, one in order to break into a criminal gang operating in east London – Ilford again. We think the aforementioned Lemotov and the leader of this gang are one and the same person and it's the same outfit, but perhaps now with some different members. Lemotov is no more Russian than I am – his father was a market trader born in Romford. Lindersland knew this and also that she had to concentrate on the gang's criminal activities. But she was concerned with his anarchist ideals and that's why we were informed and became involved. This group is dangerous. A couple were arrested last year after a tip-off and explosives and weapons were found in one of their homes. It wasn't publicized as an attack on a government minister had been planned.'

'Do you have any evidence to make you come to the conclusion that it's the same man?'

'A remarkable likeness between several photographs. You'll say that's tenuous but it's all we have.'

There was a short silence and then Patrick said, 'What is the purpose of this meeting?'

'To see you face-to-face and dissuade you from rash behaviour. Richard Daws always thought highly of you, although I understand he sometimes became extremely exasperated by your methods. This was all in my predecessor's day, of course – I've had no first-hand experience. I have read all the relevant files and reports very carefully.'

I had written some of them.

Patrick said, 'I admired and respected Daws. Whatever *anyone* says I shall track down his killer. I intend to start by eliminating Haldane, or not, from the investigation. You said you've read the files but I'll remind you: he was a bent civil servant who was paid by a banker to wreck D12 and the pair of them ended up trying not only to kill Daws but several people associated with him, including Ingrid and me. And as you've just said, he's not right in the head. There's a possibility he's determined to carry on and do what he might think of as finishing the job, with or without the help of Lemotov's group. If so, Lady Rowallen's in great danger.'

'Haldane organized the burning down of your cottage in Devon and kidnapped your young son, I understand.'

'I didn't put that in my report.'

'No, but Daws did. Is it revenge you're after?'

'Not in the way you're thinking. He ought to be put behind bars for the rest of his life.'

'I can't stop you. But it'll probably cost you your job.'

Patrick shrugged and there was a short silence.

'No, all right. I've changed my mind. Go after him. Daws was rather special to us too. But it's unofficial and I shall deny all knowledge of this meeting if you kill him in cold blood or are yourself killed.'

Patrick said, 'I don't think you've been completely honest with me. Someone in my neck of the woods had heard that it was suggested I go after Daws' killer.'

'From whom did you hear that?'

'Someone who can be trusted.'

There was no response to this.

'And Lindersland?' Patrick continued. 'She rang and spoke to Ingrid. Said she didn't know where she was and as far as anyone in the NCA's concerned she's missing.'

'You must appreciate that this is nothing to do with me at all. If I were you I should aim your enquiries at the director of the NCA.' He moved to leave and then said over his shoulder, 'Come to think of it, it would do your CV a power of good if you found the wretched woman.'

'Are others from MI5 or MI6 working on *any* of this?'

'No.' A tight fleeting smile. 'Not now.'

He turned and walked away but paused and said over his shoulder, 'Jules and Harry will take you wherever you want to go.'

'No, thanks,' Patrick said.

But for Patrick baring his teeth in a humourless grin at the two in the taxi, we ignored them and the huge metal gates swung open at our approach. We soon found a more conventional cab and were taken back roughly to where we had started from.

'Is this genuine?' Patrick asked a waiter in the Italian restaurant, showing him the voucher.

'Is the name Gillard?'

'Yes.'

'Indeed, sir. The best champagne in the house and anything you want. Anything!' He lowered his voice. 'There is a special arrangement.'

We were shown to a table discreetly situated in a corner and the champagne was immediately placed before us, opened and poured. The waiter presented us with menus and withdrew.

I said, 'I get the distinct impression despite all the smoke and mirrors stuff from that man that you've been given actual orders to find Daws' killer.'

Patrick pulled a face. 'That bloody dope has given me a headache. Yes, it's a bit like being in LinkedIn. And of course now there's this new accountability mindset the man's terrified of being associated with anything the politicos might regard as unethical.' He picked up his glass. 'We deserve this. Your health, battleaxe.'

'Do you mean you're still working for MI5 – sort of on call?'

'No. But once you've been involved . . .' He added, 'Call it the Daws factor.'

'And – er – salary?'

'Dunno. Probably a sack of spuds at Christmas.'

'He was very cagey about Lindersland.'

'Um.'

'I don't like the idea of her out there somewhere and nobody's . . . *bothering*.'

'I thought you loathed the woman.'

'I do.'

Patrick frowned at me for moment or so – it's well known that men can't understand female logic – and then said, 'We don't know that nobody's bothering. Someone almost certainly is from the NCA.' He eyed the menu.

'Are you going to bother?'

'I . . . might. I'll tell Matherson about that wine bar, though. It'll give him something else to think about.'

'From what we've been told tonight Lindersland's criminal connections were in the course of her job. Whoever was Daws' source of intelligence, especially a very senior officer, should have been aware of it.'

'We'll have to ask Martin Grindley about that.'

'When I can get hold of him. What the hell are you going to tell Greenway?'

'The truth – when the time is right.'

'Next move?' I ventured.

'To eat. I'm famished.'

I had a horrible feeling about this whole business and did not enjoy the meal at all. It persisted the next morning and was reinforced when Patrick, on his way to work after breakfast, obviously distracted and carrying his overnight bag, asked me to do what I had planned – seek out Martin Grindley, let him know what the man said and then, unless I had something else to do, go home.

'D'you want the car?' I called after him as he went away from me down the hotel corridor.

'No, you have it. It's too conspicuous for what I shall be doing.'

I packed, thinking, not rushing, and then, having received a call from DI Barton with an interesting update, made my way down to reception to check out. I had almost reached the counter when I noticed a man hurrying from the entrance's revolving doors, almost tripping over a woman's suitcase in his haste. He came towards me, I felt not because he had seen me but to make an enquiry at the desk. I knew what that was.

'D'you want Patrick?' I asked, he hardly more than an arm's length away from me by this time. Focused on his errand? Desperate?

'Oh,' said Superintendent Matherson. 'I didn't see you standing there.'

'D'you want Patrick?' I repeated. Of course the fool did.

'Is he here?'

'No, he's gone to work. But he's not staying in the building very long.'

'He'd just left. Damn!'

'How did you know we might be here?'

'I asked HR where you stayed when you were in town.'

OK, I thought, fair enough. I said, 'Hasn't he rather given you the impression he doesn't want to see you?'

The man sort of subsided.

'Shall we have coffee?' I suggested. 'Then you can tell me all about it.'

'Look, I'd rather not, if—'

I butted in. 'Right now I'm your only method of contacting him.'

He shrugged and I led the way to the small self-service café just off the atrium. Nothing was to be gained by making an enemy of this man, but that did not mean I had to give him an easy time.

'How's your liaising with Sussex Police getting on?' I asked as we seated ourselves.

Matherson took a deep breath but before he could say anything I pressed on with, 'I seem to recollect that the last time you met DI Barton you told him to sod off.'

'I was interviewing a man in connection with the murder inquiry.'

'Who has subsequently admitted that he was only a front man for the security company that installed the castle's alarm system and had previously managed a betting shop. Tell you all about that, did he?'

'No,' Matherson admitted. 'But I did have an idea he was lying. If you and Barton hadn't interrupted, I—'

'He's also been charged with assault after throwing a mug of coffee over me when we questioned him in his office. Another thing – I had a phone call from Barton a few minutes ago and it appears that there's a definite link between the clients of this company and properties where break-ins have occurred in the past few months. I don't suppose Barton felt bound to apprise you of that after you spoke to him in such a fashion.'

The superintendent tiredly rubbed his hands over his face. 'I don't suppose I've slept properly for a week.'

Diddums, I thought, but said, 'When did Lindersland go missing?'

'Just after we went to Sussex to get the computer. I carried it into her office and then went home for the night. I live in Clapham.'

'Do you know what she wanted the computer for?'

'She said Daws had been working on important matters but didn't explain.'

'Did she give you any idea how she knew that?'

'No.'

'Why the hell didn't you have a search warrant?'

'She seems to think she has carte blanche.'

'Superintendent, she might be a powerful woman but she still has to stick to police protocols.'

'I tried to explain that to her. It didn't seem to penetrate.'

'Are you her official minder?'

'No, she grabbed me to assist when she thought she needed it. I'm supposed to be the NCA's contribution to the castle murders' investigation, which I don't have to tell you is bloody complicated. She doesn't have a minder.'

'So you went home from work that evening and that was the last you saw of her.'

'That's right.'

'No phone calls?'

'No, nothing.'

'Where does she live?'

'She has an apartment in West Kensington, near Olympia.'

'She rang me wanting to talk to Patrick. She said she didn't know where she was and was then cut off. I couldn't return the call.'

'Does anyone else know this?'

By this he meant a police department and I answered

accordingly. 'Patrick would have reported it to Commander Greenway. Patrick's very efficient at what he does.'

My anger must have been apparent for Matherson said, 'I regret hitting him now. I thought that if I got in first . . .'

'He might not take you apart for behaving in such oafish fashion *again* having already bowled you down the stairs?'

'Something like that,' the man responded unhappily.

'And now?' I queried.

'There's a theory she's been grabbed by a London mob she got into in her early police days – this was years ago obviously.'

'Ah.'

'You sound as though you might know something about it.'

'What or who is the source of this information?' I asked, ignoring his remark.

'Just a snout. You're supposed to call them something more polite these days but to me they're just snouts.'

'And you want Patrick to find her.'

'His reputation suggests that he's well qualified to do so.'

'Oh, come off it! You haven't an idea in your head and no one else has either. Everyone's terrified about the bad publicity for the NCA if the story gets out and you're aware that Patrick undertakes assignments in such a way so as not to be on anyone's radar.'

'People *are* working on this.' He added, defensively, 'I was asked to speak to your husband – it wasn't my idea.'

'Well, as you know, Patrick's looking for someone in connection with Richard Daws' murder,' I told him. 'He's bound to give that priority.'

'I think I'm on my knees to you here.'

'Ye gods, surely you can refer to some cop branch in the Met which must know something about this outfit.'

'We have. Apparently there's a bloke in charge of this gang now who calls himself a Russian but isn't.'

'Dimitri Lemotov. He's an anarchist, or was, and they commit crimes to pay the rent and keep themselves in fast food and booze that'll probably kill them long before they get arrested.'

'You don't mince your words, do you? I'm not surprised you get coffee thrown at you.'

'Look, you're panicking. If it's any help to you I'm going to suggest you go back to whichever group's dealing with this and work with them. *With* them. Liaise with DI Barton, having apologised. For all we know there's a connection between the castle murders and Lindersland's disappearance. It could be Lemotov's lot and we have one case here instead of what looks like two or even three. I'll give you the name of the man Patrick's looking for because he might be the real kingpin. It's Nicholas Haldane. He's recently been seen with a man MI5 was watching. This was at an Ilford wine bar in South Street that's opposite a small public park. Don't underestimate Haldane. He looks like the spoof Gestapo officer in *'Allo 'Allo* but there's nothing remotely funny about him.'

'OK,' Matherson muttered, drained his coffee cup and went away, shoulders drooping.

I changed my mind about checking out and took my case back to the room.

EIGHT

That my theory, hastily concocted, as in seriously on the hoof, might make sense only occurred to me a little later. There followed doubts – it hung together nicely but a lot of downright wrong theories often do.

My mobile rang.

'For some reason I'm doing amazingly well this morning,' said DI Barton's voice cheerfully. 'I've more news for you. The so-called consortium that owns the security company only appears to be a name plate on a locked door in a rundown building in Ilford, east London. There are other companies listed there but they're also untraceable. I've got the local nick on it and they're going to break down the door for me. The sergeant I spoke to sounded as though he could do with a good smash-in job.'

'Progress,' I commented.

'I also popped in to see Lady Rowallen and she appears to be much better now the alarm system's sorted out and the new butler's started work. I met him. I didn't know the previous one but from what she said I rather got the impression he might have been a gentleman's gentleman, a sort of Jeeves. This guy's a much tougher cove altogether. But he makes great coffee!'

I thought it was about time I told him that Patrick was looking for Haldane.

'Yes, I've been digging in to him too,' Barton replied. 'There's quite a lot in records about the last time he was involved in criminal activities at the earl's home. It was before I was posted here, of course. There are holes in the info which I assume was due to the MI5 connection.'

'That was because Richard Daws worked for that security service at that time. I should imagine that the only link now as far as Haldane's concerned would be revenge.'

* * *

That afternoon I finally managed to contact the Grindleys, who gave me directions how to find them. This was handy as they now lived on a barge moored at Teddington, on the River Thames. Even with directions it took me a while to locate the *Alice May*, which turned out to resemble a flower show more than a boat. They had mentioned to look out for plants.

'Sorry it's a bit of a walk from where you can leave a car,' said a tall, tubby man who was bald on top and probably in his sixties. 'Martin Grindley. Come aboard.' He held out a hand should I need steadying, there being quite a chop on the river in the stiff easterly breeze.

'If we sit in the stern we'll be out of the wind,' he continued in his rather loud and somewhat affected voice. 'June won't be a minute – she's making some tea. I'll tell her you're here.'

Although aware that this man's name was not actually mentioned in Daws' file, I had driven a convoluted route just in case my movements were being monitored. Who might wish to do so right now was anyone's guess but I always believe in being careful.

There was just enough space for a teak garden table and four chairs on the rear deck, which had an awning over it. With climbing plants in troughs backed by trellis on either side to provide privacy and to act as a windbreak, it was like sitting in a garden room. There was an open view at the stern.

'You mentioned that you were with the NCA,' said Grindley, returning carrying a tray. 'It wasn't even in existence when I was working, although SOCA was. I take it you want some information on a cold case.'

I said, 'Your friend Richard Daws, as he was known professionally, was working on something before he was murdered. It's about that.'

'Terrible business! I hope Sussex Police are pulling out all the stops.'

'They are. I'm without my colleague but he's in the locality and happy for me to talk to you.'

Why had I said this? What was it about this man that I found unsettling?

I continued, 'My problem is that I want to talk to you in private as it concerns very sensitive information.'

'No problem, my dear,' he boomed. 'We'll have tea and a short chat with June and then I'll tell her it's a bit secret and we'll go for a pint. I think The Red Dragon's open all day.'

I began to wonder how I would achieve what I had set out to do without Grindley advertising to the whole of south-west London what it was.

June, though, homely and all smiles, soon sorted it out, telling him to wear his hearing aid as he was shouting. I discovered that she was an artist and painted watercolours of the river that found ready sales with tourists in a local gift shop. Ending up staying far longer than I had intended, I was given a guided tour of their home, actually a double-width narrow boat, and bought a small and charming painting that we could give Elspeth for her birthday.

And, naturally, a little later in the pub, I bought Grindley a pint.

'Fire away,' he said, mercifully quietly, after a couple of gulps of his drink.

'There were files on his computer,' I explained, having shown him my ID. 'No names mentioned but a retired assistant commissioner was mentioned as a source of information about a woman by the name of Marcia Lindersland.'

'Marcia! My word! Yes, that might have been me. Good of him not to drop me in it.' He frowned. 'But now you have.'

'It'll go no further than me and my working partner, unless, of course, this comes to a court of law. But Lindersland removed the computer from the castle before we could delete the files.'

'I expect she wanted to protect herself. Why would you want to delete them anyway?'

'We needed to so she wouldn't know she was under suspicion. The files concerned people Daws thought had criminal connections. But in her case he didn't say what.'

'He was the kind of man who only committed things to paper, or a computer file, if he was a hundred per cent sure they were accurate. She was working for me at the time. It was before I was promoted a couple of times so he probably trusted my judgement.'

'But he was with MI5 in those days. She wasn't within his remit.'

'Umm. I have to tell you that Richard's role was always a

bit blurred at the edges. He knew a lot of people and sniffed gossip out for them. It suited him and he learned a lot of things himself that sometimes gave him the wider picture.'

Yes, he had been described as the tender of all grapevines.

'Marcia,' Grindley continued, 'had infiltrated this gang to the extent of going out with – she actually lived with him – the criminal leading it, a Russian anarchist, or at least, that's what everyone thought at the time. That's why Richard was interested initially – because of him. But then it was discovered he wasn't Russian at all and probably little more than a common criminal.'

'Dimitri Lemotov,' I said.

'Oh, you know about him. Anyway, that's what he calls himself and it's almost certainly a stolen identity. Puts on a phoney accent when it suits him. An absolute poser if you ask me.'

'So there's likely to still be a real Dimitri Lemotov out there somewhere?'

Grindley shrugged. 'No doubt. Getting on with his life, I'm sure. It can't be an uncommon name and I wouldn't be surprised if he's a crook too. Or there's a possibility he's dead and the gang killed him. It's irrelevant now.'

'I'm wondering how she found out that Daws had information on her.'

'God knows – you'd have to ask her that.'

'She's disappeared.'

'Disappeared? Good grief!'

'This is entirely confidential.'

'Of course. Good grief!'

'Where exactly does this gang operate from? All I know is that it's Ilford.'

'Lemotov used to have what I suppose must be called an HQ in a private house there but people like that have got much more careful now, as I expect you're aware. I could probably get the address from a contact I have but I doubt if they still use it and it would be wasting your time. Criminals move around now. The boss might have a base here in the UK but orders are given in emails, texts and phone calls. Modern communications have seen to that. Some even live abroad.'

'So she worked undercover. What as – do you know?'

'Oh, just some female who'd got chucked out of home and was living rough.'

I extracted from him a promise that he would forward the address to me if at all possible and then said, 'I still can't understand why Daws was so bothered about her if he knew she worked for you.'

'She got to be madly in love with the fella.'

'Who, Lemotov?'

'Yes.'

'Did you suspect her?'

'Only of having an affair with a criminal. I thought she was behaving most unprofessionally and might have even joined forces with him – that's why I mentioned her to Richard. Just in conversation, you understand. Lemotov might have turned her head. Nothing personal but that's the trouble with women. I didn't really want them on the job and in my view she should never have been promoted.'

'So male undercover cops have never slept with the enemy?' I queried.

'Oh . . . er . . .'

'Is there anything else about her that might have made you, or Daws, suspicious?' I continued as he floundered.

After a pause, Grindley said, 'That was as far as my reservations about her went and I have to tell you I thought it serious enough at the time. As far as Richard was concerned I reckon there must have been something or he wouldn't have still been working on it, would he? I've no idea what it was although there was a side to her that made me uncomfortable. A bit ruthless – that's it, ruthless.'

I bought him another pint.

My first impression was that talking to Grindley had hardly been an amazing success, having merely introduced a couple of interesting nuances, but at least he could be taken out of the investigation.

Then I sat in the car and really thought about it.

The file in Daws' computer on Lindersland had actually said very little, containing only her career history and a few paragraphs to the effect that she was, in view of information received, suspect. This had to be the tip-off from Grindley, although he was not named, and Daws had gone on to note that further information could be obtained from him. There was no mention of Lemotov.

Something wasn't quite right.

Was Grindley withholding information from me because it reflected badly on him? Was he still in the pub? I had left him there yarning with other men he obviously knew.

Then I realized I had left the watercolour on the boat as June had promised to find something to wrap it in for me.

'He'll be there until almost dinnertime,' she told me when I stepped back on board.

I thanked her for the neat parcel with which I was presented.

'Does the name Marcia Lindersland mean anything to you?' I enquired on a whim as I turned to go.

Her face lost its smile. 'Why do you ask?' she said stonily.

'She's mentioned in something I'm working on, that's all.'

'You'd better come below.' And when we had seated ourselves in the saloon, she continued, 'Is that what you wanted to talk to Martin about?'

I said it was.

'He was besotted with her.'

I could think of nothing helpful to say.

'I understand she worked for him when he was in charge of some undercover operation, which, rightly I suppose, he never really talked about. He sometimes mentioned that she was the best one on his team but I knew that he phoned her whenever it was safe to do so. He might even have had an affair with the woman for all I know when they were sent on training courses.'

'Surely not,' I said quietly but thinking that there was every possibility.

'He certainly went off me for the duration. I endured a horrible time during which he hardly spoke to me at all. And then it was over and we made a fresh start. It was never really discussed but when he retired at fifty he suggested selling the house and buying a boat to live on instead. We had planned to move to the South Coast but we'd been on lots of canal boat holidays over the years and really enjoyed it. I thought it might make things better between us.'

'Did it?'

'Yes, I suppose so. But once something like that has happened it's never the same, is it? I still hate him a bit. And you're probably wondering why I'm telling you all this but I've told no one else and . . . I just had to somehow. Perhaps it's because Martin's been a bit odd lately and I'm worried it's dementia.'

All I could do was commiserate and thank her for the picture.

'Oh, but you did pay me for it,' she said with a smile. Her pleasant face then darkened again. 'I've just remembered something. I overheard a conversation between them one weekend but only because he was shouting – he was going a bit deaf then. He told her to go back to her bloody Russian in bloody Tottenham.' She smiled thinly. 'I think she must have ditched him.'

'Good,' I said stoutly, thanked her again and left.

Tottenham?

Fully expecting not to be able to contact Patrick – he tends to keep radio silence when on a job – I rang him and he answered.

I told him what had just transpired, adding, 'In my view, and I might be quite wrong, he shopped her to Daws, told him she was suspect because she wanted nothing to do with him in her personal life. Daws, at the time, might have thought Lemotov had Kremlin connections but subsequently discovered that he was a British yob and that's why there's nothing about him in the file. There's no knowing whether Lindersland really fell for Lemotov or just said she had in order to rid herself of Grindley's attentions.'

'What did you make of Grindley?'

'His eyes are far too close together.'

Patrick didn't laugh. He takes my unorthodox theories about people seriously and said, 'But is he on the line?'

'I don't think he's clever enough not to be. Just an old-fashioned cop with seriously outdated views about women. His wife's now worried that he's going a bit strange in the head. I did find him a bit peculiar.'

There was a short silence and then Patrick said, 'I'd rather you didn't start poking around in Tottenham.'

'That was my plan,' I fibbed coolly, he just having given me the idea.

'Ingrid . . .' He stopped speaking for moment and then said, 'I'll come with you if you like.'

'That would be medium tolerable,' I told him.

He did laugh then.

'Hit the wall with Haldane then?' I went on to ask.

'Temporarily. I went to his last known address in Roehampton, which as we already knew had been sold, and spoke to an insufferably snobbish couple whose attitude was that a policeman polluted their doorstep. They said they knew nothing about the previous owner of the house except that a neighbour had told them he was in prison, shock, horror, and would I mind going away right now as they were watching tennis on TV.'

I commiserated suitably. Patrick is no snob but ex-lieutenant colonels are not wired to expect rude brush-offs from people who must be regarded as ordinary members of the public.

'Where shall I meet you?' he said.

'There are other developments I need to tell you about.'

'Make it the hotel then or did you check out?'

'No.'

He made no comment on my apparent mutiny.

In our room and after I had related to Patrick what Matherson had said – he had snorted with derision over the regret at hitting him – and DI Barton's latest findings he gave me an update on Dimitri Lemotov. He was wanted in connection with two recent armed robberies committed at small street corner convenience stores in the Woodford area, these latest seemingly solo crimes unless he had had a getaway car somewhere nearby that no one had seen. On both occasions, five weeks apart, the perpetrator had worn a black hood fashioned out of what appeared to be a large woollen sock with holes cut in it for eyes and mouth, the one for the latter inevitably revealing uneven and discoloured teeth with a lot of fillings. On each robbery he had fired the handgun he had recklessly been waving around, smashing wine and spirit bottles in exactly the same fashion.

'Not just the teeth – he has heavily tattooed hands and didn't wear gloves. Therefore easy to identify.' Patrick then added, 'This man is not very bright.'

'You still have to have evidence to prove he's committed the crimes,' I pointed out.

'Agreed. But I spoke to someone in the Met earlier today and they don't think he's an anarchist, or isn't any longer. They have an idea his outfit's been hijacked by people who as well as being serious criminals are stringing him along somehow and merely using him to add to their funds. It's these others the Met are really interested in. I don't want to spoil my colleague's fun and stampede their suspects to all points of the compass but now we're here we need to work on this a bit.'

On reflection I had not thought through what I was going to do on my own. In my working partner's view the quickest and easiest way to track down criminals of what he refers to as the blue-collar variety is to visit the kind of pubs, clubs and other similar places they frequent. He also suggested that we postpone hunting for Lemotov in Tottenham, where it appeared he might live, and instead hang around in Ilford from where the gang was reputed to operate.

The first two nights of doing just that were a complete waste of time.

The third evening we were leaning on one end of the public bar in yet another such establishment in Ilford. In my view this one was the real pits, as although smoking has been banned inside pubs for years now it still had that stale beer and tobacco ambience, enhanced by gusts of stink from the gents' every time that particular door was opened. As I have observed in the past, I cannot understand how British men can drink in such frankly disgusting conditions.

'I don't know how this place survives when so many are closing,' I muttered.

'The beer's all right,' said Patrick. 'And cheap. That's how.'

As on previous nights we had dressed appropriately – he in old jeans, a blue T-shirt that he digs out for decorating at home that has quite a lot of white paint on it that won't come out, a faded denim jacket and the belt he wears for luck that boasts a brass skull buckle with red glass eyes. Most of the effect of low-life, however, was provided by the hunched-over posture and the scowl as he surveyed the rest of the crowd. There is something about him, harking back no doubt to an inglorious and hairy ancestor who was hanged at a crossroads, that makes him occasionally hanker after a fight. I don't unduly worry about this as he is very good at it, but our present lack of progress wasn't exactly helping his mood.

My contribution to the job in hand was represented by equally ancient jeans, a shrunk cotton top and rather a lot of plastic jewellery painted gold that I had bought at a jumble sale held in our village hall. I had scraped my hair back into an untidy ponytail fastened with a primeval-looking glittery object, part of the aforementioned plastic collection.

My phone tinkled the arrival of a text, and, as it is the most natural thing in the world to do anywhere, I read it.

'From Grindley,' I reported. 'With the address here in Ilford that was reckoned to be a sort of HQ for Lemotov's lot. He didn't think they'd be using it now though and would be more mobile.'

'It could still be being used as a crash pad for his mob,' Patrick observed.

On this third evening we were in the fourth pub we had visited since arriving in the town at roughly opening time and he was on his fourth half pint of Marstons Pedigree. Wisely, and certainly regretfully, he hadn't finished the others.

It was now getting on for closing time and I never wanted to see the inside of a pub again.

'Do you know what this man looks like other than his snaggly teeth and tattoos?' I was driven to ask a few minutes later.

'There's an old mugshot in records that's not a lot of use. But I think I'd know him,' Patrick replied absent-mindedly.

After another glutinous period of time had elapsed I ventured, 'Perhaps we should try to find that wine bar where Haldane was spotted. I mentioned it to Matherson but he didn't seem to attach much importance to it.'

Patrick seemed not to have heard what I said, his attention apparently focused, in gaps between the surging clientele, on a gorilla-like, hirsute individual with an impressive beer belly on the far side of the room.

'D'you remember Ricketts?' Patrick then said in a whisper

under cover of nuzzling my ear in a sexy fashion. He turned towards me, his back to the throng.

'Haldane's chief hired thug who called himself Jardine to begin with?'

'That's him over there. He's grown a beard but that doesn't hide the fact that he has part of the middle finger of his left hand missing.'

'Surely not!' I hadn't noticed the damaged digit at the time.

'It was discovered afterwards that he'd bolted before the shooting started.'

'What's the plan then?'

'To tail him.'

Ten minutes later we found ourselves, together with just about everyone else, out in the street. Ricketts had been one of the first to leave, finishing the rest of his drink, and then almost had an altercation with a man on the way out who had been unwise enough inadvertently to block his path. Another man – the one who had been standing next to him – went with him and they hurried off, yanking up the hoods of their sweatshirts against the thin drizzle.

The man who had crossed Ricketts' path grabbed my arm.

'Comin' with me then, darlin'?'

'She isn't and you're drunk,' Patrick said to him. No, snarled.

'Andeeee . . .' another man standing nearby nervously warbled. 'He's bigger than you-ooo.'

In receipt of a smirk, Patrick roared in the face of the first man, 'I never hit stupid drunks!'

He didn't say that. I couldn't write down what he said.

At a careful distance, we followed Ricketts and his friend. No one in our wake decided to have a go at Round Two.

In an undertone, Patrick said, 'What's the address that Grindley's just given you?'

'Fifteen, Haggard Street.'

'Can you find out where it is on your phone?'

'Of course, but I can't do it while marching along like this.'

'I'll steer while you do it.'

He put an arm around me and held me by the elbows to make sure I didn't walk into anything or trip up kerbs. Once, there was an emergency stop when our quarry paused under a streetlamp to light cigarettes, and I was taken in a sudden passionate embrace in a shop doorway by way of concealing our intent. I then had to start all over again on my task as that particular website had not taken kindly to a multiple finger assault on the screen.

Finally, when we had cautiously dropped back so the pair were around thirty yards in front of us, I said, 'As far as I can tell it's about half a mile from the pub, somewhere along here on the right.'

'That's a bit vague,' Patrick complained. 'Aren't you looking at a map?'

'Yes, on a very small screen while I'm on the move,' I retorted.

'Let me look.'

True enough, he had to stop to see it properly.

When we looked up again Ricketts and friend had gone from sight.

'That's the one,' Patrick said, shoving my phone back at me. 'They've turned down the next on the right.'

The houses, semi-detached, were odd-numbered on the left-hand side of Haggard Street, and by the time we arrived and had noted number one, the road was empty but for parked and a couple of passing cars.

'Eighth house along,' I whispered and we carried on walking.

All was dark and quiet at the house, the only sign of recent entry the garden gate slowly swinging closed. We went straight on past and stopped a little further along.

'He's wanted by the police,' Patrick said to himself. 'Decision time.'

NINE

The decision was a difficult one as Ricketts had only been head henchman and it would be crazy to go after him when others who might be in the house could be more important. Even if we called up help there was the risk that not everyone on the premises would be arrested, having escaped.

All this was going through my mind as we stood in the shadow of a small kerbside tree. Another point to be aware of was that it was obvious the police knew about this address, as Grindley had obtained it for us, so perhaps a wait-and-see policy was in operation.

'We'll hang around for a while,' Patrick decided.

We crossed the road and went a short distance away to another tree that had the added advantage of being a bit larger. A vehicle parked right by it would partly conceal us from view.

I did not look at my watch but at least half an hour went by and, except for passing cars and a few pedestrians, nothing moved.

Patrick glanced at his and muttered, 'Sometimes I really fancy a smoke. Give it another ten minutes.'

He had barely finished speaking when three figures appeared on the path leading up to the front door of the house having apparently come from around the side of it, two taller individuals and one shorter. In the illumination from a street light it quickly became obvious from the way they came through the gate that those on the outside were male, neither appeared to be Ricketts, and they had hold of the smaller one in the middle. They approached a parked car nearby.

The person in the middle, a slim girl with long blonde hair, started to struggle.

'No!' she shrieked. 'Let me go! You can't do this! I've done nothing wrong! Please let me go. I swear I won't tell anyone.'

One of the men twisted round and slapped her face, hard. 'You were told to shut up and do as you're told!' he growled.

This had quite the wrong effect as far as the men were concerned as she burst into noisy tears. Distracted, they did not notice Patrick walk across the road and lean on the car to which they were heading, and then gaze at them over the roof of it.

'He wants her,' he said in a harsh voice with a thick mid-European accent.

The three juddered to a standstill.

'Who does?' was all one of them could think of saying.

'Dimitri, you imbecile. Who else could I mean?'

'But—'

'He wants her for himself for a little while. Then he will kill her.'

'But . . . who the hell are you?' the other man blurted out.

'A friend of his. You don't know me. He sent me because people don't argue when I'm around.'

They suddenly realized that they were looking down the wrong end of a handgun.

'Release her,' Patrick ordered. 'And you, Tracy, come with me. Now.'

I held my breath and felt as though my heart had stopped beating. Would she flee if they released their grip on her arms?

'Round here,' Patrick said to the bewildered girl when she found herself freed. 'Quickly!' he barked.

She scuttled around to his side, still sobbing.

'Get back inside,' the two were told. 'Stay there. If you don't you're dead meat as I shall wait for a while.'

They went and as soon as they were out of sight Patrick put an arm around Tracy Finch's shoulders, firmly in case she tried to escape, and walked with her towards the junction with the main road. I shadowed them, my job to watch for any repercussions. None came.

'Please don't let anyone hurt me,' Tracy was begging Patrick when I caught up with them.

'No, you're quite safe,' I assured her.

Following this piece of inspirational thinking on Patrick's part – cops had had nothing to do with it, had they? – we were then presented with the problem of what to do with her. One solution was to take her back to our west London hotel for the night before driving her to Sussex in the morning. She was an important witness. But she might try to escape as soon as our backs were turned. There was no warrant out for her arrest so to take her to a police station where she would be put in a cell if no safe house was available seemed grossly unfair in the circumstances. She was shivering with cold, being very flimsily dressed, and probably from shock and hunger as well, even with my jacket around her shoulders.

In the end we deferred any decisions and took her to a motorway service station on the way back to the city. After telling her the truth: that we were from the police and her only hope of safety was with us, Patrick exacted a promise from Tracy that she would not try to run off. The sight and smell of hot food seemed to clinch this and she had soon demolished a large meal. There was something very naive, if not childish, about this young woman which made me wonder if that was why she had been employed by the security company – another person who could be manipulated, out of their depth, easily frightened.

Patrick did finally contact Sussex Police who promised secure accommodation that was not at the nick. He then pulled strings – in other words involved other police forces – as his credentials allow and it was arranged that a car from the Met would drive Tracy to Horsham. Having made the rendezvous we then went back to our hotel.

'I should have tried to find out if Haldane or Lemotov were in the house,' Patrick said on the way there.

'If you'd asked questions they would have become suspicious,' I told him. 'The important thing at the time was to get Tracy away without any hint that the police were involved.'

'They'll soon find out that the phoney Russian wasn't behind it, though.'

DI Barton was expecting us to arrive mid-morning the following day as I had rung him at a time when I thought he could reasonably be expected to have turned up for work. He had apologised for a slight tardiness in answering the phone, saying that he had encountered a cloudburst on the way, the roads awash, and was just struggling out of his wet bike leathers. He had gone on to say that he had been informed that we had found Tracy Finch as soon as he had walked through the door, was about to arrange for her to be brought to the nick and we were welcome to interview her first as he had a meeting he had no choice but to attend. I reminded him, gently, to tell her mother that she was safe and well.

Patrick, I knew, was still fretting about what he regarded as his failure to establish whether our real targets had been in the house; the likelihood that they could have been literally within reach but not arrested was haunting him. It was a waste of breath to try to convince him otherwise, the main reason for his depression lack of sleep and only having had time for a skimpy breakfast. He is not one to be able to subsist on muesli.

As I drove he did, however, make contact with Michael Greenway to report what had happened, requesting that the commander relay the news to the Met as they may have the house in Ilford under surveillance. If not, he added, it would be a damned good idea if they did.

'I just want to go in there and sort it,' Patrick said to me, still angry with himself after the call.

'We need to talk to Tracy before we do *anything*,' I said.

Barton was on hand when we arrived. 'She's still pretty upset,' he told us. 'I think it would be a good idea if Ingrid chats with her first to put her at ease.'

Patrick gazed upon his battleaxe gravely and I gave them both a big smile. Of course I would.

'Oh, and nothing was found in that room in the semi-derelict building in Ilford,' Barton added. 'Completely empty, just layers of dust and dead flies. Funny sense of humour – somebody said they'd fingerprinted them.'

Tracy had been provided with a thick cardigan into which she was huddled although the morning, and the interview room, was quite warm. At Patrick's suggestion I left the door slightly ajar, partly in order for him to hear what was being said as he was standing just outside, and also to show the girl that she wasn't banged up.

'You were with that bloke last night,' she said in little more than a whisper when I had introduced myself and told her who I worked for. 'He really, really scared me.'

'Yes, but the idea was to intimidate the others into letting you go. He'll talk to you in a short while.'

'Look, I haven't done anything wrong,' Tracy whimpered. 'And shouldn't I have a solicitor or something?'

'You're not under arrest and haven't been cautioned or charged with anything.'

'Oh.'

Why hadn't somebody already made that clear to her?

'Would you like your mother to be here?' I asked.

'No! A cop asked me that. No. She's always said I'd get into real trouble one day and now I have.'

'All it looks like from where I'm sitting is that you got in with the wrong crowd.'

'They came and grabbed me, you know. When I'd left Mum's and was on my way round to Susie's place.'

'How about you telling me the story right from the beginning?'

'I'll still get into trouble. I knew they were crooks almost straight away but was too scared to say anything.'

'Would you like something to eat first? Some tea?' This young lady was perfectly fit to be questioned as long as it was done with care.

She settled for coffee and buttered toast with jam and, after a few minutes during which I got her to talk about the night life in Brighton – 'They're all gay, you know, it's epic' – the refreshments arrived, including two extra mugs of coffee.

Patrick put down the tray, unloaded it, put it somewhere else, closed the door and seated himself with a happy sigh. 'Good morning,' he said to Tracy.

She mumbled a greeting and then in the manner of someone who really needed to get something straight in her head, said, 'So you're nothing to do with this Dimitri character?'

'Only insofar as I'm going to arrest him,' Patrick replied with a smile. 'Take no notice of me and tell Ingrid the story right from the start.'

Giving him a dubious look as though he might suddenly shapeshift into the scary figure of the previous night – did she wonder if he was a bent cop? – she began, 'I hadn't been able to get a job before. I didn't do very well at school but was sort of OK with IT and stuff like that. And games and PT, only that wasn't much use. Then I saw this job advertised in the *Argus*, our local rag. Girl Friday wanted, it said. I've never been exactly sure what that means but it was dogsbody stuff actually. I didn't care to begin with as it was a job. Money! Not many of my friends have jobs.'

'You went for an interview at the security firm's office near Brighton railway station?' I enquired when she paused to eat some toast.

'Um,' she said through a mouthful. Then, 'With Harding. I should have walked out there and then as he's disgusting. Like something creepy in a soap – a bloke who looks at dirty pictures on the Internet.'

I felt like telling her that it was highly likely she was bang on target but thought better of it.

'But it was a job,' she continued sadly after a sip of coffee. 'It meant so much to me right then. And I got it. Now I'm beginning to wonder if I got it because they knew I was thick.'

'No, I expect it was because you were young and inexperienced.'

'But I soon got to know that something dodgy was going on, which makes me just as bad as them for staying there.'

Softly, Patrick said, 'It was just as well you did stay and said nothing as the people involved with this are very dangerous.'

'So they'll get me now – again,' Tracy responded dully.

'No, you'll be given police protection. One thing: at no time when we visited the company's offices did we see you there. Why was that?'

'I'd been off sick with the flu. Well, a bad cold really. I was trying to work out how I could get away from the disgusting place for good.'

This tied in with what we had already been told.

'What made you first suspect that something illegal was going on?' I enquired.

'Jason told me. He said he'd been told to mess up people's security systems and it was easy to see the reason behind it – so people could break in. He walked out. Another guy was working there when I started but he walked out a fortnight later. Jason's all right, I like him.'

I glared at my working partner in an effort to prevent him

from telling her that Whitley had been murdered and was met with a Botticelli angel lookalike. OK, he wouldn't.

'And there was another bloke,' Tracy went on, having dealt with more toast. 'I'm feeling much better for having had this.' She buried her nose in the coffee mug.

'Another bloke?' I prompted when she appeared to have gone off into a daydream.

'Yeah, just trying to think who he was supposed to be. Some kind of boss man, I suppose. He came round just the once but that was enough. Scared me silly. Said he hoped I would follow instructions. He didn't say "or else" but might just as well have done by the way he spoke to me. I never got to know his name.'

'What did he look like?'

'The opposite to Harding, who's fat, sweaty and red in the face. He was much thinner and his clothes were old fashioned – a black suit that was even worse than the stuff my grandad wears.' And then, realizing that we wanted a bit more information, went on, 'His face was dead looking, especially his eyes.'

'Glasses?' I queried.

'Yes, those metal-rimmed ones that make some blokes look like serial killers.' She actually shivered. 'He was like death warmed up really. Kept in a cupboard overnight and switched back on again in the morning.'

An absolutely perfect description of Nicholas Haldane.

'D'you know why he turned up at Brighton?' Patrick asked.

'No, he went in Harding's office and they spoke quietly. I think Harding was scared of him too.'

I said, 'Did Dimitri turn up at Brighton?'

'Not that I know of. I'd never met him until . . .'

'Until?' Patrick prompted.

'I don't know why I said that really,' Tracy muttered.

She did.

He let that go for a while. 'The name was never mentioned?'

'Not at work. I heard them talking about him when I was taken to the house in Ilford. It's his house, they said.'

'Who were "they"?'

'A big ugly bloke with a beard called Billy and his pal Vince.

They grabbed me on my way to Susie's, said they were from the police and I was in danger. I didn't believe them but they pushed me into a car and took me to London.'

'That wasn't who brought you out of the house last night.'

'No. Those blokes lived in the house but I don't know their names. They never spoke and I didn't want to speak to them. They slept during the day and either loafed around at night and drank or went out drinking. Always stank of booze and there were bottles everywhere.'

'Any idea where they were taking you?'

'No, but I had an idea they were going to kill me.'

Patrick said, 'Yet, before that, you ran off when Harding was arrested, went home, packed a suitcase and headed for a friend's house. Why did you not go to the police then with your story? You must have been really glad that the law had caught up with what was going on.'

'I thought the crooks, the dead-looking man, would send people to get me first to stop me talking.'

'Did you receive money over and above your salary?'

'No.'

'I know that Harding's a creep but he did say that you were part of the pressure against him and, in his words, "she keeps tormenting me about it". I suggest you were given extra money for doing things like that.'

Tracy tossed her head. 'Perhaps I did. He deserved it.'

'How did you know he'd been picked up by the police if you were off sick?'

'Someone rang me on my mobile.'

'Who?'

'I don't know. Just a man's voice. It might have been the bloke who runs the coffee bar across the street. I think he likes me.'

'How did he know your number? Had you given it to him?'

Tracy went a little pink. 'Yes.'

'Your mother seemed to think you'd gone back to work after being ill.'

'No, I was at Susie's house. We were talking about me leaving the job. I dashed home and got some more of my stuff.'

'Was there anyone else at the Ilford house except you and the four men who went in and out?'

'No, not then.'

'Not when?'

'When you got me away.'

'Who was there other times?'

'Just a few other blokes. They sort of drifted in. Perhaps they got paid. I tried not to look at them in case they thought I fancied them or something.'

'Did you see the dead-looking man there?'

'No.'

'What else did you do for extra money?' Patrick went on imperturbably.

'Nothing. I didn't do anything for extra money.'

He folded his arms. 'Look, I'm very good at knowing when people aren't telling the truth.'

'I am telling the truth.'

'You're not.'

She looked at me appealingly. 'Tell him I'm not lying.'

'I can't,' I replied. 'Please cooperate.'

'May I see your hands?' Patrick requested.

Reluctantly she placed them on the table, palms up. The tips of several fingers looked red and sore. Patrick mimed at her to turn them over and, even more reluctantly, she did. The injuries were worse on the backs: scabs on badly grazed knuckles, a nail torn down to below the quick that had been filed as short as possible.

'How did this happen?' Patrick asked.

'I tried to escape, climbed out of the window of a bedroom they shut me in. But they caught me.'

'This isn't that recent,' he observed, 'and I can assure you that, having once been in the army, I'm fully familiar with this kind of thing. Tracy, it's so important that you tell the truth because by not doing so you're protecting serious criminals. If you were threatened with violence, or worse, if you didn't do as you were told then a court will take that fully into consideration.'

She snatched her hands away out of sight and burst into tears. I gave her a few tissues from my bag and we waited patiently while she recovered a little. Nobody was going to shout at her.

'But I did do it for money,' Tracy finally managed to say and then sobbed afresh. After about half a minute she blurted out, 'Harding gave me two hundred pounds in cash.'

Patrick executed a triumphant thumbs up – the girl had her face buried in her hands – and whispered in my ear, 'Got the greasy bastard!' Then he continued, 'Let me guess, you and a couple of others drove out into the countryside one night where you went on foot over fields and then up a bank into a garden. After going down a steepish slope you were then required to stand on someone's shoulders and climb the rest of the way up an ivy-covered stone wall. You were carrying a rope with a grappling iron of some kind on the end that you had to hook over the stone ledge by a wooden hatch in the wall. Although you were lightweight and that's why you were chosen, the ivy tore away and you ended up suffering those injuries.'

He had not been halfway through saying this before she removed her hands from her face and stared at him, aghast.

'Am I right?' he asked her.

'How can you possibly *know* all that?' she said in an appalled shriek.

'I'm a great fan of Benedict Cumberbatch.'

After a pause, she said, 'I didn't know they were planning to attack someone. I promise I didn't.'

'So you didn't see any weapons in the car.'

'No, and it was dark.'

'What on earth did you think they were going to get up to?'

'I tried not to think about it. All they'd said was that they wanted me to help them get into an old warehouse. Nothing else, and they'd take me back home afterwards. Look, please, I couldn't not do it, he was—'

'Who?' Patrick whispered when she clammed up.

'Just, just a . . . bloke.'

'Please tell me.'

'I can't.'

'Was it Dimitri?'

She just stared at him, her eyes brimming.

'He threatened you if you said a word to anyone,' he suggested.

I could easily imagine Katie sitting there, dragged into this kind of situation by befriending the wrong people, told a pack of lies and having a wad of notes waved under her nose . . . Towards buying a horse perhaps, for a riding holiday . . .

Tracy nodded. 'He said he and all the other men would rape me until I was dead. And when you turned up last night and said . . .' She cried again.

'Oh, God,' Patrick said quietly. 'I'm so sorry.'

Around a quarter of a minute later or so Tracy peeped at him through her fingers. 'But you couldn't have known,' she said with staggering generosity and after a big sniff.

'No.'

'His other name is Lemo-something. He bragged that he was Russian. I didn't believe him – he's as common as dirt.'

'Lemotov?' I offered, really loving her thinking.

'Yes, I think that's what he said.'

'Had you seen the other man in the car before?' I went on to ask.

'They had hoods on. I only knew it was Dimitri from his voice. I lied. I did see him at the house. That's when he . . .' She couldn't go on.

'Do you know if he actually lives at the house sometimes?'

'No.'

'Did you see a woman there?'

'No.'

Patrick took a deep breath. 'Forgiven me?'

'Yes,' Tracy said with the smallest smile.

'So you waited outside, standing in the bottom of the moat and—'

'Moat!'

'Yes, it was a castle, not a warehouse.'

'They had little torches but it was really dark and they put a hood over my head too. From the smell I reckon it was made out of a horrible old sock and the eyeholes weren't exactly where my eyes were. I had to keep moving it to see.'

'Go on.'

'I stood on the other bloke's shoulders and climbed up and put the hook thing on the end of the rope over the ledge. Then he moved suddenly and I fell off. But they didn't care, just tied the other end of the rope around my waist and left me there.

All the wind had been knocked out of me and I'd bashed my hands on the wall as I fell.'

'And?'

'Dimitri climbed up the rope and sawed at the door, or whatever it was, and after a bit they went in. Ages and ages went by and I heard two shots and then another one. Not close by but in the building – er, castle – somewhere. Quite quickly they came back, slammed back the door thing, threw down the hook and almost dragged me back to the car. And swearing! They'd forgotten I was tied to the rope and the hook kept catching in everything really hurting me. The other man said he'd wring my neck if I didn't get a move on. I had to tell him what the problem was. Talk about stupid!'

'You heard him speak then.'

'Yes, he had an American accent.'

'I'm so glad we got you out of there,' Patrick said.

'But they lied to me, didn't they?' Tracy said, getting upset again. 'They didn't take me home, they took me back to that house.'

'Without stopping?'

'Yes. No! I've remembered now. I was hurting all over, especially my hands. They were bleeding everywhere so I wasn't taking any notice really. We parked outside another house first and Dimitri got out and went in. He stayed for what seemed like ages and then reappeared and got back in the car.'

'Where was this house, Tracy?'

'I really don't know. Sorry. It was dark and everywhere in London looks the same to me.'

'Do you remember any road signs?'

'There were millions of them.' Her eyes welled up again. 'I was crying.'

'No landmarks?' I queried.

She pondered for a few moments and then said, 'A big sports stadium, all lit up. That's why I noticed it.'

'Please think carefully. Was anything written on it?'

'Tottenham? Oh, that's a football club, isn't it?'

We questioned her a little further but she could remember nothing about the house they had parked outside other than it had a big Christmas tree in the front garden.

TEN

After their incursion into Hartwood Castle we had contacted the New York Police Department about Irvine Baumgarten and Clancy Elferdink, giving their descriptions. We had heard nothing. Patrick fired off another email with the news that the NCA was now fairly sure the pair were involved with serious crime in the UK and we urgently needed details of them regarding possible criminal records. But how on earth had the Americans linked up with Lemotov, if indeed it wasn't just a fantastic coincidence and the man Tracy had heard speak wasn't one of these men?

'Harding lied when he said he'd never met Haldane, didn't he?' I said. 'Tracy said he came to the office.'

'He lied about quite a few things,' Patrick replied. 'About giving her the two hundred pounds for a start.'

DI Barton had had no choice, after talking to Tracy Finch himself, but to charge her with being an accessory to murder. In a phone call to Patrick he had gone on to state what we already knew: that she could not be released for her own safety and was a very important witness. Due to the fact that it appeared she had been virtually dragged, under false pretences and threats, to the scene of the crime, the charges could eventually be dropped if nothing else came to light. Barton had asked when she had been given the money by Harding and she had replied that it had been afterwards and, unless someone else had removed it, it was still locked in her desk drawer at work. She hadn't wanted it; it was connected with some kind of violent crime. The DI had promised that he would send someone to speak to her mother.

He had finished by saying that these latest developments had encouraged him to arrange to question Harding again. I doubted whether he would obtain any really useful further information from him, except perhaps mobile phone numbers if they hadn't already been deleted. Harding had merely been a stooge.

The security company remained closed.

Although Patrick had alerted the Met immediately and they had raided the house in Ilford, they found precisely nothing and no one, the whole place having been stripped of anything remotely valuable. The furniture and fittings remaining were little more than rubbish. A forensics team had been sent in; the whole place being filthy and likely to contain a wealth of fingerprints and also, no doubt, DNA.

We had returned to London where Patrick reported to Greenway, including our being hijacked by MI5. The commander had been incandescent about this and had sworn to complain at the highest level. Patrick had had to use all his charm to try to talk him out of it and had finally resorted to threatening that if he did he wouldn't report everything that happened in future. Some things are better left off the record.

News came from the United States remarkably quickly this time, with apologies for the delay, the reason being that enquiries had been complicated and involved other agencies. Irvine Baumgarten, the issue outside marriage, as he was described, of Samuel Zettinger, was Daws' very distant relation, his only surviving relative. Records showed that his mother had been Martha, who'd been married to Jake Baumgarten, and the boy had been brought up in that household. Irvine was now a pastor in a small town in Wyoming, had married the local schoolteacher and they had eight children. There was no criminal record – not even a speeding ticket.

Clancy Elferdink, on the other hand, was a one-time attorney who had represented top mobsters – this the wording used – in cases where witnesses and jury members had been intimidated and even killed. It had been discovered that he had several aliases and there was a warrant out for his arrest due to his now known association with criminals and criminal activity. He had been thrown out of the American Bar Association and it was thought he had left the country using a false passport.

There were no known links between the two men.

A couple of hours later photographs were emailed to Patrick when we were in his office and I was about to leave to go home for the weekend, leaving Patrick behind to carry on with his search for Haldane. He was still of a mind that the disappearance of Marcia Lindersland was not his problem and I couldn't really blame him.

'As we suspected earlier, it's not the Baumgarten we've met,' Patrick said, gazing at the computer screen in front of him.

I looked for myself and beheld a slim, middle-aged American of clean-living appearance wearing clerical dress with his folksy wife, cute kids and fluffy dog – everyone, even the dog, smiling. The photograph had come from a local newspaper, the occasion being the town's centenary celebrations, and had been taken eighteen months previously.

'It is Elferdink, though,' I said, the chubby face of the so-called lawyer seeming to stare accusingly back at me.

'The man calling himself Baumgarten is definitely a phoney then and his sidekick's a crook.'

'But what's the link? How come these people are associated with Lemotov? Or even Haldane?'

'My theory's still that Haldane's the link. He's the type to burn for revenge and could have undertaken research into Daws' ancestry. He might have done it years ago and found that there was only the one relative who wasn't likely to live for much longer. There was then the snag of discovering the existence of Baumgarten, who was a priest and highly unlikely to want to become involved in the murder of an English aristocrat. But through heaven knows what dodgy contacts, Haldane could have turned up Elferdink, who's probably always ready for anything like that. All they had to do was manufacture another Baumgarten, hire whichever honchos they needed and plan to split the proceeds. They've committed the crime but the rest has gone wrong due to their incompetence and ignorance of the English inheritance system. On top of which Harding's been arrested, we rescued Tracy and she appears to be telling all she knows.'

I said, 'You may be right but I'm finding it difficult to believe that Haldane failed to research the rules of our inheritance system.'

'But he's an arrogant bastard, isn't he?'

'Whether you're right or wrong I'm worried what they might do now.'

'I'll inform Barton immediately in case they turn up in Sussex again.'

'And Pamela?'

Patrick thought about it. 'Well, her bodyguard ought to be told.'

'Then she should.'

'Yes, you're probably right. Not a lady to keep things from.'

'I think we should go there first and then I'll decide whether I'm going home for the weekend.'

'A whim, O oracle?'

'No, Haldane gives me the horrors.'

Superintendent Matherson rang me just as we were leaving, saying he was at HQ and had some news. When I told him that I was also in the building he asked if I could meet him in the canteen in ten minutes.

'He doesn't know you're here,' I said to Patrick when I had agreed to this. 'Perhaps you'd be so good as to refrain briefly in pursuing your war of attrition against him.'

My husband clicked his heels together and gave me a comic opera salute.

Matherson was huddled around a mug of liquid that from its appearance could have been tea, coffee or the run-off from a silage pit. Judging by the way he performed a nervous shimmy when we sat down at his table he had not noticed our entry, but in all fairness he did have his back to the door. I felt driven to apologise for startling him.

'I arranged for a low-key raid on that wine bar in Ilford last night,' he began without further preamble, making a point of speaking only to me. 'By that I mean we didn't smash down the door in the early hours when they were supposed to be closed. I was told they hardly ever are but we went in at just after eleven p.m. The excuse was drugs as it's been successfully raided before. We found a known dealer who was carrying and duly arrested, and I questioned the manager about his customers. I showed him a mugshot of Haldane. He owns the place – bought it several months ago.'

'Congratulations,' Patrick said, obviously meaning it.

Matherson acknowledged this with a brief and chilly glance in Patrick's direction. He then went on, 'I reckon that was about the time he was released from prison. It could follow that he acquired that outfit and could have bought, or bought into, the Brighton security company at about the same time.'

'More likely the latter,' I said. 'He's only been out of prison for four months and Harding had been working there for around six.'

'Better than that,' Matherson continued, 'is that I'd taken the precaution of having a full search warrant and in a locked store room that the manager insisted was nothing to do with him we found a quantity of stolen property: computers, antiques, jewellery and stuff like that. I've had no time to contact Barton about it yet but reckon it could be the proceeds of burglaries in his neck of the woods following the security systems of properties there being buggered up by the technician who ended up being murdered.'

'That's an incredible breakthrough,' I enthused and a smile actually cracked the man's somewhat rustic features. 'Did this manager know where Haldane can be found?'

'He said he didn't but I don't believe him. I threatened him with the National Crime Agency.'

'In the shape of?' I gently prompted.

A thumb jerked in Patrick's direction. 'Him.'

Whereupon Patrick started to laugh. He has a very infectious laugh and I found myself grinning broadly. Others in the room turned, smiling, to look at us, at which point Matherson too began to chuckle and amazingly accepted the hand that Patrick offered him. The two ended up slapping one another on the shoulder.

'Is he under arrest?' Patrick enquired finally.

'Just taken in for questioning,' Matherson answered. 'Which as you know can only be for a certain length of time. He's at Ilford nick on suspicion of handling stolen property – has a previous conviction for being a fence.'

'And the wine bar's been closed?'

'Yes, it has.'

'I will talk to him if nothing's achieved fairly quickly. I suggest that you let your Ilford colleagues get on with it meanwhile and apply to hold him for longer if necessary. Ingrid and I are concerned what Haldane's next move might be and are on our way to Hartwood to check on security. I'll be free after that.'

Patrick then went on to give the superintendent the information

Tracy Finch had provided us with, ending by asking if there was any news of Marcia Lindersland.

'No, and I reckon they'll soon find a body,' Matherson replied gloomily.

'D'you have her address handy?'

He wrote it down in my notebook from memory.

'You've been there?' Patrick asked.

'Half the bloody Met's been there. I understand they're dragging a pond in a park that's not far away from her place right now.'

'How do we get in?'

A couple of keys on a ring with a red tally was produced from the top pocket of his jacket with the warning, 'Don't lose them; I don't have another set.'

'Where did these come from?'

'The residents leave spares at security in the block where she lives in case of emergencies.'

'Do we need to ask further permission from anyone?'

'No, I'll tell my contacts you're going to have a look round.'

'By the way, what happened to that computer?'

'I think they're still trying to discover the password.'

'No, I don't think she's at the bottom of a pond,' Patrick said, answering a question I hadn't asked him.

'She could be in Tottenham,' I offered.

'Could be. And someone must know where Lemotov lives.'

Records didn't, however.

Other than this brief exchange we said very little on the journey to Sussex.

Christopher, the new minder-cum-butler, answered the door. We had made a point of going to the formal entrance at the front of the private wing as Patrick wanted to meet him. We beheld a fair-haired man of medium height, probably in his mid- to late-thirties, who looked extremely fit.

'With Lady Rowallen's permission I engaged a local craftsman and his son to replace the rotten hatch in the outer wall,' Christopher told us as we walked up the main staircase with him. 'It's been done in green oak and is around five inches thick. I reckon it'll withstand anything short of artillery.

The door furniture, the hinges and lock, have to be done to heritage specifications and that will take a while so there's a temporary bar and padlocks on the outside and bolts to be fitted on the inside while they're made. I think Her Ladyship's going to leave the bolts in place whatever anyone tells her about authenticity.'

'Good man,' Patrick murmured. 'Any dodgy visitors?'

'Yes, yesterday. A man called saying he represented the security company who put in the system that had been tampered with. He said he wanted to apologise to Lady Rowallen and make amends.'

We reached the wide area at the top of the stairs.

'I sent him packing and informed Detective Inspector Barton,' Christopher continued. 'I understand they're going to increase patrols of their area cars locally.'

'What did this man look like?'

'Like something that might haunt the cellars, sir.'

'If you so much as catch a glimpse of him in the locality again please call me immediately.'

'Oh, thank you for coming!' Pamela cried on emerging from her sitting room. 'Christopher, it's almost lunchtime but I'd love some of your wonderful coffee and I'm sure Patrick and Ingrid would too.'

'There's been progress,' Patrick said to her when we had seated ourselves. 'We now know who killed your husband and Jordon and there are warrants out for their arrest.'

'Oh, dear,' Pamela whispered. 'But it is good news, of course.'

'And until they're apprehended I would like you to take Christopher with you every time you go out. Every time, without exception. I shall give him the handgun that's in a drawer of the desk in the study and make sure he familiarizes himself with it before we go. He won't get into trouble as he'll be acting under my orders.'

I sincerely hoped this would wash, as the saying goes.

'I didn't know Richard had a gun! Even take Christopher into the garden with me?'

'I'd rather you didn't just wander around the garden.'

'Oh dear,' Pamela said again.

'And those Americans *are* phoneys. And criminals.'

'I think we all knew that, didn't we? What about that dreadful woman?'

'She's disappeared.'

'Good!'

Amanda having gone back to university, Helga, a smiling Valkyrie in chef's clothing, had taken her place in the kitchen. She presented us with warm vegetable quiche and various salads, followed by homemade ice cream. Afterwards, Patrick and Christopher went off into the woodland with the SIG Sauer handgun and pieces of a large, torn-up cardboard box to use for target practice. Christopher proved not to be a particularly promising shot, but Patrick at least ended up satisfied that he could safely use the weapon in an emergency.

'I'm most reluctant to go,' Patrick said to me quietly as we were leaving late that afternoon and were crossing the entrance hallway, having said we would let ourselves out. 'They're still very vulnerable. Haldane – and from what Christopher told me earlier I'm sure it was him yesterday – or Lemotov, whoever, could rig up someone to look like a postman or some other kind of delivery bod in order to gain entry and Christopher's hardly likely to answer the door with the gun in his hand.'

'Pamela's a wealthy lady,' I pointed out. 'She can hire someone else as back-up on a temporary basis.'

'Who would come at such short notice?'

'Terry Meadows.'

'He'd probably feel he ought to do it for nothing.'

'Let *them* sort that out.'

Patrick went back upstairs and Terry was contacted immediately, Pamela insisting on paying him a fee. He promised that he would come over as soon as he had tied up a few ends at work. This left me wondering, as it was the start of the weekend, if this would risk domestic discord, but it wasn't really any of my business.

I too abandoned going home for the weekend. The decision was a difficult one as I wanted to see the children and always feel guilty about the added pressures on Carrie and Elspeth and John when we're away. Knowing that there is a very efficient routine in place – for example, Matthew and Katie always have

dinner with their grandparents on Friday evenings – did not
make it any easier.

'Lindersland's place?' I queried, having informed Patrick
of my intention.

'I always have this yearning to find something that the Met's
missed,' he said.

'Look, she hasn't just locked herself in the loo.'

'Some clue as to Lemotov's address,' he corrected, straight-
faced, turning the key in the ignition of the Range Rover.

It was approaching dusk by the time we arrived in West
Kensington and we agreed that we would have a quick look
round the flat and return for a proper search in the morning.
Our hotel was only a short distance away.

Lindersland's apartment was in a newish modern development in a side street off the Hammersmith Road. There was
an entry system that entailed us having to summon a security
man. He barely glanced at our warrant cards and then directed
us towards the lifts, telling us that we needed the top floor.

'Heaven knows who he's let in,' Patrick grumbled as we rode
upwards.

'As usual, I urge caution,' I said.

'Too right. But let's think about it for a minute. The whole
thing simply doesn't make sense. Why has she disappeared?
Why would Lemotov want to kidnap her? What good would it
do him? No ransom has been demanded so far as we know.
Why would she abandon her job and go to him? Was she under
some kind of duress to do so?'

'Martin Grindley said she was madly in love with him.'

We arrived at the top floor.

'But you thought she might have said that to get rid of him
– Grindley, I mean.'

'It's only a guess. The woman's probably a thousand miles
from Lemotov.'

Having noted that we needed to turn left down a corridor to
reach the number of the flat we wanted, Patrick stopped and
said, 'Have a go at another theory. As I've just said, everything
we have already just doesn't add up.'

'I'll do that when I've had a look round her home.'

Before we went right in Patrick walked around very cautiously. In the past we have come across nasty explosive surprises more than once in premises we have searched. Everything here, though, seemed normal.

I decided that the place hadn't been burgled – it was just that the police had looked everywhere for clues as to her possible whereabouts. While it was true that nothing appeared to be damaged they hadn't replaced stuff in drawers but just dumped them on the nearest flat surface or even the floor. Piles of good art and travel books removed from shelves had been so carelessly placed as to avalanche into untidy heaps.

'She'll go mad when she sees this,' I muttered to myself, going into one of the two bedrooms.

This proved to be the one – a double – that Lindersland herself used. In here too thoughtless cops had spread her possessions everywhere, even her underwear. Seemingly they had given up on the dressing table, incorporated in a row of fitted wardrobes that filled one end wall, as the drawers had been pulled open and only bore the signs of a swift rummage. Perhaps the sight of ladies' razors and similar highly personal effects had defeated whoever it was. There were a few items of cheap jewellery, bangles and pendants mixed up with the rest in one drawer, possibly gifts as they didn't look quite her style.

Patrick switched on a light somewhere in another room. 'Found anything?' he called.

'No. But she's on the pill.'

'Must be Lemotov then.'

'Somehow I don't think so.'

He came into the room. 'How's that?'

'I simply cannot believe she's gone back to him willingly unless she's regarding him as unfinished business and is hell-bent on getting him behind bars. She appears to be a perfectionist so might regard his still being at large as professional failure on her part. She's also fastidious. Lovely underwear, beautiful and expensive clothes. That man simply isn't her scene, if he ever was.'

'And?' Patrick prompted when I paused for thought.

'Grindley told me that when she was on his team she worked undercover as a woman living rough. Going on from what I've just said, she may well have done it then but wouldn't now. She has a career a lot of women would envy. You asked me for a theory and it's that Lemotov has nothing to do with her disappearance at all.'

Patrick frowned. 'She obviously has a boyfriend.'

'Not necessarily. She might just believe in being prepared.'

'Who else then?'

'I still have a funny feeling about Martin Grindley.'

'Shall we come back in the morning?'

OK, he thought I needed to sleep on it.

ELEVEN

A night's rest did not result in my changing my mind, although I was looking forward to a daylight search of the apartment for any further ideas. We were having a quick breakfast when Patrick's mobile rang.

'Terry?' I queried at the end of the call, having heard Patrick promise to go somewhere immediately.

'No, Christopher. He's taken over walking the dogs early morning for Pamela. They both take them out late afternoon and spotted a car parked in a farm track near the southern boundary. He's not absolutely sure but thinks the man in the front passenger seat was the same one who called at the castle the other day. They drove off at speed when they saw someone approaching.'

'Whoever it was hasn't been positively identified as Haldane,' I observed.

'I know but I'm a bit worried by their behaviour. He's worried. He said Terry annoyed him a bit by making a joke of it and suggested loading the falconet and, as it's quite small, running it out on the ramparts.'

'That's exactly the sort of thing Terry would say.'

Patrick finished his coffee. 'Yes, God knows how he thought they'd get it up there and we know him better than Christopher does. I'll go back. D'you want to do the proper flat search and let me know if you find anything? I've established that there are no hazards.'

I agreed. We arranged that he would stay if he thought it necessary and inform Barton with a request for an extended police presence, again if it was thought necessary.

It was decided that Patrick ought to have the Range Rover this time so I caught a taxi to the apartments where Lindersland lived, or had lived if she was indeed at the bottom of that pond. I felt a bit ashamed that I did not care one way or the other about this, but what had she ever done for me except seriously frighten an elderly friend and fail to prevent a subordinate from knocking my husband to the ground?

I was fully aware that people like Lindersland do not have address books that they leave lying around. That was the habit of previous generations before the days of smart phones or computers – those who weren't spies and government agents, that is. These days a large proportion of older people do have mobile phones and devices like iPads – my mother-in-law does – but she still writes down people's addresses. She doesn't trust the modern electronic age and, frankly, I think she has a point. Hackers and viruses apart, these things can die on you.

Lindersland then would either commit important addresses – personal ones, that is – to memory or have them in her phone, neither of which was available to me right now. Sensitive work-related information would be stored in her computer at work or in paper files in a safe.

I wandered from room to room, my thoughts completely adrift. There was one largish living room that overlooked the rear of a hotel, a kitchen/diner of minuscule size, then two bedrooms and a bathroom in which one could not have even swung the proverbial cat. Like her office, there was nothing here that gave a hint of her character, no family photos, pictures of pets, nothing. It was as if this living space was merely a room in a hotel.

Looking at the same dreary view from the spare bedroom window I saw a row of garages. Did she have a garage? It seemed unlikely as there were only the two keys for the front door on the ring, one of which, the security man had wearily told us, also opened the main door of the building.

No, my mind sort of waffled, addresses weren't kept in garages. Neither of the keys were the right sort for a garage anyway.

'This is stupid,' I said out loud. 'I didn't think she was with Lemotov yesterday, I still don't today, so why am I wasting my time here?'

I had glanced at the keys that were in my hand and now looked again, this time at the writing on the red tally.

The Red Dragon, Teddington. The key rings had been for sale on the bar.

True to my mission, I had a last quick look through the piles of books on the floor and then, more carefully, at paperwork spread across the sofa. There were receipts from fashion shops locally, one from Shrewsbury – a family home or holiday cottage? Plus the usual council and income tax stuff that everyone has at home. Again, nothing useful.

By the time I got to the houseboat at Teddingon the Grindleys had just finished lunch. There was a certain tension in the air and they didn't offer me anything. As I had bought myself a coffee and a sandwich and eaten it sitting on a seat on the riverside this was perfectly all right, but the situation was interesting.

Martin Grindley seemed agitated and his colour was rather high. His wife, June, on the other hand, appeared subdued and pale. They had had a row.

'What can I do for you?' Grindley snapped.

I decided to chuck petrol on their embers and produced the keys. 'These are the keys to Marcia Lindersland's flat,' I said. 'As you know, she's disappeared.'

'Where the hell did you get them from?' he demanded to know.

'The police gave them to me. It's a spare set that's kept in the security officer's room where she lives.'

'Oh – oh, sorry. I – I thought for a ghastly moment you meant they'd been found on her body.'

'As you can see,' I went on, 'the tally's from the pub up the road. Have you seen her there lately?'

'I haven't seen the woman at all!' he exclaimed. 'For years. There's nothing to say she didn't go there with someone and buy herself a key ring.' He glanced frantically at June, who pursed her lips, gazing at him questioningly, but said nothing.

I wished Patrick was here to question him. I said, 'It appears that she has a boyfriend. D'you know anything about him?'

'No! Nothing! Why should I?'

'I'm wondering if it's where she might be, that's all,' I replied quietly. 'With *him*.'

'As far as I knew she was only going out with that confounded crook when she worked for me. God knows what she's been up to since. And I have to say I think it's damned bad manners to turn up here like this and interrogate me in front of my wife, making out I'm somehow involved with this woman and her disappearance.'

'I don't think I suggested that for one moment,' I said. 'Sorry to have bothered you.'

I left.

As my dear father used to say: if the cap fits, wear it.

It is not easy to watch someone who lives on the water and I did not dare to leave the area for the time required to go back to the hotel and change my clothes and appearance. His reaction to my questions had been interesting and I remembered what June had said about him being a bit odd lately. Previously, my own reservations about him had been more vague, together with the fact that I had got the impression he had shopped Lindersland to Daws for no better reason than that she appeared to be attracted to Lemotov. It was the kind of thing a woman might do out of pure bitchiness. This had prompted me to sow a little jealousy by mentioning the possible existence of a boyfriend.

Did this man know where she was?

I had seated myself on the same bench that I had used to eat my lunch, about eighty yards from the houseboat in the opposite direction to Grindley's route to The Red Dragon. I positioned myself carefully so that a couple of lampposts prevented a clear view unless I moved my head slightly. It seemed unlikely that they would spot me. Luckily it was a warm and sunny afternoon, pleasant to wait around, the Thames sparkling in a very light breeze, a little traffic of the pleasure craft variety and people paddling canoes.

The Grindleys stayed on board for the next two hours and I began to get a crick in my neck from constantly glancing in that direction. Then, when it was almost four o'clock, June Grindley appeared on the afterdeck of the *Alice May* and sat down. I was too far away to see properly but I had an idea that she had been carrying something, perhaps a mug of tea, or a book. Her husband stayed out of sight.

The afternoon dragged on, the sky partly clouded over, and it began to feel as though it might rain. I was desperate for a mug of tea myself by this time. At four fifty-five, June having gone below, I was on the point of giving up when Martin Grindley stepped quickly off the boat on to the riverside path and headed away from me, towards the pub.

To avoid walking directly past their home and appear to be snooping in the event of June spotting me, I went down some steps and followed a path that bordered a small park. It was quiet – just a few people with dogs and mothers or nannies with small children in a play area. With a pang I thought of Carrie taking Vicky and Mark to the playgroup.

In order to remain out of sight of the houseboat I had lost visual contact with Grindley and, although I was fairly sure he was going to The Red Dragon, I hurried. Sure enough, he soon came into view and followed the exact route we had done, only this time entering the public bar. He had directed me into the lounge, perhaps thinking that might be more acceptable to a female strange to the area. He was a bit old fashioned like that. The thought went through my mind that I might be in for a long wait, as hadn't June said that he usually stayed until dinnertime? It occurred to me that his strange behaviour might be due to drinking too much.

The pub was quite close to the river and nearby there were another couple of benches in a tiny square with a tree in the centre. I seated myself. A chilly breeze was now blowing off the river and I shivered. A spot of rain hit my hand and, a couple of minutes later, the rain rapidly working up to a downpour, I was forced to move into the shelter provided by a larger tree across the road. I began to yearn for a hot shower followed by a hot meal. My mobile rang.

'All OK at this end, in case you were wondering,' said Patrick's voice. 'I get the impression that Pamela's engaged Terry to stay until Haldane's arrested and made it worth his while as he has that kind of smile on his face. But one can't ask. She actually begged me to stay for the weekend at least, and I can't really refuse. If you want to come along I can pick you up at the station.'

I said I'd let him know.

'Where are you?'

I told him.

'Please don't wander around there after dark. Even Teddington has its rougher element.' He paused and then said, 'For what it's worth I don't think Grindley's a key player in all this.'

I promised him solemnly that I wouldn't take any risks and he finally rang off, having given me the impression that he was rather fed up. Not with me, though. He too would have preferred to go home for a short break from this wretched case and all the to-ing and fro-ing it entailed.

Around fifteen minutes later when the rain had eased off somewhat, Grindley left the pub, turned a sharp left and walked quickly down a road that appeared from what I could see of it to be a residential area with just a few shops. There was purpose in his manner; this was not just a man trying to keep fit. I followed at a discreet distance but suddenly realized that he probably wouldn't notice if I was driving a horse-drawn brewer's dray.

After two hundred yards he turned left again and set off down a narrow side road that probably did date back to the horse and cart era. There were even a few sections of cobbles in the centre of it. I had to be careful here as we appeared to be the only people around and there were few places where I could conceal myself should he turn to look behind him.

The lane twisted and turned a little and finally came out on the riverside where there was a row of boatsheds-cum-garages. I paused, concealing myself as much as possible in a doorway. He did glance round once, but fleetingly and nervously, and then went down towards the far end of the row, rummaging in a pocket for something as he went. This proved to be a key of some kind with which he appeared to open a padlock rather than a lock in the door itself. Both doors were opened wide and he disappeared within.

I went a little closer, to the end of the row nearest to me. Then I heard a car door slam, an engine start and a small saloon car of some kind emerged. Grindley got out, refastened the doors and drove away. The lane obviously turned right at the end as the vehicle went from sight. Guessing that he would rejoin the road, I ran back the way I had come and was just in time to see him turn on to it around two hundred yards from me and head towards me. I ducked into a shop doorway just before he went by.

He wasn't driving very fast and I tore after him, not caring if he saw me in his mirror. By massive good fortune a taxi approached from the opposite direction and my frantic body language of belting along waving worked: it swung round and drew alongside me.

'Police,' I snapped, or rather panted. 'Please follow that grey car but not too closely.'

We drove roughly east and then I was relying on my somewhat sketchy knowledge of London. We turned and followed a seemingly convoluted route roughly in the direction of New Malden, finishing up on the A3.

'What's the bugger done?' asked the taxi driver in a foreign accent.

'Nothing yet,' I replied.

We went on for another few miles, going through the smarter outskirts of the town and then through a seemingly endless area of high-density housing and what appeared to be dozens of South Korean restaurants. Still Grindley pottered along. Then, just past a huge supermarket, he turned left.

'Careful, please,' I urged. 'I don't want him to know he's being followed.'

Ironically, we then almost lost him when we had to stop at traffic lights, but were just in time to see him turn again, right. By the time we arrived, having been forced to stop to let a lorry out of a side road, I saw that his car had been parked outside a house about a quarter of a mile along it. Of Grindley there was no sign. The taxi driver managed to find a space to park nearby, keeping the vehicle in view and, at my request, we waited for a couple of minutes.

When Grindley failed to emerge from either that house or another nearby, I asked the driver to wait and got out. The houses were clones of the countless semis in which a great proportion of Londoners live. My experience of those which are inhabited by people who, if not already helping the police with their enquiries, ought to be, told me that the one nearest to Grindley's car definitely had a lot going for it – that is, dirty, scruffy and with foot-high grass and weeds in the front garden. There was a certain similarity between this place and where we had found Tracy Finch in Ilford.

This was no time for lurking around inconspicuously. I marched down the sideway, almost fell over a couple of full black rubbish bags dumped on the path and then hurled myself in through the back door of the house into a kitchen. Two things happened simultaneously: a man slouching against the frame of an inner doorway started so violently that the can of lager he was just about to drink out of shot upwards and hit him on the nose, sloshing liquid all over his face, and a woman standing near the sink dropped a largish stack of pots and pans she had been holding into it with an enormous crash.

Some of the lager must have gone into the man's mouth and down the wrong way as he was bent over, coughing and spluttering. I barged past him, dashed into every room on the ground floor, found nobody else and then ran up the stairs to repeat the process.

Grindley was just exiting a bedroom looking furious but stopped dead when he saw me and tried to go back in and slam the door against me. I yanked him out of the way – since working with Patrick I've discovered that adrenaline is wonderful stuff – and he tottered off-balance and almost fell down the stairs.

'I heard a rumour in the pub that a woman was being held against her will here,' he shouted at me. 'I decided to investigate. Don't you remember who I am?'

'Only too well,' I replied, went into the bedroom and shut the door in his face. 'You appear to need Mrs Gillard after all,' I said to the woman who was sprawled on the bed as though she had just been violently shoved there.

Marcia Lindersland just gaped at me.

The Smith and Wesson in my hand had the effect of ensuring we met no resistance on the way out. This was helpful as I had great difficulty in getting the woman down the stairs – being imprisoned had seemingly rendered her legs temporarily reluctant to do anything. We left Martin Grindley still trying to collect his thoughts on the landing while no doubt working out a plausible story to give to the police.

'He's mad! Raving mad!' Lindersland cried when I'd success-fully got her into the taxi. 'I can't go home; he got my address from someone in the Met. Now he knows where I live he might come after me again if he's not arrested!'

'She has nothing, nothing whatsoever, to do with Haldane and the Americans,' Patrick assured Pamela the next morning over breakfast. 'Lindersland came here because she knew that some-thing on your husband's computer blackened her character. As we know, she went right over the top.'

I had taken her back to the hotel where I had rung Matherson. He was at home but had immediately organized transport to collect the woman to take her to a place of safety. This had arrived remarkably quickly. I had handed her over with the same kind of emotion that one might a parcel, having established that she would make a full report about what had happened and also made it perfectly clear to her that I would claim the very large taxi bill on expenses.

When she had calmed down she had given me some back-ground information but there had not been one word of thanks from her – not one.

'Her old boss in the Met had a fixation about her bordering on an obsession,' Patrick continued for the benefit of Lady Rowallen. 'And it would appear that out of jealousy he told his old friend Richard that he suspected her – this was in her early police career – of unprofessional behaviour because she was going out with a man initially thought to be a Russian anarchist, therefore possibly of interest to MI5, in order to gain the man's trust so she could find out about his criminal activities.

'Lindersland's old boss appears to have completely lost the plot. Lindersland told Ingrid he tricked her into meeting him for a chat about old times and took her to a house that he said was his home, ostensibly for her to meet his wife. It wasn't his house. He'd hired a couple living in New Malden, who someone in his local pub had said would do just about anything for money, to keep her prisoner and that's all I know so far. Any idea what he wanted from her, Ingrid?'

'Yes, her. He was going to divorce his wife and they were going to live on his houseboat happily ever after. He actually thought he could achieve that by force. Deluded, to say the least.'

'Especially as the woman can hardly be described as a good catch,' Pamela sniffed.

'There's more that I didn't tell you last night,' I said to Patrick. 'While we waited for her transport to arrive she told me that she's still keeping an eye on Dimitri Lemotov. As we'd thought, she regards him as a job she ought to finish. Quite recently, just before the Grindley business, she rang him – he hasn't a clue who she really is – and he told her that he'd got rid of all his anarchist mob and is involved in what he called the big time.'

'That's very, very interesting,' Patrick said.

'He'd always bragged, Marcia said. She had managed to get several of them behind bars when she got to hear of anything that was planned but had to be very careful not to be suspected by them of supplying information to the police. I'm not quite sure how she got away with that.'

'Stupidly naive,' interposed Her Ladyship, somewhat unfairly.

'This lot he's got in with now,' I continued, 'and she understands it's mainly in connection with supplying them with hitmen, is as a result of his, Lemotov's, talking to a man who for some reason he thought she knew – Ronnie Shaddock, the trade unionist MI5 were watching. Shaddock, Lemotov said, had been fixed as he had threatened to go to the police when he realized that the men he had thought of as anarchists, keen to join violent demos and so forth, were actually a bunch of violent criminals in it purely for the money. As I said, he was fixed, but Lemotov didn't say by whom, if it's even true, and she didn't like to jeopardize obtaining future information from him by asking.'

'Did you ask her if the name Nicholas Haldane meant anything to her?' Patrick enquired.

'Yes, and it didn't. I told her that he been seen in a wine bar with Shaddock but Lemotov hadn't mentioned the name to her.'

'Does she know where Lemotov lives?'

'Only that he used to have a house in Tottenham. She's no idea if he's still there and didn't like to ask that either.'

'We still don't know how she knew that Daws had information about her in his computer.'

'I asked her about that too but all she said was that someone had dropped a hint to her at work. She wouldn't say who it was and I got the impression that resentment at her promotion was involved.'

'Better not stir that one up then,' Patrick muttered.

'I had a phone call yesterday from the Sussex Tourist Board,' Pamela said, having fleetingly been in a world of her own. 'A man asking when I felt I would be able to re-open the place to the public.'

'It's too soon and would be far too dangerous,' Patrick said.

'I did say I thought it unwise in the circumstances as the police hadn't caught Richard's killer and the motive was still unclear.'

'Is this a person you've dealt with before?'

'I've no idea. Every time they make contact it's someone different.'

'Then how do you know he represented what he said he did?'

'Oh, dear.'

'Did you tell him anything about the situation here?'

'No – at least, only that I had plenty of support.'

'That wouldn't have done any harm. But please be careful in future. Do you still have that so-called attorney's business card?'

'Oh! I don't know. I probably threw it away,' Pamela said with a toss of her head, cross at being told off.

'Please look for it.'

A few minutes earlier we had learned that the owners of the house where Lindersland had been taken had disappeared but neighbours had been most helpful – apparently the couple had at one time kept a dog that had bitten several people until the police had taken it away to be destroyed – and they were arrested at the woman's mother's house a couple of miles away. At the moment they were refusing to say anything about the person found at their house.

Martin Grindley had been released on police bail, having stuck to his story that he had heard a rumour in The Red Dragon that a woman was being held against her will in a house in New Malden and decided to investigate. Asked how he knew the address, he had said that he had approached a snout he knew of but hadn't wanted to break the man's cover by revealing his name. He had then tried to pull rank on the strength of his one-time career but still been charged with kidnap because of a statement made by Marcia Lindersland the previous night. Grindley had told the investigating officers that he was going back to his houseboat. It would serve him right, I thought, if June had meanwhile chugged off into the sunset with all his assets.

After quite a long search Pamela discovered the business card in the same drawer in which she kept the key to her late husband's study but could not remember putting it there. Any plans Patrick might have made were then put on hold when he received a call from Superintendent Matherson asking if he would interview the manager of the wine bar in Ilford. The man was refusing to answer any more questions. A request had already been made, and granted, to hold him for longer but that was due to expire in ten hours' time.

We promised Pamela that, if possible, we would both be back for the rest of the weekend.

TWELVE

We had already decided to use one of our favourite scenarios for this interview.

To be fair, the wine bar manager, whose name was William Evans but was thought to have other aliases, did not really look like a common-or-garden criminal, although I have learned over the years that first impressions mean little. He was dark-haired, around forty-five years of age and was sitting as though slightly stooped. From his smart suit and tie one might imagine him to be an executive of some kind.

Shifty looking, though.

'What's this, the big gun I've been threatened with?' he said derisively as we seated ourselves in the dingy interview room. His voice was twangy and pure East End, which rather negated his something-in-the-City image.

'A bad reputation isn't necessarily an advantage,' Patrick said absent-mindedly.

'Don't you mean a good one?'

Patrick surveyed him. 'No. When I worked for MI5 they let me loose on people who used to be referred to as traitors. But I have to work under a different set of rules now.'

'That's good to know.'

'The feeling here is that you know a hell of a lot more than you're prepared to say.'

'No, I don't and I'm glad I don't as I've been framed before. The police are all corrupt round here. Anyway, what's *her* role in all this?' This with a nod in my direction.

'This lady will take notes on behalf of the National Crime Agency. I'm required to have her present to act as a witness in order for her to provide proof that it isn't true when you complain afterwards that I tried to remove your head from your shoulders.'

'Look, have a care – this is all being recorded, you know.'

'But you say the police are all corrupt.' Patrick, who I had an idea had mentally labelled this man as someone who might do exactly that, chuckled to himself unnervingly and resumed, 'Look, I'm not interested in you or your wine bar, or for that matter whether the corrupt cops you say work here who will probably charge you with receiving stolen property reckon you're a waste of space, put you in a weighted sack and chuck you in the river. The premises you rent have been used to store certain items and I really want to have a little chat with you about those.'

'A chat,' Evans echoed.

'Yes. I'm not arresting you and have no intention of doing so. And, as I've just said, I'm only interested in the man you identified from the mugshot as who owns the business.'

'I only rent the wine bar part. God knows what anyone does with the rest.'

'I was under the impression that the store room in question *was* in the main part of the building and not in a number of shacks and sheds at the rear.'

'Well, er, it is in a manner of speaking. But it's no good questioning me about all this – you need to speak to him.'

'I need to know where he lives.'

'No idea.'

'And his name?'

'Call him Nick, he said. He's not the kind of person I pester with questions.'

'Haldane?'

A look of alarm shot across Evans' features before he could prevent it. 'No idea.'

'It's Haldane. Scared of him then, are you?'

'He brings this bodyguard character with him. Looks as thick as a plank but they're always the most dangerous.'

'Umm. Billy Ricketts.'

'You know about him too then.'

'Haldane's not long out of prison and wanted in connection with a murder investigation. Why are you protecting this man and his odious thug?'

'I'm not, I just don't know any more.'

Patrick now gave the impression of a man hanging on to

an extremely bad temper with difficulty. He wasn't acting. He said, 'Do you know a man who calls himself Dimitri Lemotov?'

'Never heard of him.'

'How do you contact Haldane?'

'I can't – he's very careful is Nick. He just drops in or sends along his minder, or some other bod, when he needs to tell me something. If I want to tell him anything I just have to wait. Look, I've explained this to other cops already.'

'Like the other night when the police raided you. You couldn't warn him.'

'I . . . er . . . no.'

'The police round here are all corrupt,' Patrick muttered, staring at the surface of the table between the two of them as though it had just given him inspiration. He got to his feet.

'Where are you going?' Evans asked, unable to keep the alarm from his voice.

Patrick did not answer, just shot a filthy look in his direction and left the room.

'Always like this, is he?' Evans said to me uneasily.

'He's called in as a last resort,' I replied, pretending to jot down notes.

'But cops have to stick to the rules these days.'

'Yes, of course,' I answered, making my tone insincere.

'You look a nice sort of girl. How can you stand working with someone like that?'

I just smiled at him in what I hoped was a cold-blooded fashion and then said, 'You know, it was really stupid of you to say that the police are all corrupt.' When he remained silent, I added, 'The station commander's listening in the next room.'

Was he? I hadn't the first idea.

'Perhaps that was a bit over the top,' Evans said with a worried look in the direction of the door.

'It's not true then, as far as you know.'

'Er, no.'

'You have a record for handling stolen property. Did this Nick tell you that most of what was found had come from the Sussex area?'

'He didn't say anything about it.'

'Just put it in that store room.'

'That's right.'

'I don't believe you. You're not an ordinary run-of-the-mill henchman. He wouldn't employ you as anything like that anyway because you're not strong looking. Nor merely to run a wine bar, which I'm assuming is a front for your other activities. I think you organize the sale of stolen goods, manage the finances of those and that was why he bought the business: he really wanted your contacts as an outlet for his criminal gains.'

This was right off the top of my head but sounded plausible to me.

'That's preposterous!' Evans protested.

I continued, 'Evidence suggests that Nicholas Haldane also bought a security company in Brighton for no other reason than to gain access to a large property in Sussex in order to murder the man who lived there. It was a revenge thing and needn't concern us right now. We think he bribed and/or threatened a burglar alarm system technician who worked for him to tamper with the system at this property to enable a couple of gunmen to enter. The technician was subsequently murdered, but the police are working on the theory that the criminals involved had already discovered that it was a lucrative business as easy entry to other properties where the owners had valuable possessions had already been orchestrated. Perhaps at that stage they were having rehearsals. Some of those stolen items will almost certainly be among those stored at your wine bar. You're Haldane's Mr Fixit. Correct?'

'No!'

After the short silence that followed this denial Patrick exploded into the room with murderous intent written all over his face.

'Yes!' Evans shrieked. 'All right, I admit it!'

Patrick sat down, relaxed, gazed at me and said, 'What the hell have you been saying to him?'

He had of course been watching and listening, courtesy of the video link, in a room close by.

'Listen,' Patrick said to Evans. 'I'm perfectly aware that people like Haldane don't hand out their addresses and mobile numbers to their employees. I want Haldane. Very badly. Where do you meet up with either him or one of his henchmen when things have to be discussed?'

'I've told you – he drops round or sends someone.'

My husband took a deep breath. 'No, when *you* want to discuss something with him. Where does he hang out on certain days of the week at certain times? Is it a pub? A club? We've seen Ricketts in the Cat o' Nine Tails but I reckon that's a bit down-market for Haldane and the house the gang he appears to be involved with were using nearby has been abandoned.'

'He doesn't live here in Ilford.'

'How do you know that?'

'He remarked once that the traffic had been terrible and it'd taken him an hour to reach me. Wasn't at all pleased.'

'OK, where's he to be found?'

There was a long pause while Evans agonized.

'You'll almost certainly be remanded in custody. He won't be able to get at you there,' Patrick encouraged.

'I hate him really,' Evans said in a low voice after another silence. 'At the end of the day its people like me who take the punishment, isn't it?'

'Yes, it is.'

'He doesn't live on the same planet as me. You won't believe me but he seems to live two lives.'

'You mean he has two identities?' I asked.

'Something like that. Perhaps more than two.'

'Please be more specific.'

Evans sighed deeply. 'He told me when I first knew him and he was in an unusually chummy mood, you know, talking out of the corner of his mouth like people who are posing do, that he used to be a top civil servant and wheeling and dealing had always appealed to him. But that wasn't enough – he wanted more interesting stuff. He got in with some banker who had a real grudge against a lord someone or other who also worked for the government. He didn't say who. The banker paid Nick a pile of cash to blacken this bloke's character, ruin his Whitehall department and kill him and some of his friends. Personally, I thought that last bit excessive. But something went wrong, the cops found out and he and the bloke were arrested before they could finish it. I got the impression he's been bitter and twisted about it ever since.'

'I'm sure he is,' Patrick murmured. 'Go on.'

'I think he was trying to impress me, despite the fact of having been caught and sent to prison. To make up for it somehow, if you get me, look big. He said he'd run gangs from inside through people he met there and blokes he'd used for the original Lord Whoever job. He had money, he said. Something about stocks and shares and banking scams that he'd been into for years. I have to admit I was impressed. That takes brains.'

'And the other lives?' Patrick queried.

'I saw him on the telly a while back. At Ascot, you know, the races. In his topper. I always bet a few bob on the horses.'

'Are you sure?' I asked incredulously.

'Positive. He was being interviewed as his horse had just won a race. I didn't catch what he was calling himself as I hadn't really been paying much attention but the nag's name was Hartwood Castle.'

'I'll kill him,' Patrick whispered. He shot to his feet and smashed his fist against the door, then turned, grimacing with pain. 'Kill him,' he repeated in a kind of sob.

'You're quite safe,' I quickly assured Evans.

'Sorry,' Patrick said, reseating himself, his hand obviously in agony. 'Most unprofessional.' He went quiet.

'It's personal then,' Evans said, his voice a little trembly.

'It looks as though he's responsible for recently arranging the murder of the same Lord Someone or other,' Patrick replied quietly. 'A very respected friend of mine.'

'Well, can't say that I hold with lords and all that but . . .' Evans ran out of things to say, unsettled by his questioner losing his temper.

'No, he was someone from another planet as far as you're concerned. Senior decorated army officer, Army Intelligence in Northern Ireland, MI5, Serious Organised Crime Agency, National Crime Agency and due to retire soon in order to carry on with his hobby of growing roses.'

There was another long silence.

'I heard a good word to describe someone the other day,' Evans said. 'Again, on the telly. Toxic. That's Nick, or whoever the bastard really is. Toxic. But he pays well.'

Patrick smiled thinly but said nothing.

Evans appeared to come to a decision. 'This business of him having two or even more identities . . . I thought of screwing him down a bit over it or sell the info to any interested party who might want to take over his outfit but . . .'

When he again stopped speaking I said, 'You were hoping to blackmail him, you mean?'

'All's fair in love and war, isn't it?'

'You wouldn't have lived long if you'd tried that,' Patrick informed him crisply.

'No, I think you're right and I now see that I could do with getting shot of him out of my life altogether. You could trace him through the horse, couldn't you?' With a sickly smile he added, 'And perhaps put in a good word with the cops here for me?'

Patrick leaned forward, both elbows on the table, glared at the other man and barked, 'Have you anything else to say?'

Evans recoiled slightly. 'Oh, er . . . I – er – didn't tell you the truth just now. He has rooms in a house in Tottenham that belongs to that bloke you mentioned – the Russian, Lemo-whatever. I overheard them talking once when they were having a drink in my bar. I can't believe that's his only place, though, not if he's got a racehorse, for God's sake.'

'Address?'

'No idea. Honest. I really don't know.'

'How do you contact him?'

'I leave a message in a crack in a wall on a footbridge over the railway line. Other bods of his might use it for all I know.'

This sounded to me like something out of a far-fetched spy thriller but it could easily be verified. In receipt of detailed instructions from Evans we duly did verify it, just as it was getting dark that same day. It was raining so we were able to huddle into our anoraks, just Mr and Mrs Joe Bloke walking home from the pub. Making sure that no one else was in sight Patrick used his tiny torch to locate the cranny between two concrete blocks, actually concealed behind a bush at one end of the bridge.

'There's something in here,' he said, having to speak louder than he would have done as a train thundered along the main line beneath us.

'Evans didn't say anything about receiving messages here,' I said.

'No. However . . .' Having brought it towards the comparative shelter of our waterproofs he unfolded the single sheet of paper he had pulled out, which appeared to have been torn from a notebook.

'Heard you'd got yourself arrested,' he read out by the light of the torch. 'If you're out on bail watch out for Billy.'

'Is it signed?'

'There's just an N and we know who that is. I'll phone the nick and confirm that Evans is being remanded in custody for his own safety.'

'If we could camp out and watch this place we could put a note in the slot and follow who collects it. Sorry, just thinking aloud – it's not practical.'

Patrick glanced around. 'No security cameras in sight either.'

'And seeing that I'm supposed to be your consultant I'm going to say that it was a pretty stupid thing to do to your hand, the one that was injured recently.'

'Even otherwise absolutely perfect blokes can be stupid sometimes,' he replied, in all seriousness.

His mobile then rang and he swore under his breath, having intended to switch it off while we were in this locality. He answered it, signalling to me that we should carry on walking in the same direction. Quite; it was not a place to hang around.

Even with the hood pushed right off my head I could not hear who the caller was or what they were saying other than that it was a woman either speaking very quietly or the reception was bad. Something told me, however, that it was not Pamela. Marcia Lindersland? Again?

Patrick listened for a minute or so and then said, 'Thank you, but I really think you should leave it there . . . No, don't dial nine-nine-nine. I work for the National Crime Agency too and

I'll contact the Met and . . . Yes, I promise, but give me the address . . . Yes, I'll deal with it straight away.'

I grabbed my notebook and pen from a pocket, having to hunt for it a bit, and then ran to catch up. By this time Patrick was shoving his phone away, fuming.

'Believe it or not, that was Marcia Lindersland's *mother*. Lindersland's been staying with her since the Grindley business and she overheard her talking on the phone to a man she knew she went out with years ago, someone called Dimitri, and who she admitted to her at the time was a criminal. The mother, who's going up the wall with worry, knows she got his address out of him as she wrote it down but left it behind in her rush. Apparently Lindersland's on her way over there now on the pretext of renewing her friendship with him and, after checking that he really is at home, hopes to get him arrested. What the hell have I done to deserve this bloody woman?'

Feeling that no answer ought to be forthcoming from my direction, I merely asked if he'd been given the address.

'Four, Juniper Row, Hatton Street.'

'Tottenham.'

'Yes.'

'How on earth did her mother know your phone number?'

'In her hurry Lindersland left behind her mobile and purse as well. She said she accessed the phonebook and I sounded promising.'

You are, I thought.

We had left the car a few minutes' walk away in a residential road that had, miraculously, a parking space. When we got back to it a couple of youths were eyeing up the vehicle, one actually with his hand outstretched towards the driver's door handle.

'I wouldn't do that if I were you,' Patrick called. 'A circular saw comes out of the wheel hub and slices both your legs off.'

It has a nifty alarm instead, an imitation of a one-time destroyer steam whistle: *whoop-whoop-whoop!* Almost as loud as the original too.

The youths hurried away without a backward glance.

I drove while Patrick set the sat-nav and organized back-up.

'This might be the end of it,' he mused, having then called

Matherson with the news as a courtesy after contacting the NCA hotline. 'If Haldane's there he can be grabbed as well.'

I said, 'As ever, your oracle is urging caution.'

'Absolutely. I wonder if it's entered her head that Lemotov might now know who she is.'

The traffic was heavy and after a while I began to feel that I had been driving for hours. The route the sat-nav had chosen seemed to be a tour of every narrow back street in east London. Range Rovers are not really engineered for narrow urban back streets and I got a tut or two from my partner when I demolished some dustbins left mostly in the road that scattered uncollected rubbish over a wide area.

'You drive then,' I grumped.

'No, I just adore your style,' Patrick said, laughing.

When I saw the football stadium I knew we were nearly there and, a few twists and turns later, the sat-nav indicated that we had arrived. We had, at Hatton Street. I pulled into a section of road that had double yellow lines and stopped. There was a lamppost nearby but there's nothing about our vehicle that would make people realize that police were present in the area.

'A big Christmas tree in the front garden,' Patrick recollected. 'That's what Tracy said.'

'Shall I drive the length of the road?' I asked. 'Heaven knows which group of houses is Juniper Row.'

'Good idea. Nobody will be able to see who we are now it's dark.'

This I did, then turned around at the end, with difficulty on account of parked cars, and drove slowly back.

'No Christmas trees by the look of it,' I said. 'But there's one tallish conifer that's probably an ellwoodii of some sort on one side of the road and a monkey puzzle tree about the same size on the other roughly opposite to it.'

'Which one looks most like a Christmas tree to a young woman who probably knows nothing about gardening and was very upset at the time?'

'The monkey puzzle – the branches are more pronounced. The other is just an oval blob in the dark.'

We went back to where I had first parked, which was on the same side of the road as the house we suspected was the one we sought, and stepped out. It had stopped raining but was very murky, the smell of smoke in the air but not the pleasant scent of a simple garden bonfire, more like a building, as though there had been a serious fire. In fact, I could hear sirens in the distance, but then again one can almost always hear the sirens of various emergency vehicles in a city. Somewhere nearby cats were fighting.

We waited by the vehicle and the back-up did not materialize, Patrick muttering something about the traffic. A man walked past and commented rudely on our illegal parking. He was sent on his way with an earful delivered in a cockney accent. No, we were not the police.

'So has she actually arrived or not?' Patrick went on to say in an undertone.

'Are you sure it was Lindersland's mother who rang you?'

He gazed at me in surprise. 'How can I be expected to know that?'

I gazed back. 'Kindly activate your professional assessment programme.'

'OK, she did sound genuine, as I said, a mother half up the wall with worry.'

'Nevertheless, I do not like this situation *one bit*.'

'So we go in doubly careful.' With a grin he added, 'Your cat's whiskers are always my first line of defence.'

Only if you take heed, was the thought that immediately trotted through my mind.

He had already told me that this was not going to be an all bells and whistles raid but low-key. That matters were already in hand became obvious a couple of minutes later when an unmarked car drew up alongside ours but skewed round, blocking the road, and two unmarked blokes got out. Even with what I can only describe as savagely short hair they looked like cops.

'Gillard,' Patrick said to them tersely.

When it became clear from their hesitation that they had no idea who he was, he produced his warrant card and there was a short whispered consultation. I was content not to be involved with it as I leave this kind of choreography to those who know what they're doing. Although they were speaking quietly I made out that there were others at the other end of the road, an armed

squad, their vehicles also blocking it. All that was needed was
for Patrick to pinpoint the house for them. It was arranged that
he and one of the undercover men would stroll unobtrusively
down the road and he would indicate which one on the right-
hand side it was, then a message could be given to those at the
far end.

'I won't be long,' Patrick said to me. He gave me a thumbs
up and the two set off.

'I hate the waiting around part,' the remaining man muttered.
He eyed me up and down. 'What's your role then, love?'

I told him, politely, and he said, 'Oh,' and went quiet.

The waiting around part stretched into an eternity. Trains
hummed in the distance, planes flew high overhead in the dank
clouds which were seemingly a matter of feet above the
chimney pots of the houses, traffic hooted and roared on a
nearby main road. Incongruously, a fox yapped.

The sound I was waiting for, when it came, was louder than
I had expected: the battering open of the front door. Boots
thumped, people shouted. Three shots were fired. My companion
snatched a gun from under his jacket as someone came running,
pell-mell, along the road towards us.

'Stop! Armed police!' he bellowed, jumping out, ready to
fire.

I had positioned myself in the lee of the 4×4; this wasn't
really my gig but I now took the Smith and Wesson from my
pocket and cautiously stepped out just as the man, whoever he
was, stopped dead. He then tried to bolt between the vehicles
but didn't notice me until it was too late. Performing an emergency stop, his feet slipped from under him and he ended up
half under the Range Rover.

'Your suspect,' I said to the cop.

THIRTEEN

Another car drew up, a taxi.
'The police have closed the road,' I said, going closer as the driver's window opened and he stuck his head out.

Marcia Lindersland got out of the other side of the car. 'I *am* the police. Let me through.' She appeared to be dressed in old clothes, her hair all mussed up, no make-up and she looked at me without a trace of recognition.

'You're not and you're staying right there,' I told her, nerves making me speak more sharply than I might have done in normal circumstances. 'Shots have been fired.'

'How has all this happened?'

I turned my back to her.

The remaining policeman ignored her too, oblivious of the true state of affairs, busy handcuffing the runaway who was complaining that it was all a big mistake and he was an innocent bystander. A small handgun of some kind was then found in one of the pockets of his leather jacket.

A further two shots were fired somewhere down the road and everyone instinctively ducked down. Truly, the police would want to bring this to an end as soon as possible before members of the public were injured or even killed.

Lindersland was still standing, undecided, by the taxi, and I was bracing myself for her trying to make a dash for it. Not that I was responsible for the confounded woman's safety. Right now, with anxiety gnawing at my insides like rats, I think I could have serenely contemplated her being led out in front of a firing squad.

An ambulance preceded by a squad car then arrived in a blaze of flashing blue lights and the taxi driver had no choice but to move his vehicle and park it somewhere else. The detained man was bundled into the unmarked vehicle, which was also moved, and the two newest arrivals speeded off into the distance.

But not out of sight – their brake lights blazed and I guessed they had been stopped from proceeding further roughly outside the targeted house.

Forgetting about Lindersland, I set off down the road, desperate for news. I was cautious though; this was not going to be where Ingrid Langley blundered into a police raid and got herself shot between the eyes by a holed-up desperado. So I walked well to the right-hand side, using hedges and trees as cover wherever possible. I came to a woman standing by her front gate trying to see what was happening.

'What's going on?' she asked.

'Please go back inside and stay away from the windows,' I told her. 'You'll be told when it's safe.'

A little further along I paused and watched from the comparative safety of an overgrown hedge. Nothing moved; it was if everything and everyone was frozen under a spell. I couldn't see Patrick.

A voice suddenly boomed through a loudhailer, making me jump. 'Come out now! Armed police! We have the rest of your gang under arrest and you're achieving nothing by hiding in there and may be seriously injured when armed police again storm the building in one minute.'

Silence but for police radios chattering and my heart thumping. I would rather have been where the action was and know what was going on than marooned here. Inside a police van a dog barked. All this – that is, nothing much – went on for what seemed rather a long time.

A shot cracked indoors, and then another.

'God, the bastard's topped himself!' I heard someone exclaim.

Roughly fifteen seconds later two figures came into my line of vision, the one in front staggering with his hands on his head, the second having him scruffed by his clothing, shoving him along. He broke away but was pursued and caught.

'Was it you?' Patrick yelled in the man's face, having gripped him this time by the front of his sweatshirt. 'Did you pull the trigger at Hartwood?'

'N-n-n-no,' the man yammered.

Patrick shook him. 'Who then?'

'Some . . . some . . . Yank.'

'What Yank?'

'He – he wouldn't say.'

The spell broke, people hurried forward and I lost sight of the pair in the resulting melee.

'Get a cordon rigged!' a uniformed cop called, walking towards me. 'Madam, I must ask you to—'

'NCA,' I said and when he look dubious, showed him my ID.

'Is she with you?' he went on to ask, looking somewhere behind me. I turned. 'No, but she is official,' I told him.

Marcia Lindersland strode off and into the crowd. I caught up with her as she came upon a group who included a man who had to be the one Patrick had just brought out of the house. Someone in plainclothes, no doubt a CID officer, was formally arresting him. He wasn't receptive – he was drunk.

'I had to be present for this,' Lindersland said to him haughtily. 'You were my cold case. With a bit of luck you'll die in jail.'

Dimitri Lemotov, for it had to be him, bared horrible teeth at her in an expression that wasn't remotely a smile. 'Oh, the skinny cop. Stupid of me – I must have been hitting the bottle when I told you where I was. Can't remember now. Quite come on in the world, haven't we, now we're a top cop? Don't think for one moment that you fooled me, duckie, but it was real fun to string you along.' He leaned right up close to her and, slurring his words, bawled in her face, 'You looked like the filth, you smelled like the filth and you screwed like the filth.'

Someone yanked him away; he swayed and almost fell.

Lindersland turned and walked off.

'I have to refuse your request and you shouldn't have gone in alone like that,' the CID man was saying to Patrick.

'I was out the back and heard him fall down the stairs,' Patrick said, clearly fighting to control his temper. He held out a handgun of some kind. 'I'm afraid my prints are on the barrel. And why the hell didn't you find him when you first went in?'

The detective gave him a look and departed, leaving him with the weapon.

'No Haldane or Ricketts, just sundry hired yobs,' Patrick said to me after taking several deep breaths. 'And they won't let me go back indoors to check Haldane's rooms for clues as to where he might be until scenes-of-crime people have finished.' Then he shouted, 'Is *no one* interested in this piece of evidence?'

A man came forward and took it from him.

'He fired two shots at you then,' I said as we walked back to the car. This did not seem to register so I stopped and added, 'Patrick, please calm down.'

He too stopped and turned to face me. 'Sorry.' A quick gaze skywards. 'No, not at me – I wasn't indoors then. He must have been seeing things and was probably too drunk to have hit anything even three times the size of Ricketts.'

'I wonder what happened to his Russian accent.'

'As someone said, an utter phoney. The prisons are full of 'em.'

Lindersland was standing by the Range Rover. 'I'm afraid I came out without any money,' she said, not quite meeting our gaze. 'The taxi driver has a prior booking and is refusing to take me back to my mother's. Would you mind paying him and giving me a lift?'

Lying in bed that night – what remained of it, that was – I could imagine the various responses to Lindersland that must have gone through Patrick's mind, all the way from a straight refusal to a very soldierly, if not blistering, concoction with due reference to Lemotov's remarks a little earlier. But he had not said anything; neither of us had spoken to her all the way to her mother's and merely done as requested, better comment perhaps. She simply wasn't worth it.

And now he sat, half turned away from me, at the little desk-cum-dressing table in our hotel room, writing his report. He was doing it in longhand as he doesn't get on with my laptop, finding it too fiddly, so I would type it and email it to Commander Greenway in the morning. I had an idea this would not be just his usual bare facts account followed by a summary and brief professional comments, but include a damning critique of Lindersland right from the beginning.

Not being able to get hold of Haldane, again, had been a bitter blow to him.

I lay there for some reason trying, and failing, to think of other, more polite, phrases for *she bloody well screwed up* and then, very suddenly, fell asleep.

As previously noted, since he's been promoted Patrick's brief means that he can call upon whichever police forces are necessary in order to investigate his cases. The next morning this involved landing on the doorstep of the Met CID officer, one DI Baker, who had given him short shrift the night before. Although only nominally with the rank of constable to enable him to arrest people, Patrick gave him a verbal haircut. The result of this was that he was given permission to go into the Tottenham house with the scenes-of-crime personnel and wearing full anti-contamination gear on condition that he searched for evidence only in the two upstairs rooms that Lemotov had admitted Nicholas Haldane rented from him.

I was not present during any of this. It wasn't necessary and I recognize it's sometimes better if Patrick works alone as the presence of a woman can cramp a man's style. What with one thing and another he did not arrive back at the hotel until just before six thirty that evening, where I had made a point of waiting for him in the reception atrium.

'Nothing useful,' he reported, seating himself tiredly on the other end of the leather sofa. 'He'd taken nothing to Tottenham that gave any clue as to his main address, what he calls himself if indeed he does have another identity or the names of any associates he might have. Lemotov apparently has a colossal hangover and although talking to save his own skin is insisting he knows nothing about Haldane's personal life nor where he lived. DI Baker is inclined to believe him as the man is obviously scared half to death of him and even begged not to be released on police bail.'

This was more than disappointing but real-life policing isn't like TV cop shows.

'What have you been up to?' Patrick went on to ask.

I said, 'Not a lot. I wrote out your report, emailed it to Mike and then decided to take a paper copy to him personally and fill him in with the details as he likes to get those too.'

The commander hadn't had time to access the email but had read the hard copy while I was there. His hair hadn't quite stood on end but there had been a couple of muttered expletives and his final comment had been, 'When this gets out she'll probably wish he'd lit a fire under her instead.'

If it ever did.

I continued, 'But before I went out I checked that everything was OK at home. It is except that Justin's badly grazed both knees falling off his bike.'

'Again!'

'You know, he's exactly like you at that age. I also rang Pamela. Christopher's going to contact you sometime today with an update only I don't think from what she said that much has been happening. I then endeavoured to track down that racehorse that Evans reckons Haldane owns. There is one and it's in training at a racing stable near Newbury. It's a six-year-old chestnut gelding belonging to a Mrs Constance Danton-Hall. A certain similarity with the name, wouldn't you say?'

'Danton-Hall,' he echoed. 'No address, I take it?'

'No.'

'It shouldn't be too difficult to track her down. That's if it's her real name. Oh, and I've arranged for someone to put a note in that crack in the wall on the footbridge. I can't believe anyone from Haldane's lot is keeping a round-the-clock watch on it but I don't want to be seen anywhere near the place.'

'What will the note say?'

'That Evans is out on bail and wants to meet Haldane as he's heard on a grapevine that Lemotov's been arrested and is talking. Evans has more information and expects to be paid for it.'

'And this someone is going to wander by later to see if there's a reply?'

'With his mate – safety in numbers. If they spot Ricketts, and I've given them his description, they're going to grab him.' He got to his feet. 'I'm famished but I'll have a quick shower before we eat.'

'It's still the weekend and Pamela reminded me that you said you'd be there if you could.'

My husband wilted slightly and then said, 'Please phone her and check that everything's still OK. I'd really prefer not to have to drive down there if there's no important reason for us to be present. Yes, I know I promised. Tell her there might be developments at this end and I'm utterly knackered.'

Well . . . not exactly in those words perhaps.

'Elferdink,' I heard Patrick say as he walked off. 'He's going to get impaled on a railing up his arse.'

Pamela sounded disappointed but said she understood if Patrick was tired. Shortly afterwards, while he was getting dressed, he got a call from Christopher to confirm that all was well and that Her Ladyship had invited him to keep her and Terry company for dinner.

Meanwhile, I had rung our DCI friend, James Carrick, in Bath as I knew it was his and Joanna's wedding anniversary. Joanna was under training as she was going back into the police.

'I'm just about to set off for home,' he had said after I had given them my congratulations and, on the spur of the moment, added that I had a query for him. 'D'you want to call me there in around twenty minutes?'

'Just a quickie and then I won't introduce work into your evening,' I had said. 'We have a lead in the form of a racehorse belonging to a Mrs Constance Danton-Hall called Hartwood Castle that's being trained somewhere in the Newbury area.'

'Hartwood Castle! That's too much of a coincidence.'

I had then repeated the details for him to write down. 'I know it's not your patch but does the woman's name mean anything to you?'

'Not off the top of my head. I'll work on it. But is tomorrow morning all right? Only a mystery person's treating us to dinner at the Crypt at Batheaston. Would that be you and Patrick by any chance?'

'It might be,' I joked. 'Have a lovely time. And look, as you obviously haven't heard of the woman Patrick can phone Thames Valley Police.'

'It's no trouble. I can contact someone who works full-time at Bath racecourse. He knows everything and everyone connected with horses in the South West and beyond and gives me the nod sometimes about certain people. And thanks for this evening.'

* * *

The morning brought no news from whoever had planted the note in the footbridge and we had no choice but to have a later than normal breakfast, hoping that James Carrick could locate the racehorse owner for us before we tried other channels. I was glad of the leisurely start to the day for Patrick's sake as he had not been joking over the knackered remark. Unusually for him, the man had slept like something dead, not even waking when I had snuggled up to him more than a trifle hopefully at seven thirty, and there had been no alternative but to get up and make myself some tea.

'Something on your mind?' he enquired, looking up from his full English breakfast.

'No, I was merely recollecting feeling wildly randy this morning and you were like the log pile at home.'

'I hope you're still on the pill.'

That had to be the most unromantic remark ever, and I told him as much. I got a broad smile in response.

Carrick didn't contact me until just before eleven, by which time Patrick was fretting that he ought to be doing something other than reading newspapers.

'Sorry about the delay but I had to get my source's home phone number from the management as he's off sick today and his mobile's died on him,' the DCI said. 'He's heard of the Danton-Hall woman and her husband. They live close to Newbury, he thinks either near or in a village by the name of Market Fyfield, and there's nothing dodgy about them on *his* radar. According to gossip they're typical country set, live in some kind of manor house, support charities, host village fetes and hunt balls, that kind of thing. They have just the one horse in training but keep two at home for hunting and what he described as hacking, whatever that is.'

'Riding around enjoying the scenery,' I explained.

'I get you. There's nothing on them in Criminal Records either.'

Market Fyfield was one of those villages that appear to have been invented by *Country Life* magazine. Neat thatched cottages with pretty gardens lined the wide village street and little bridges giving access to them spanned a stream that ran

the length of it on one side. There were a few shops: an interior decorator's, an antique shop that also sold expensive gifts
and a couple of ladies' fashion boutiques. Another small shop
sold local organic produce and greengrocery at eye-wateringly
expensive prices. The Danton-Halls' home, if it was indeed a
manor house, could only be the one large property at the
western end of the village which must, at one time, have
indeed been the home of a sequence of Lords of the Manor
and their families.

After having a late snack lunch we arrived at the entrance to
the house, which we had passed on the way into the village.
One had to announce one's presence over an intercom which
at least established that it was the right house. Eventually, the
wrought-iron gates, one of which had a BEWARE OF THE
DOGS notice on it, swung slowly open.

There was a short curving drive to the Regency-style property, the appearance of which was rather spoilt by a large
covered swimming pool to one side of it. This was spoilt
even further by visible patches of black mould growing on
the inside of the clear plastic roof. The garden was neglected
in a tidy sort of way; in other words someone cut the sweeping
lawns and that was about it. The dogs, a couple of Labradors,
bounded up to us barking in not particularly friendly fashion
as we approached, but Patrick bellowed, 'Down!' at them and
they obeyed. He then told them to sit and they did that too.

'Oh!' said a woman hurrying from the front door, having
seemingly had trouble wresting it open. 'I was expecting a
police car.' She eyed us as, it appeared, in her view people on
foot were suspect.

I could hardly tell her that we do not usually take our private
transport close to the homes of those we are about to interview
if they are potential suspects.

'Mrs Danton-Hall?' Patrick enquired. 'Was it you I spoke to
just now?'

She confirmed that.

Patrick introduced us and we presented our warrant cards.

'It is Sunday, you know.'

'This is very important,' Patrick told her.

'And the dogs!' she cried. 'They never do as they're told.

What on earth have you done to them?' She gazed at us accusingly, as though we had sprayed them with something nasty.

'Just told them to sit,' replied the man who prefers cats.

'Oh,' she said again. 'Perhaps you ought to take them in hand. They chew the tyres of the postman's van.' She gazed around vaguely. 'You'd better come in, although I can't imagine what you want with us. Unless it's about that incident at the hunt last week.'

'No, it isn't,' Patrick said.

'Thank God for that. It *is* a drag hunt now and we're perfectly law-abiding but the saboteurs still turn up. One of them frightened Margie Thomas's cob and it swung round and trod on his foot.'

We entered a spacious hallway. Coats, boots, sticks and other outdoor gear was everywhere, an old-fashioned hall stand and a hat stand loaded with more waterproofs and headgear. Mrs Danton-Hall thrust open a door to our immediate right and we followed her in, the dogs bringing up the rear. Whether still under the Patrick effect or not, they wandered over to a couple of baskets and flopped down into them.

'Hartwood Castle,' Patrick said when we had seated ourselves on a faded and rock-hard ottoman. The entire room looked faded and uncomfortable, the walls lined with gilt-framed oil paintings, most of which were portraits of corpulent and bewhiskered gentlemen and ferocious old ladies wearing black silk gowns and jet jewellery. Forebears? All the paintings looked in need of a good clean.

'Oh, God! He hasn't killed anyone, has he?'

'Not so far as I know.'

'Oh, you *did* frighten me. He's very naughty. Chestnuts often are, you know.'

Being introduced merely as an assistant who will take notes – our normal procedure – gives me the opportunity to study whoever is talking while their attention is on the one asking the questions.

Constance Danton-Hall was probably in her early fifties but gave every indication of defying fate by all means possible. She had that slightly drawn and underweight look of women who go to the gym far too often and don't eat enough. The tan was not genuine although not overdone, and her shoulder-length hair, expertly highlighted, was immaculate. Her clothes were expensive and in good taste: black trousers with rather a lot of dog's hairs on them and a white T-shirt. Did she garden without wearing gloves? I wondered as her fingernails were grimy.

'Why did you call him that?' Patrick was asking her.

She looked a bit flummoxed. 'No idea. That was Charles' idea. Why do you want to know?'

'I can only tell you that we're investigating a serious crime and the name has a connection.'

'Sorry, that sounds a bit silly to me but I'll ask him.' She got up, went over to the door, which had been left ajar, and shouted, 'Charles? Charles! Are you there?'

There was some kind of hurrumphed male response from a distance away.

'He's coming,' Mrs Danton-Hall reported, reseating herself.

Her husband duly appeared and I practically gasped out loud. Here was a near replica of Nicholas Haldane. The likeness was uncanny but not exact. This man was older, fuller in the face, had more hair, was not wearing glasses and lacked the dead look of Haldane. He had to be the individual William Evans had seen on the television racing programme.

'Why did we call the horse Hartwood Castle?' his wife asked him. 'The National Crime Agency want to know.'

Well, put like that it was more than a bit silly.

'What a ridiculous question,' said the man of the house.

Why had I shivered when I heard him speak?

'Please answer it,' Patrick snapped.

'In Sussex, isn't it?'

'Yes.'

'I can't really remember but I think it may have been on account of my wife and I having visited the place when we were on our honeymoon. Seemed as good a name for a horse as any.'

'When was this?' Patrick went on to ask.

The man turned to his wife. 'How long have we been married, Con?'

'Twenty-five years,' she answered. 'No, twenty-six.'

'It wasn't open to the public in those days,' I told them.

'Well, it wasn't that then,' he said. 'Sorry, in that case I can't help you.'

Patrick made himself more comfortable. 'Mr Danton-Hall, people usually call racehorses by names that mean something to them. Was it called that when you bought it?'

'Er, no. I have an idea he was called Gingernut.' He uttered a false laugh. 'On account of his being a bit loopy sometimes, you see.'

'Are you the sole owners?'

'Er . . . yes.'

'Do you know a man who calls himself Nicholas Haldane?'

'No.'

'He looks very much like you.'

'I know nothing about a man of that name. Look, I'm busy. Have you finished with your questions?'

'No cousins several times removed, long-lost brothers?' Patrick went on impeturbedly.

'No, none,' Danton-Hall snapped.

'Haldane's wanted for murder and I'm sure I don't have to detail the penalties if you withhold information from the police.'

Constance put a hand over her mouth.

'Well, the wretched man's not here!' Danton-Hall shouted.

'I don't believe I suggested that he might be. Tell me, is this a family home, handed down through the generations?'

'I don't see what business it is of yours.'

'Charles,' said his wife nervously in a low voice, 'the man's only doing his job.'

After a pause Danton-Hall took a deep breath and said gustily, 'No, I bought the place lock, stock and barrel about ten years ago from a business associate when his company failed. That was about the time I retired and we'd always fancied living in the country. It wasn't a family home for him either; I think he'd bought most of the stuff here at auction.'

'What were you before you retired?'

There was the merest hesitation. 'A stockbroker.'

'And before you came here you lived where?'

'In London.'

'Perhaps you'd give me this man's name.'

'There's no point – he killed himself shortly afterwards.'

'Nevertheless . . .'

The man looked at his spouse. 'Remind me, Con, my mind's a blank. John someone or other?'

She shook her head. 'It's no use asking me. He wasn't someone we entertained and I don't think I ever actually met him.'

'It's on the house deeds, though, surely,' Patrick prompted.

'Which are with my solicitor,' Danton-Hall said.

'Be good enough to find out for me.' Patrick stood up and gave the man his business card. 'You can contact me on that number.'

We left and neither of them showed us out.

'What did you make of that?' Patrick asked me as we made our way down the drive.

'On the surface, perfectly normal,' I replied. 'Vibes, though . . .'

'What?'

I shrugged but something was bothering me. 'I can't really explain but, nevertheless, stinking fish.'

FOURTEEN

Not far from the main entrance there was a little iron gate that gave access into a small, overgrown meadow that I had an idea might at one time have been devoted to wildflowers. Quite a few were struggling to top the tall grass and rank weeds that grew there now and I remembered the names of a few that were growing nearest to where I was standing: Corncockle, Meadow Crane's-bill, Viper's Bugloss.

I remembered something else.

'Nice view,' Patrick said, gazing into the distance.

'The coat!' I exclaimed.

'What coat?'

'It was hanging on the hall stand and exactly like the one Irvine Baumgarten was wearing when the pair of them turned up at Hartwood.'

Patrick thought about it for a few moments and then said, 'Elferdink had that dreadful yellow-and-orange tartan outfit. Can't recollect what Baumgarten had on other than that it was also pretty lurid. Plus a handbag.'

'He wore white trousers and a bright green-and-pink-checked jacket. Big checks. It was a manbag, by the way.'

'Not quite Charles's thing then.'

'I think it's safe to say that.'

'We need to watch the place even if it's just to eliminate them from enquires, as cops are supposed to say.'

'Or get the local police to do it,' I suggested

'I can't risk them parking somewhere terribly obvious and being seen. Even if they use an unmarked car they might be noticed. *I'll* do it. Tonight.' When I gave no reaction he stopped looking at the view, which was wonderful, a couple of horses grazing in another field beyond, and gave me his full attention. 'You're really worried.'

'I think that man is related to Haldane – it's just too much of a coincidence. D'you mind if we move away from here? I can almost feel eyes boring into the back of my neck.'

We went back to the car where I continued airing my fears. 'Or even, when you think about it and I really hope I'm not being neurotic here . . . Haldane's older now; it's a while since we saw him. Then, he was stick-thin, his hair used to be smarmed down with some kind of gunge, he wore glasses, his expression was dead. Did he put on weight while he was inside, has since changed his hairstyle and got contact lenses? I wouldn't have thought he's had time to have plastic surgery done.'

'But Tracy Finch said she had seen a man fitting Haldane's description as we knew him not all that long ago.'

That had slipped my mind. 'Then he's perfected both personas. One is his natural self and the other, or others, are acted, make-up, clothes, whatever. She said he was thin. Just about anyone would look thin standing alongside George Harding.'

'It's all possible,' Patrick said, but sounding as though he doubted it. Then he added, 'I agree, this man looks very similar to him.'

'I hope you're not going to sit up a tree all night.'

'I might have to break in.'

'Patrick, this isn't some kind of gizmo-ridden movie!'

I was subjected to a cherubic gaze. 'Trust me.'

It seemed pointless to remind him about the dogs.

It had been agreed that I would stay with the Range Rover, which right now, several hours later, was parked in a woodland track some fifty yards from the main road, or rather the minor road, that led to Market Fyfield. It was ten past ten and had just got fully dark. I dared not switch on the interior light in order to read so had to sit in the darkness. This was because I did not wish to be investigated by the local constabulary, game-keepers or any henchmen of the Danton-Halls/Haldane should they be as suspect as I thought.

Although it was a clear night with brilliant stars it was extremely dark as there was no moon. Most of this magnificent stellar display was blocked to me due to overhead vegetation, but as I sat there quietly my eyes got used to the deep gloom and I discovered I could easily make out the details of the little glade off to my left into which Patrick had disappeared. I tried to concentrate on it, watching for wildlife, to stop myself from dozing off. It was difficult.

Patrick had left the vehicle a few minutes previously and had issued no requests or instructions, just asked me to wait. He had returned a few seconds later to check that I had locked all the doors and to say that his target was a matter of a quarter of a mile away. He would ring me if he got into trouble. This, I knew, was just a sop to my worries as when you've been shot from point-blank range a phone's not a lot of use, is it? So I sat there, the window wound down, trying to make out anything of interest moving in the glade. This did not mean that I neglected to check what was going on in all other directions.

An hour and a quarter went by and I had gone beyond the stage where I could tell myself that a lot of police work involves waiting around. I felt that the local cops could have done this and earned themselves some overtime. Seemingly, just after this thought went through my mind I woke with a start, hitting my head on the door frame, when there was a loud shriek somewhere on the other side of the glade. Heart thumping, I sat quite still. After a short silence but for the distant sound of a couple of cars passing on the road, I heard a hissing sound. There was then another shriek. I relaxed; it was a barn owl. Seconds later I glimpsed it through the trees, a ghostly white shape gliding away, presumably in the direction of the open fields beyond.

Three-quarters of a million years later, when it was getting on for one thirty a.m., my mobile, which for obvious reasons I had silenced, vibrated.

'I can't get Patrick,' Mike Greenway said without preamble. 'Is he with you?'

'Not too far away,' I replied cautiously, not quite sure if it actually was him as the reception was bad. Didn't this man ever sleep?

'I need him back here right away. Lindersland's been found dead – murdered.'

Ye gods. I said, 'Mike, I can hardly hear you. Do you have a landline phone handy?'

'Yes, I'm at home.'

'I'll call you on that number and see if the reception's any better.'

This I did, still keeping watch and, his voice clearer but not much, he confirmed the news. As I was speaking to him a shadowy figure came into my line of vision across the glade. When Patrick arrived I handed him the phone, whispering who wanted to speak to him. But he told me to tell him he'd speak to him in a few minutes as we urgently needed to move from where we were.

'Were you seen?' I asked when I had driven a couple of miles away from the village and parked in a lay-by.

'No. Baumgarten *is* there. I spotted him talking to Danton-Hall, or whoever he is, through a window where the curtains hadn't been closed. I have to say Danton-Hall didn't look too delighted with his guest, who seemed to be overdosing on the whisky.'

'Lindersland's been murdered and Mike wants you back in London straight away.'

'Oh, bloody *hell!*' Patrick groaned and rang the commander. He listened but said little. After the call he sat quietly for a few moments and then said, 'Although Lemotov's in custody it looks as though he somehow got a message to someone and put out a contract for the woman – in revenge.'

'Is that what Mike thinks?'

'No, right now it's what I think.'

'What are you going to do?'

'What can I do but obey Mike's orders and get the local police to raid the house and grab Baumgarten? "No more solo heroics," Daws once said to me, "no more tilting at windmills. Be your age, Gillard." I just pray that I can still squash Haldane and Elferdink underfoot like the lice they are. Shall I drive?'

'*I'll* drive,' I said firmly. I hadn't expected him to be devastated by grief. 'She didn't deserve to die,' I went on to say, hoping I didn't sound reproachful.

'No, she didn't,' Patrick muttered.

A senior officer at Thames Valley Police initially expressed reservations at instantly being expected to raid a property involved in a case about which they knew absolutely nothing. It took a phone call from Commander Greenway, who repeated what Patrick had told them, that Baumgarten was wanted on suspicion of being an accessory to murder and of having a false identity. The American, if indeed he really was an American, was subsequently arrested in his pyjamas. He appeared to be the only occupant of the house and said he had no idea where the Danton-Halls had gone. We gathered that someone from the CID department was remaining in the immediate area to keep an eye on the place.

'What day is it?' Greenway asked tiredly when we finally found him in someone else's office. Since the creation of the NCA and the move to a new location he had been campaigning relentlessly to be given a bigger room. He is a big man and this had come about but it was being redecorated.

'Monday,' I said.

'What happened to the weekend?'

My thoughts precisely. We had reclined our seats in the Range Rover and snatched a couple of hours' sleep in the lay-by, then, a little later, stopped at a motorway services station for breakfast.

'No, it's no good,' the commander then muttered. 'Coffee. Not here.'

Twenty minutes later in a nearby bistro, the caffeine having satisfactorily kicked in all round, he continued, 'Question. How did they know where Lindersland was? She wasn't at home but still at her mother's.'

'They could have got the number of the taxi she arrived in at Tottenham,' Patrick offered. 'Or noticed the name of the firm on the illuminated sign on the roof and blagged the address out of them somehow. I'm pretty sure no one tailed me when we took her back.'

'Lemotov's stopped talking now he's sobered up – refuses to say a word about anything they throw at him,' Greenway said. He then went on to explain that the woman had been on her own in the flat at the time – her mother, Mrs Elaine King, having gone to see a local friend. This may well have saved her life as it appeared that Lindersland had been gunned down, shot in the face, killing her instantly, the moment she had opened the front door to a caller. But the mother was full of remorse as she and her daughter had had words and she had gone out to get away from her for a while. They had never, apparently, been very close.

To me, this had a familiar ring to it. 'King?' I queried. 'Was Lindersland married?'

Greenway shook his head. 'No. But her mother had married again after her husband, Lindersland's father, died. Mr King's dead too now, killed in a car crash.'

'Did Mrs King see anyone hanging around when she went out?' Patrick enquired.

'No, but she did on her return. She says she met a man on the stairs who wished her good morning. Questioned a little further, she added that she couldn't be sure but when she first clapped eyes on him he might have been putting something under his jacket or checking that something was still safe in an inside pocket.'

Patrick nodded briskly. 'No doubt a hand weapon of some kind in a shoulder holster. What were his actual words?'

'That's the interesting bit that I was just coming to. He said, "Good morning, ma'am." She thought he might be an American. And before you jump in again and ask me that too, Patrick, I'll tell you that I've emailed that photo of Clancy Elferdink to the relevant investigating officers.'

I said, 'That doesn't really make sense. Why would Elferdink kill her?'

Patrick said, 'Ingrid has a point. He's possibly implicated in Daws' death but I would have thought not likely to do Lemotov's bidding.'

'Whatever the truth, I hope Mrs King's being given police protection,' I said. 'The killer might want to tidy up that particular loose end.'

'She's going to be taken to her sister's in Tunbridge Wells after she's had a look at the photo – she should be safe enough there,' Greenway disclosed.

There was silence for a few moments and then Patrick said, 'So what do you want me to do, sir?'

The business of Patrick calling the commander sir had been dropped a while back – 'You used to be a lieutenant colonel, for God's sake!' – so its inclusion here was a bit like running out a gun battery on a man o' war.

Greenway fleetingly looked slightly taken aback and then said, 'You *had* been working on the business of Lindersland's disappearance.'

'Which I can't believe has bugger-all to do with the fact that she's now been murdered. Besides, it was Ingrid who found her. I've been concentrating on finding Daws' killer. I'm getting close – one of the American suspects was arrested early this morning.'

'Martin Grindley's been released on police bail,' I reminded them, not at all convinced by Patrick's pronouncement.

Both men looked at me as though I'd just arrived in a spaceship.

'He's bananas,' I added helpfully.

'Well, I suppose we ought to keep that possibility under consideration,' Greenway said slowly. 'But for now I think we ought to assume that those investigating her death will have thought of that.'

'I feel I owe it to you to come clean,' Patrick said. 'MI5's asked me to find Daws' murderer.'

'*Who* in MI5?' the commander queried heavily.

'The boss when we were hijacked.'

'You might have mentioned it in the first place.'

'I wasn't sure of the best way to play it then.'

'I don't like the possibility of conflicts of interest.'

'There's absolutely no conflict of interest as far as I'm concerned. In my view, as Daws was head of the department we used to work for in SOCA, then it's up to his one-time colleagues to find his killer. And please don't tell me that it wouldn't look good on your CV.'

If that wasn't a broadside . . .

Greenway actually smiled, genuinely amused, and then, eyes in the direction of the ceiling, said, 'Daws hired you because you were different. I have to keep reminding myself that the man in front of me was once an army officer and, when he subsequently worked for MI5, was let loose on people suspected of selling their country down the river. This man, let's face it, is like working with something that ought to be in a cage.' His gaze snapped back on Patrick.

'He told me I'd probably end up behind bars,' Patrick recollected.

'You're a family man,' Greenway observed gently.

'Look, I have no intention of indulging in some kind of bloodbath, thereby bringing any number of cherished national institutions into disrepute. I shall *arrest* him. But should he happen to threaten me with any kind of weapon I'll have no choice but to retaliate . . . because I'm a family man.'

'It'll be the last time I give you my blessing for anything like this,' Greenway said after an edgy silence.

'I understand that.'

'It'll serve you right if they give you a bloody knighthood.'

Irvine Baumgarten had been gleefully scooped up by Sussex CID, who had taken him back to Horsham. Interviewed, he had played the innocent American tourist and refused to budge from that. Questioned a little later by DI Barton himself, he had gone on to admit that he did have a friend by the name of Clancy Elferdink, with whom he had been travelling. Clancy, he had snivelled, had gone off somewhere, having dumped him with some English friends of his who clearly did not want him. He hadn't the first idea where Clancy was, nor where his hosts had disappeared to. Worse, Clancy was looking after his passport for him so he had no proof of identity.

'And that's as far as we've got with him,' Barton said, having related this information to us. 'I felt that it was important to do the groundwork and leave it to other investigators to continue with the questioning. But at that stage we were duty-bound to give him food and some rest.'

We had driven down from London and it was now mid-afternoon. I was in need of a proper meal and several hours' sleep myself by this time, even though we had grabbed a sandwich and coffee en route. Patrick appeared to have gone into a state of suspended animation, eyes half closed, like a dozing cat watching a mouse hole, and I think the DI was finding this a bit disconcerting. I wanted to reassure him that this was merely someone trained to recharge his batteries while on the job, but didn't.

'Can we talk to him now?' Patrick asked.

'Why not? He's just sitting in his cell nursing a big sulk.'

On being brought into the interview room Baumgarten slumped into the chair provided for him, rested his chin on his hands and stared straight ahead at a point somewhere between our heads. He could not be described as a good-looking man but would be improved with a better haircut than he was sporting at the moment and a shave. The latter was hardly his fault. Able to have a close look at him in a less difficult situation than previously – for us, that is – I noted down that he was of medium height, had mid-brown wavy hair, a swarthy complexion, small blue eyes and, as I had already observed, was considerably overweight.

Having put his document case on the table, Patrick introduced us – the man had shown no sign of having seen us before – and formally opened the proceedings, adding that everything was being recorded. This elicited no reaction other than Baumgarten meeting Patrick's gaze and then rather wishing he hadn't.

'The fact that we've already met at Hartwood Castle has no great bearing on this,' Patrick began by saying. 'And I'm bound to advise you that you may have a legal representative here if you wish.'

'I had a guy present when I was last questioned. I didn't get the feeling he could do a lot for me as I'm not a Brit.'

'I'm not quite sure why you got that impression but you can have him back at any stage. I also want you to know that we were at Hartwood in our capacity of old friends of Lady Rowallen and therefore were accidental witnesses to your unannounced arrival with Elferdink.'

'We were engaged in a perfectly legitimate enterprise,' Baumgarten snarled, startling me with his sudden anger. It might have been something to do with the insufferably smug look on my husband's face.

'No, it wasn't, or rather isn't, but we'll come to that in a minute. What is your real name?'

'It *is* my real name.'

'No, again. The real Irvine Baumgarten is a priest living in Wyoming.' Here Patrick took the photographs sent over from the United States from his document case and pushed one across the table. 'That's not you, is it?'

'Hardly – it's obviously some goddam imposter.'

'No, for the third time. That is the real Irvine Baumgarten, illegitimate son of the late Samuel Zettinger. And this,' Patrick handed over the other photograph, 'is your chum, Clancy Elferdink. Right?'

'Yes, that's Clancy,' the man conceded.

'Who is a dodgy ex-lawyer to the extent of having been chucked out of the American Bar Association. Were you aware of that?'

'No.'

'Not only that, there's now a warrant out back home for his arrest as he appears to be tied in with criminal gangs. He's wanted on suspicion of murder here, as are you. Any thoughts on that?'

'It's all hogwash. And my name *is* Irvine Baumgarten, despite what this idiot priest in Wyoming says.'

'The man hasn't said a word. He doesn't even know about it. All this information came through authorized channels.'

'It's still hogwash. You're framing me because the cops over here are useless.'

'Everything's becoming much, much clearer. A criminal calling himself Dimitri Lemotov was hired by an ex-civil servant by the name of Nicholas Haldane. Haldane was fresh out of prison and eaten up with the need for revenge because his desire for prestige and wealth had been thwarted by the 14th Earl of Hartwood, together with the police. In short, he subsequently planned to murder the earl. Through some kind of criminal grapevine he contacted Elferdink and they cooked up a plot to get his money, property and title. You were the poor sap hired to impersonate the earl's distant relative's son. Lemotov's been arrested and being questioned, so it's no use your denying any of this because it's all out in the open.'

Some of the bravado seeped away from our suspect.

'Where did you meet Elferdink?' Patrick went on to ask.

'In New York.'

'That was where Mr Zettinger was in a nursing home, wasn't it?'

'Yes.'

'Elferdink told you that?'

'No – er – I mean, yes.'

'Make up your mind.'

'Clancy told me.'

'Tell the truth. Who are you really?'

'I'm not saying any more. I demand to speak to someone from the American Embassy.'

'I'm sure that can be arranged eventually. Handy with guns, are you?'

'No! I don't hold with violence.'

'Isn't being unarmed rather unusual in your country?'

'It may well be. I just don't hold with swaggering around with shooters.'

I thought a deceptively softer touch might be useful here, caught Patrick's eye and he nodded. I said, 'How did Elferdink get hold of the names of Mr Zettinger's solicitors and information like that?'

'God knows.'

'Did he pose as his legal representative?'

'No idea.'

'But details of that kind of thing would have been in the nursing home's records, wouldn't they?'

'You tell me, lady.'

'And, of course, Mr Zettinger would have been far too confused to be able to remember things like that.'

'He wasn't that bad and a nice old man really.'

Silence but for Baumgarten swearing under his breath.

'You worked there,' Patrick stated flatly. 'You got all the information Elferdink wanted.'

'I'm not saying any more and I mean it this time.'

His interrogator sighed contentedly. 'So the witness we have was right. The man with the American accent who went with Lemotov to kill the earl was you after all.'

'*What?*' the man gasped incredulously.

'Well, it was one or the other of you. We know that and I'm sure it'll shortly be confirmed by what Lemotov says. He's not Russian at all by the way, just a London mobster.'

'But . . .'

'OK, so what *really* happened?'

'Look, I wasn't in on this homicide!'

'There were two actually as the bodyguard was killed as well. Give us the full story.'

There was a long silence and then, 'I suppose I'll have to think about it.' For what must have been a full minute this time, the man went quiet. Then he said, 'OK, I'm not doing time for that jerk.'

'What happened after you left the castle?'

'Clancy drove to the place where those folk live and said to stay with them until he gave me the word he'd got the money and I'd get my share.'

'And you *believed* that?'

'Yeah,' the man muttered.

'Where did you hire the car?'

'Heathrow.'

'I have news for you. What you were told at the castle is quite correct. Right now Elferdink knows that. He was probably aware there was no title for you or the rightful son at the start but strung you along hoping to bully the widow into buying you off. As far as titles go bastards can't inherit and that's not an insult, it's English heraldry.'

Although his last remark had not been aimed directly at him, Baumgarten, or whoever he was, winced.

'Presumably Elferdink has your passport. Or have you destroyed it?'

'No, he has it.'

'Forged?'

'I guess so.'

'You know so. You won't get it back. You've been left high and dry over here and are an illegal immigrant. When you've done your stretch for murder or being an accessory to murder you'll be deported if your countrymen don't extradite you first.'

'Shit,' the man muttered.

'Where is Elferdink?'

'No idea.'

'Have you heard from him since he left you there?'

'Yeah, just the once. He sounded happy and said everything

had gone to plan. I said, "For God's sake get me out of here
– they hate my guts.'"

'Who d'you reckon was calling the tune – him or them?'

'Them. The guy wanted to talk to Clancy so I handed my
phone over and although I went away a bit I heard him shouting
at Clancy to get me out of his house. Nothing happened though
and it began to get a bit nasty.'

'And you say you know nothing of what he's been up to
since you arrived there?'

'Nope. You reckon he killed those guys on a previous trip to
the UK?'

Patrick ignored the question. 'Tell me exactly where you met
him.'

'At the funeral. I always go to the funerals of folk I helped
look after. He came up to me and first of all said he'd traced
Mr Zettinger's ancestry and found I was related to him. I might
inherit, he said, as the old man had had no living kin. He was
all friendly but I didn't believe him to start with.'

'But how did he explain his involvement?' I enquired.

'He just said he was an interested party. That's not out of
order in the US as some attorneys are like that – always looking
for the chance to make money. Ambulance chasers, I think you
call them over here.'

'A hearse chaser,' Patrick murmured. 'Then he told you of
his plan.'

'I didn't feel good pretending to be someone I wasn't and
had no idea where he'd gotten the name from – just thought it
was off the top of his head. But Clancy said the money'd all
go to your government if we didn't put in a claim.'

'Did you really think you'd end up being the 15th Earl of
Hartwood?'

'Yeah, to start with after he'd given me all this bullshit. I've
been a sucker, haven't I?'

'You could say that.'

I was glad that Patrick appeared not to be harbouring a
huge resentment against this man, for as he had himself said,
he had been a sucker. In my opinion he was lucky to be alive,
given the inclinations of the people with whom he had been
associating.

The questioning went on for a little longer and Patrick finally got him to say that his real name was John Pogue. He pressed him for Elferdink's whereabouts but he still insisted that he didn't know. As by then Pogue was in a mood to make Elferdink eat his yellow-and-orange tartan trousers, we thought he was telling the truth. He was charged with being an accessory to murder, with possibly more charges to follow, and remanded in custody.

Yes, the picture was becoming clearer but the only real progress was that a watch was put on airports, ports and bus and railway stations for Nicholas Haldane, the Danton-Halls – the two men had to be regarded as different people until we knew otherwise – Clancy Elferdink, plus any number of dubious associates who might be travelling with them.

FIFTEEN

'What happened to those dogs?' I asked when we were on our way to Hartwood and Patrick had just been speaking to whoever had been watching the Danton-Halls' home in Berkshire. From the one side of the conversation I had been able to overhear it was obvious that they had not returned.

'As they appeared to have been abandoned they got the RSPCA to take them away. There was no sign of a housekeeper or other staff but a local girl who keeps an eye on the horses turned up and was questioned. She doesn't know where the Danton-Halls might have gone either.'

Another thing we had learned was that after his arrest Dimitri Lemotov, foul-mouthed and violent, had been taken to West End Central police station. He was already wanted in connection with other gangland crimes, but after a telephone conversation with DI Barton Patrick called Commander Greenway and asked him to persuade the Met to take Lemotov to Horsham on the grounds that the Sussex murder case was more pressing. We had not heard the result of this request by the time we reached Hartwood.

Lady Rowallen knew we were coming and was delighted with the news that one of the Americans was in custody. We had previously discussed it and did not feel it the right time to tell her that Marcia Lindersland had been murdered.

A little later, and unlike in movies featuring sleuths who neither seem to eat nor sleep, Patrick and I enjoyed a substantial and excellent dinner with her, including several glasses of wine, then fell into bed and slept the sleep of the exhausted.

'Real life is better and sometimes worse,' I found myself mumbling to myself as I awoke. I was rather shocked to discover that it was a quarter to nine.

Real life in the shape of my husband didn't seem to be around but he came into the room, fully dressed in what he refers to as his rough gear, half a minute later.

'I heard gunfire just as it was getting light,' he reported. 'So I roused Christopher and we went outside carrying shotguns. I asked him to patrol by the house looking as though he meant business while I reconnoitered. No one was around that I could see but there were fresh tyre marks on a track in the woods, a 4×4 of some kind, not far from where we saw that bloke with binoculars hiding in the tree. I then found a couple of half-smoked cigarettes nearby, which suggests they left in a hurry, and put them in an evidence bag.'

'It could have been poachers or just local yobs.'

'It could but it wasn't. What I had heard was small-arms fire, not shotguns, and you probably wouldn't hear air rifles from this distance. I didn't wait around to look for any more evidence, whether they'd been shooting at trees for target practice, for example, but came straight back here in case. I don't like things like that.' He tossed off what he was wearing and hunted out something a bit more formal from his bag. Then, mostly inside a shirt, he went on, 'Today we might even get from Lemotov where Haldane's hiding.'

This was not to be as when we were just finishing a practically on-the-hoof breakfast of toast and coffee Patrick got a call from DI Barton. His face went very grim. At length he asked, 'Are *you* OK, though? . . . Thank God for that . . . Yes, we'll come straight over.'

'Bad news?' I said.

'The van bringing Lemotov was just pulling into the nick's forecourt when a Land Rover Discovery rammed it and three or four armed men – he's not quite sure – jumped out. A constable crossing the area was immediately shot at and wounded. They then burst into the nick, grabbed a woman and her daughter who were waiting to report something in reception, dragged them back outside and held guns to their heads, demanding Lemotov be handed over. When nothing happened immediately they fired at the windscreen of the van, seriously wounding the driver. The man with him froze with shock so the gang blasted off the locks of the vehicle and released Lemotov. Another car was waiting by this time and they piled into it, having shot out all the front windows of the nick on the way with what sounds like some kind of sub-machine gun. Quite a few people have been cut by flying glass.'

'The 4×4 you saw the tracks of in the wood?'

'Well, the one used at the nick was stolen. Won't be difficult to find out. I'll ask Barton to send someone out to take some impressions.' He sat down on the bed. 'I feel responsible for this as he was brought to Horsham at my suggestion. But who else knew?'

Ambulances and police from Worthing were at the scene when we arrived, the latter assisting members of the resident CID in taking evidence, the whole of the forecourt cordoned off with incident tape which hung limply in the soaking drizzle. Inside was a different story, shocked people giving every impression that they intended to carry on with their normal duties yet seemed unable to remember clearly what these were.

The open-plan staircase was strewn with broken glass and here and there on the floor were spots and smears of blood. The story was the same in the main CID office, which faced the front of the building, only with more glass and a lot more blood. One woman, seemingly uninjured, sat at a desk looking shell-shocked, a colleague talking quietly to her.

Barton was in his office, horribly pale, holding a blood-soaked handkerchief to his neck, a small red puddle on the desk in front of him.

'God, this all happened in seconds. And the DCI's in Barcelona,' he said, or rather mumbled.

'Do you want him brought back?' Patrick asked.

'No.'

'Who the hell knew Lemotov was coming here?'

'Pass. But it might be nothing more complicated than knowing he'd been arrested and someone with half a brain thinking it through and realizing he might be brought here for questioning.'

'Can I assist in any way?'

'Tell 'em you have my authority.'

Patrick immediately organized a paramedic for the DI, who

took one look at him and the gash on his neck and called up a team with a stretcher. The pair of us then went through the entire building looking for other people who were injured and I found a woman in the toilets trying to stem a large bleeding cut on her hand under warm water. Patrick stationed a PC who insisted that he was all right on the main entrance and shepherded everyone else not actually doing anything into the canteen, which was undamaged, and asked the staff to provide free hot drinks. When they demurred he slapped his NCA credit card on the counter and uttered a few choice expletives. They got on with it.

Outside, a few minutes later, we were told that the scenes-of-crime people had been held up. Patrick assumed the DI's role while I questioned onlookers and other members of the public who were waiting around in the rain, as some had pictures of the crime on their mobiles. Others had noted registration numbers of the vehicles involved and some even had descriptions of the gang that could be determined despite the fact that they had been wearing masks. And Horsham, of course, a quiet one-time market town, is not the kind of place where honest citizens would be frightened of retribution from any resident mobsters, because there probably aren't any.

An hour or so later, a DCI and a DI from Sussex Police HQ at Lewes arrived and took charge, together with my notes, the former giving us a cursory nod by way of thanks.

'One assumes a full-scale search is also underway for those responsible,' my working partner murmured to them before we took our extremely damp selves off to the car. 'And you might try to discover how the gang knew Lemotov was being brought here today.'

It emerged when we located him in A&E, having had his neck wound stitched, that Adrian Barton had already put a manhunt into operation. He was still as white as the bandage around his throat and definitely not fizzing.

'I'm waiting for my wife to give me a lift back to the nick,' he then told us in little more than a whisper.

'The hell you are!' Patrick snorted. 'A DCI Bigfeet from HQ has temporarily taken over. You must go home and rest.'

'*Who?*' the DI asked weakly.

'Size elevens at least. He didn't bother to introduce himself.'

'My bike's at work,' Barton agonized.

'It'll be quite safe in the middle of a crime scene, won't it?' The DI shrugged sadly.

'Have you remembered any more of what happened?'

'Only that there were four of them and one was of heavy build. I think he was the one who shot and wounded Constable Blake in the forecourt. He's not too bad by the way – I asked. The woman and her teenage daughter are here too being checked over for shock. No idea about the guy in the van but I'm guessing it's serious. Where was I?'

'You told me earlier that the other bloke in the van just froze up.'

'Yes, they dragged him out and yelled at him to open up but he just froze and then sank down on to his knees. They kicked him a couple of times then gave up and started firing at the locks on the back doors. This had taken only a few moments, you understand. I was moving away from the window by this time to grab a phone and they must have got the suspect out just seconds later when the windows crashed in. A sub-machine gun. As you yourselves saw . . . the whole of the front of the station was shot up. I can't understand . . . why nobody was killed, either from the shots or flying glass. It was blasted through open doorways . . . went everywhere. Sorry, but you must . . . have seen that too. And sorry again . . . I really feel a bit too weird to say any more.'

We stayed with him until his wife, Margo, arrived, when it became necessary for Patrick to provide considerable assistance to get him to their car. He had, she informed us, eyes skywards, refused to be admitted for a possible blood transfusion, and she had been told it was a miracle the piece of glass had not sliced through any of the vital blood vessels.

'So what will they do with Lemotov now they've got him?' Patrick wondered aloud when we were having a mini debriefing in the car.

'Kill him,' I said.

'That would be right on trend, wouldn't it? Too dangerous to leave him alive to grass on them when he's caught up with again.'

'It worries me that it might have been them having target practice near the castle.'

'It worries me too. But it's not my job to track down an escaped suspect.'

I waited for the 'but'.

'And he's not the man I'm really after,' Patrick added after a little more mental wrangling.

But?

I said, 'I'm even more concerned about Jane Grindley. Her husband told the police he was going back to the houseboat. I'm not at all sure why they released him on bail.'

'Retired assistant commissioner and all that, I suppose.'

'But someone in an even more senior position has made a serious complaint against him.'

'Ingrid, you seem to have got into the habit of asking me questions I can't possibly know the answers to!'

'I don't expect you to but a little more constructive thinking right now would be helpful.'

We glowered at one another for a few moments.

'Domestic spats apart . . .' Patrick resumed quietly.

'You want to go after Lemotov and I need to check on Jane Grindley.'

He smiled ruefully. 'OK.' Then leaned over and kissed my cheek. 'D'you reckon Barton would lend me his motorbike?'

'No, I don't!'

I shut my mind to whichever mode of transport Patrick might use. He had insisted I take the car and I headed north. The DCI from Lewes apparently had a theory that the fugitive, in the care of his rescuers, would head for Brighton first and go to ground for a while, as that's what they usually do. I reasoned that that may well apply to local outlaws but this lot, as far as I knew, weren't.

Perhaps my concerns over Martin Grindley were flying in the face of common sense. But, as his wife had said, he had been besotted with the woman. Recently he had imprisoned her and, from what Lindersland herself had said, thought he could persuade her to live with him. Daft, but men are like that sometimes. It had happened to Patrick not all that long ago: a woman he had once known turning up and bewitching him with reminders of more carefree times before he was seriously injured, a lost youth, of days before his regiment was effectively destroyed by mergers. She had, for a short while, almost turned him against me.

'Powerful stuff,' I whispered to myself. In my wildest moments I had wanted to kill her.

Did Grindley have a gun and, if not, where would he have obtained one? Mentally unbalanced probably due to senility, his attitude could have been that if he couldn't have her, no one else would. He had old-fashioned ideas about women. And Lindersland's sprawled position on the bed in that room had spoken of having been given a violent shove. Also, he had been furiously angry, and had the facial expression of a man who had been told to sod off and release her this minute.

And if his wife had now told him to sod off as well?

Parked at Teddington, close to where I had before, I thought about it. I am no sailor but I am aware that the difficult thing about checking on people who live on a boat is that if one tries to sneak on board it rocks slightly, thus warning those below that they have a visitor. There was no legitimate reason for me to call and Grindley, if he was even there, would hardly welcome my presence.

What the situation really demanded was Patrick as the two men had not met and he could pass himself off as an official of the river authority as an excuse to have a look round. I flirted with the idea of recruiting someone from the local constabulary but reasoned that unless they were experienced at working undercover most cops tended to look like cops even in plain clothes. I could hardly borrow Terry as he was needed at the castle. There was only one other person I could call on. I found my mobile.

'You know you preferred Patrick to concentrate on investigating Lindersland's murder . . .?' I began when he answered the phone and we had exchanged greetings.

'I did,' said Michael Greenway.

'He's gone after Lemotov as he thinks he put out a contract for her killing. I'm concentrating on checking on Jane Grindley's safety for, as you know, I have a bad feeling about her husband.'

'I thought Lemotov was in custody!'

'Sorry, communications breakdown.' I told him what had happened in Horsham.

He swore, apologised and then said, 'I'm on a day off and thought I'd switched off my mobile. Is it really important?'

An extremely *rare* day off. Feeling very guilty, I said, 'I'm not all that far away from you at Teddington. I was wondering if you could spare an hour or so to call on the Grindleys on some pretext or other. Sorry again, but I simply don't know who else to ask and he knows me.' Pride perhaps prevented me from saying that this man might attack me on sight for ruining his plans.

'Must be plenty of cops in your neck of the woods.'

'Right now I don't need PC Plod!'

He must have taken this as a compliment as he changed his mind and promised to be with me as soon as was practical.

Mike, wearing what looked like his gardening jeans and a T-shirt with a couple of holes in it, arrived just under an hour later and for this reason and a couple of others: bits of leaves in his hair, a streak of oil on his face, he definitely didn't look like a cop. Before I contacted him I had checked that the *Alice May* was indeed at her berth. She was, with no outward signs of life on board. I agonized that they had probably merely gone shopping in the nearest Waitrose.

'This is much better than cutting a hedge,' the commander said, taking a deep breath of muddy-reed-bed-scented air and gazing appreciably over the water. 'Oh, some news for you. That man Mrs King, Lindersland's mother, saw on the stairs has turned out to be a Canadian who's just moved into the top flat. Where's the boat?'

I walked with him until we were just out of sight of it, told him its name and then waited. Several long minutes elapsed, seagulls swooped on pigeons being fed bread by a woman and toddler, swans glided by, a man in a canoe almost capsized and somewhere in the distance a clock struck three.

'And is there honey still for tea?' I whispered.

Greenway came into view, waved and I went to him. 'I haven't been on board but no one *seems* to be there,' he said when I got close. 'But I've got one of your funny feelings about it.'

We went on board and, as I had expected, the boat rocked a little. I immediately noticed that the plants were drooping as they needed watering. Then, somewhere below, there were muffled thumping noises. It ceased. When we moved towards the stern it started again.

'Do they have a dog?' Greenway queried.

'Not so far as I know,' I replied.

We tried the door at the stern but it was securely locked. As we went back towards the bow the banging started up again.

'Something's not right and I'm going to break in,' Greenway said, gazing at the lock on the low doorway into the saloon. The door itself was half glazed but despite the bright afternoon all was fairly dim within and we could make out nothing to give a reason for the noise. He stepped back on to what had once been the tow path – the slight movement of the boat setting the banging going again – and hunted around until he found a largish stone.

'The key *might* be on the inside,' he said hopefully and smashed the glass.

It was, and having knocked out a little more glass Greenway unlocked the door and we went down the three steps into the saloon.

'Anyone there?' he called.

Frenzied banging.

June Grindley, bound and gagged, was lying on the floor of a cabin off the saloon and had obviously been kicking against a chair so that it hit the wall. She had been there for some time and wept uncontrollably when we released her, hardly able to move her limbs. The commander then tactfully disappeared while I calmed her down and helped her undress. Then she had a wash in an adjacent tiny bathroom while I found her some dry clothes. The distressing effect of being tied up for long periods of time is not usually mentioned in books and films.

I was feeling almost responsible for this ghastly state of affairs. If only I had followed my instincts and come sooner. Really worried that she was dehydrated and minded to call a paramedic – June was not a young woman – I watched her carefully. But seeing my concern she huskily said she would be all right when she'd had a large mug of tea.

'He's quite mad,' she then mumbled.

I had recently heard that same remark from another of Grindley's victims.

Greenway had usefully busied himself by making the

much-needed tea, finding a tin of biscuits. June felt she could face the world by this time but was slightly baffled by my companion and his appearance, especially when I told her who he was.

'Where's your normal colleague that you mentioned to Martin?' she asked me, obviously quite unable to believe that I worked directly with a commander.

Greenway chuckled. 'Oh, there's nothing normal about Patrick.'

'D'you feel like talking about it?' I asked when June was on her second mug of tea.

'I feel like braining the fool,' she responded angrily.

'Are you OK?' I asked urgently when she went pale.

'Oh, God, I've just remembered! He said he would come back when I'd had time to reflect on my errors – his exact words – and set fire to the boat.'

'Don't worry, we'll take you somewhere safe,' Greenway said soothingly.

'But this is my home! Everything I own is here! Everything special.' Her eyes filled with tears again. 'He'll destroy it all!'

'It really is all right,' the commander assured her. 'Someone will be here waiting for him and arrest him when he does turn up.'

'But he might be ages. And you can't justify keeping someone here for long.'

Spoken by someone who knew the workings of the police.

'I'll stay,' I said.

'But you can't, my dear – he's old but really strong and he'll hurt you. As I said, he's mad. He ought to be in a psychiatric hospital.'

'It'll be fine, I'll call up assistance,' I said. I couldn't really tell her that if he behaved threateningly towards us I'd shoot him.

'He took me completely unawares,' June continued. 'The second time he came back – after he'd disappeared for hours, that is – and obviously I'm referring to the times when I didn't know where he'd been and was beside myself – he was furious. I took a book into the bow and tried to read. I knew he was pacing around in here and then he must have calmed down as everything went quiet. I went back, thinking I ought to get the dinner ready. I was in the galley when he grabbed me from behind. He said I was a real nuisance, actually told me I had outlived my usefulness to . . .' She broke off, her voice failing.

Greenway said something under his breath that we were not intended to hear.

'And then he tied me up,' June went on. 'Told me he'd knock me out if I struggled. At first I thought I could wriggle out of the ropes when he'd gone, that he might not do them up very tight so I could escape after a little while. That he might have some kind of feeling left for me but he . . .' She broke down again.

I put an arm around her shoulders, thinking that I might just shoot the bastard on sight anyway.

After a minute or so June made a big effort to carry on with her account and said, 'I simply don't know what's been going on. The first time he went off for hours without saying where he was going was later in the same day you came to see us, Miss Langley. When he returned that time he was in a really black mood. God above knows what'd been happening to set him off like that.'

I glanced at Greenway who said, gently, 'He'd been arrested, Mrs Grindley.'

'What on *earth* for?'

'He'd invited Marcia Lindersland to a house in New Malden on the pretext of renewing an old acquaintance so that she could meet you. A couple had been paid by him to hold her there against her will.'

'But . . .' June sat up, straightening her shoulders. 'No, that makes sense, absolute sense. It explains a lot of things.'

'Does he have a handgun of any kind?' Greenway went on to ask.

'Martin? No! At least—'

She stopped speaking because the boat had rocked slightly.

Quietly, the commander got to his feet and approached the bow doorway to stand to one side of it. There were no sounds of footsteps on the deck above but the almost imperceptible movement of the craft indicated that someone was walking above our heads. June looked at me in alarm but I put a finger to my lips and then a steadying hand on her arm. I was aware of my grip tightening on it when a man looked cautiously around the doorway.

'It's all right, it's the normal colleague,' I said.

SIXTEEN

Patrick came in, didn't look surprised when he beheld his boss and shook hands with a bemused Mrs Grindley.

'Lemotov?' Greenway enquired.

'He was found very dead at the side of the road near Henfield in Sussex,' Patrick replied. 'Shot in the head. I got a call almost as soon as Ingrid left me and so I caught a train here. The route suggests the rest may have headed for Brighton.'

If so, the DCI from Lewes had been correct.

'You were asking me if Martin has a handgun,' June said to Greenway, happily not involved with what they were talking about and needing to get back to business. 'He used to have one at one time – I saw it in a drawer in the days when we lived in a house. I challenged him about it and he said he needed it in connection with his job. I assumed when he retired that he'd had to hand it back and thought no more about it.'

'Did assistant commissioners need to be armed in his day?' Patrick asked his boss.

'No,' Greenway answered shortly.

'He would have been more junior than that when he had it,' June said.

'For a special assignment then, perhaps,' Greenway conceded. 'But everyone's very careful regarding firearms so I simply don't know how he could have ended up keeping it.'

'Has he shot someone then?' June ventured.

'He might have done,' I told her. 'But there's no evidence as yet to incriminate him.'

'*She's* been shot?'

'I'm afraid so,' Greenway said. 'Did your husband make any comment about anything like that when he returned the second time?'

'No, it was all about him. How wronged he was and it was all my fault, almost as though he was blaming me for actually existing. I have to say he bears no resemblance now to the man I married.'

Greenway rose. 'I'll organize surveillance. Please don't worry, Mrs Grindley, he'll be re-arrested and won't threaten you again. Patrick, I'd like a word with you outside.'

Whatever this entailed, it only took a couple of minutes and when Patrick came back, he said, 'He's gone home to cut his hedge but armed protection should be here in about twenty minutes. There'll be a round-the-clock watch by various people, on board if you want them to be, Mrs Grindley.'

'So I'll be a prisoner here.'

'Not at all. You don't have to stay here. If you want to go somewhere else, Ingrid and I can take you there or arrange transport if it's not local. But for your own safety you will need to keep a low profile until he's arrested.'

'No, I won't bother you any more, thank you. I'll think about it and can always call a taxi to take me to a hotel, can't I?'

'As long as it's not one where you've stayed with your husband in the past.'

'Oh, dear, the things you have to think about.'

We remained with her until a slim woman of probably some twenty-five summers wearing plain clothes appeared and presented us with her warrant card. I think the boat owner had been expecting something a little more outwardly intimidating but said nothing and we left the pair of them getting acquainted.

'I'm now off duty and fancy a pint,' Patrick announced. 'Is there a pub handy, do you know?'

'The Red Dragon,' I told him. 'Open all day.'

'Then we can get back to Hartwood.'

'What did Greenway want to talk to you about?'

'He asked me to stick closely by you in case Grindley tries to work off a bit more resentment.'

'It's nice to be loved,' I joked.

We left it at that, for now June Grindley had police protection we could concentrate on bringing Richard Daws' murderer to justice. On reflection this was probably more important to Patrick than anything he had ever worked on since leaving MI5. I was fervently hoping it would be over soon; the man still looked completely exhausted.

Pondering on this and other things as we walked the short distance to the pub I wondered if, denied the regional position, he would hand in his notice to the NCA as soon as this case was over and find a safer job that was also near to home. It was what I had wanted him to do for some time and now I thought it very likely.

I could be described as carefree then, leading the way through the entrance and towards the door into the saloon bar of The Red Dragon – carelessly, forgetfully, stupidly carefree.

Then . . .

'Won't be a mo,' Patrick said and I turned to see him heading towards the gents. For some reason he turned back. 'Everything all right?'

'I'm an idiot – this is Grindley's local,' I hissed.

'Surely he wouldn't risk hanging around here.'

I shrugged and, practical as ever, he grabbed me and bundled me through the door into his intended destination. I sought refuge in a cubicle while he availed himself of the facilities and we only met one other customer on the way out, who gave me a funny look.

'What does Grindley look like?' Patrick whispered, having paused in the doorway.

'Tall, portly, mostly bald, probably late sixties,' I replied. 'I think he normally drinks in the public bar.'

'I'd rather you stayed well away while I check but you never do.'

True, but this was the kind of thing we had rehearsed countless times. Going into the public bar in the lead Patrick paused, no doubt smiling as though looking for a mate – I don't know, I wasn't watching him. No Grindley. In the same formation we then made our way through a group of several drinkers standing yarning by the counter, the only occupants but for a couple seated at a table by a window, towards the door marked Lounge.

He was here.

'Stand aside!' Grindley yelled at Patrick the moment he saw us. 'I've no quarrel with you, whoever you are. Just her.'

The weapon that he had yanked from a pocket, a short-barrelled Smith and Wesson, was now aimed, if a little unsteadily, directly at us.

Three other people in the bar bolted through an archway and I was vaguely aware of a few more rooted to the spot over to my left.

'I'm a police officer and you're under arrest,' Patrick said. 'I warn you, I'm armed.'

'I see no gun,' Grindley jeered.

'There are other people here who may be injured if you do anything reckless. Put the weapon down.'

Grindley actually appeared to think about it for a couple of seconds and then fired.

In that short space of time I had dived to the floor. Before I had finished rolling along and ended up mostly under a rectangular table on one wall there was another shot. A hail of tiny missiles, splinters, came from somewhere, a few slamming into the side of my face. A woman started screaming and didn't stop.

A third shot had fired almost simultaneously with the previous one and there was a heavy crash.

'Shut that woman up!' Patrick's voice yelled.

That alone sufficed. She stopped.

Cautiously, I reversed my journey out from under the table and stood up. My cheek felt as though it had been stung by several bees.

Patrick was staring at me as though he'd seen a ghost and then managed to get out, 'God, I thought he'd hit you.'

'No, only the table leg,' I said.

Grindley had died before he could kill me third time lucky.

Bizarrely, the first representative of the law to arrive on the scene was Michael Greenway, breathless. Later it emerged that he had decided to sit on a riverside seat as he needed to make a couple more phone calls. Having stayed longer than he intended – it was a pleasant afternoon – he had heard the shots. Needless to say, he took charge and inevitably declared the pub a crime scene.

My priority before making a statement was to find someone to remove the splinters from my face. This manifested itself in a paramedic who arrived on a motorbike having been diverted from his intended course after a member of the public had dialled 999 – one of those who had sensibly run for their lives. He soothingly told me that he didn't think I would be scarred for ever but it did bleed quite a lot.

'Anaesthetic,' Greenway said, handing me a gin and tonic during a short break in the proceedings when the local police had arrived together with a pathologist. 'Plenty of witnesses, thank the Lord. The landlady said he'd been behaving oddly today, drinking more than usual and was rude to her, but she couldn't be expected to know that he had a gun on him. It's Met issue, by the way.'

I told Greenway where Grindley's garage was as I had a suspicion what was stored there.

A little later, a dressing over the worst of the small holes in my face, I found Patrick sitting by a window in the other bar waiting to make his statement.

'The last thing I wanted to do was kill him,' he said, staring stonily at nothing.

'I know,' I said, putting a hand over one of his. 'But I think you'll find that he was psyching himself up to torch the boat with June in it.'

'We'll have to go and tell her.'

'Mike's going to do that.'

'I ought to.'

'No, Patrick, you don't. All he's going to say is that he was shot by a police marksman when he resisted arrest and threatened people with a gun, which is perfectly true.'

'The man was ill.'

'So were people like Hitler.'

Gazing at me, Patrick took a deep breath and said, 'I'm so glad you're OK, though.'

Shockingly, he then put his head in his hands and wept.

In the next half a minute or so I mentally composed his letter of resignation.

Forestalling any protestations from Patrick – in the event none were forthcoming – I insisted I drive the pair of us home, Greenway having used his eyes and ordered him to take a week's leave.

'We're not going to Hartwood,' I had said, this one of the rare occasions when I really put my foot down. 'Pamela has

Terry and Christopher, who equate to half-a-dozen ordinary blokes, plus DI Barton and a large chunk of Sussex Police if necessary. Someone only has to pick up a phone.'

It was quite late when we arrived in Hinton Littlemore after a journey during which we had hardly exchanged a word and, having raided the fridge for something to eat, the pair of us went to bed. The following morning I got up early, at just after six, leaving Patrick sleeping, and made myself some tea. The kitchen, the Rayburn with the kettle simmering on it, the kittens, catlets now, tumbling from their basket to mew for breakfast, the view of the garden through the kitchen window – I needed this normality and peace.

The garden looked dry, suggesting that it hadn't rained here, but there was a heavy mist hanging over the village that was gradually turning to drizzle. Having fed the kittens and made tea – you have to do it in that order or you risk tripping over or treading on them – I went outside for a few moments, in my dressing gown, and felt the cool, blessed dampness on my face.

Had my wonderful, brave man cracked?

I was sitting at the kitchen cradling my mug of tea when Elspeth came in, I expect to feed the cats in case Patrick and I weren't yet up.

'You've hurt your face!'

'Just a few splinters,' I explained.

Patrick's mother is nobody's fool. 'Patrick told me that he intended to go after whoever murdered Richard Daws. I take it this was in connection with that.' Both she and John had met him; he had visited this house when Patrick worked for MI5.

'No, actually, it wasn't,' I replied. 'Although there was one small link it alters nothing.'

'And Patrick?'

I burst into tears.

'Oh, dear,' I heard her murmur. She brought a chair closer and put an arm around me.

'What has he done?'

'It's nothing like that, he's not in trouble,' I told her, knowing what she was thinking after various scrapes he's been in in the past, trying to pull myself together, the words tumbling out of me. 'Only with himself. He shot a man who tried to kill me because I'd rescued someone he'd kidnapped. He was quite old and probably mentally ill or suffering from dementia, and it looks as though he was about to set fire to his houseboat with his wife inside it as that's what he'd threatened to do.'

'Umm,' said Elspeth. 'How dreadful. Ghastly. But what else could Patrick have done?'

'Nothing. But . . .' I made myself say it. 'It was having to kill someone who was ill that he'd never even met before.'

'But he saved your life.'

'Yes, but how many times should I ask that of him?'

'No, that can't be right because I should imagine that if you work together it's . . . what shall I say? . . . all part of the job. Forgive me, Ingrid, as I really don't know how heavily you're involved with what Patrick does, but from what I've seen and heard over the years I should imagine that you're right there by his side.'

I was thinking that Martin Grindley would be alive this morning if I hadn't been present as he would have been arrested when he went back to the boat, loaded with incendiaries or not.

Patrick entered, yawning. He immediately ceased to do so when he saw his mother and kissed her cheek.

'I have a week's leave,' he informed her, seating himself while I made them both fresh tea.

'Good, the children will be so happy to have you at home for a bit.'

'And, after that, I'm going to resign.'

'Splendid. That'll make *everyone* happy.'

Very carefully, I poured boiling water into the teapot.

Being Elspeth, she then got right to the point. 'Does that mean you're going to abandon finding Richards Daws' killer personally?'

'Yes, I am. I've every faith in Detective Inspector Barton and his team from the local police.'

'Ah.'

'I've had enough, Mum.'

Silence.

'You can't,' Elspeth said softly.

I stared at her in horror.

'You'll hate yourself for ever.'

Another silence.

'Patrick, I really disliked Richard Daws. I thought him a ruthless man with scant regard for those who worked for him. That's only the impression I got from meeting him briefly a couple of times so I may be quite wrong. My instincts tell me that those responsible for his death are even more ruthless and probably international criminals. You can't leave arresting them to a detective inspector from Sussex, no matter how high the esteem you hold him in.'

'There comes a time . . .' He stopped speaking.

'Ingrid's just told me what happened yesterday.'

In the endless silence that followed this I poured the tea, too soon, and handed it out, feeling, as I usually do in difficult situations in the company of the pair of them, superfluous and an intruder.

Patrick got to his feet and, taking his tea with him, left the room.

'You hate me, but I do know my son,' Elspeth said sadly and also went, through the other door into the conservatory and towards the annexe.

I wanted to hurry after her and tell her I didn't but in the end refrained. Both she and John have always expected far too much of Patrick.

Fully occupied with five delighted young people, baby Mark putting a well-chewed rusk into Patrick's mouth by way of a Big Hello, there were hardly any opportunities for important discussions and that was just as well. I didn't want to talk about anything sensitive right now and it was perfectly obvious that neither did he. I was not aware of his having written a letter of resignation but his Glock 17 was securely locked away in the wall safe in the living room, together with my Smith and Wesson.

All this was surreal and very unsettling, but I had a novel to finish.

Feeling slightly treacherous, I had phoned Terry in a quiet private moment on the second day at home and told him what had happened. He had appeared to be completely unfazed by the news.

'Don't worry,' he had told me. 'Remember what happened

when he was working undercover as a Hells Angel in his MI5 days and those bikers tied him to a gate and thrashed him with a belt until he almost died? He went a bit up the wall for a while after that – aesthetic, thinking guys often do. I'm not a thinking guy and that's why I was hired to work alongside him. I go in and sort the buggers out.'

'I seem to remember that we joined forces and sorted them out,' I had said.

'So we did. I'll do a bit of sniffing around about these Danton-Halls Patrick told me about. See if I can discover if the bloke really is Haldane with a face transplant.'

'Please don't leave the castle.' I hadn't been aware that Patrick had discussed them with him.

'No problem. I have a lot of contacts, some not necessarily on the right side of the law.'

I was very grateful for his cheerful support, and always have been, but this was different. This time Patrick hadn't gone a bit up the wall – on that occasion he had accused Terry and me of having an affair – but was suffering from some kind of post-traumatic stress disorder. I didn't quite know what to do about it, or even if I should try to.

Finally, the oracle decided to shut up her shop and pull down the shutters.

Five days went by and I endeavoured to make everything as 'normal' as possible. The three older children were at school during the day and I achieved my ambition of taking Vicky and Mark to the toddlers' club held in the village hall. This did not go as well as I had expected. Mark was really suffering from an emerging tooth, making him fretful and grizzly. Poor little Vicky ended up being pushed over by a bigger child in some kind of disagreement over the sand pit, at which point I gathered them up, walked out and lugged the wailing pair home.

'I must be a lousy mother,' I said, or probably also wailed to Carrie when we encountered her in the kitchen and I had told her what had happened.

'You're not. Some of the kids down there are real brats,' she replied briskly and raided a tin for a couple of biscuits.

Sweet silence fell.

I hadn't thought of that. I was a lousy mother.

Patrick, I knew, had spent time with his father in John's study.
I did not comment or ask questions, not even when, one afternoon, John took him clay-pigeon shooting. The rector has won
several trophies at this and I got the impression when they
returned that my husband was completely unruffled by taking
part in the afternoon's sport – nay, enjoyed it – even though it
had been too late for him to enter the actual competition.

Would he go back to work in a couple of days or not?

The following morning, Terry phoned me.

'Result,' he said quietly, as though he did not want to be
overheard at his end. 'It looks as though the Danton-Halls are
phoneys. I checked to see if DI Barton was back at work – he
was – and asked him to check, through Thames Police, who
pays the council tax on their place. Sorry, I had to say Patrick
had told me to find out and I'm sort of portraying myself as
his assistant. Nicholas Haldane pays it. Barton then really got
the bit between his teeth. He's ready to flay alive whoever shot
up his nick and accessed the National Census. According to
that Haldane's living there with a woman by the name of
Bronwen Thomas, born in Cardiff. I'm not quite sure why they
gave their real names on that so perhaps the assumed names
and identities have come about since it was done last time.
Nothing about being tenants at the place, although that could
be a more recent development too. Thomas has a criminal record
for fraud and assault and I have a photo of her. Are you still
at home?'

I said that I was.

'I'll email it to your computer right away. Let me know if
it's the female you met.'

It was. Even though the hair was short, dark and cut into an
untidy bob, the woman calling herself Constance Danton-Hall
was undoubtedly Bronwen Thomas. When we saw her the
immaculate blonde hair could have been a wig.

Patrick wasn't around and I didn't know whether to tell him
or not when he turned up so consulted my own oracle as far
as Patrick's concerned. She was in the garden.

'Yes, tell him,' Elspeth said, having risen from weeding her
herb bed. I still regard the whole garden as hers and always
ask her if I want to plant anything or feel that a shrub's days

are over. She created it and it's lovely. 'Patrick won't expect you to tiptoe around him,' she went on. 'Besides, a few days' break might have made him change his mind.'

He hadn't.

'There are already warrants out for their arrest,' he reminded me, not really concentrating on what I was saying.

'We've been fishing,' Matthew said to me through the open doorway of the conservatory on his way by. 'We caught two trout but they were too small so we put them back.'

'Trout?' I said to Patrick when the boy had gone, not having to elaborate further.

'That's right,' he replied with a smile.

'So what's going to happen the day after tomorrow? Are you just staying here?'

'No, I shall go to London and hand in my notice.'

'Patrick, we haven't talked about this.'

'Do we have to?'

I kissed him. 'Not if you don't want to.'

This was what I'd wanted for ages, wasn't it?

SEVENTEEN

Patrick duly caught an early London train. I took him to Bath Station and, later in the morning, as I had expected, I received a call from Commander Greenway.

'What's this all about, Ingrid?'

'He's killed one man too many,' I told him.

'Who, Grindley?'

'Yes.'

'I've been told there was a whole load of stuff for starting fires in that garage, including several cans of petrol.'

'Patrick's probably thinking the same as me – that he would have been arrested when he returned to the houseboat.'

'He might still have been able to shoot his wife and her armed protection officer first if he'd caught them unawares.'

'We'll never know now,' I said.

There was a short pause and then Greenway said, 'There's not much I can do about this.'

'I don't think it would have mattered who it was and, don't forget, Patrick was a sniper in Northern Ireland when he was in the army. And in other countries.'

'This is terrible news to me, of course, but I don't think I ought to try to talk him out of it.'

'Nor me.'

When had I thought it through from Patrick's point of view, his decision was logical. A similar situation might arise again when and if another disgruntled and/or mad as a box of frogs criminal decided to vent his fury on me due to my modest success as Patrick's working partner. He has always said that he doesn't want to work without me so the situation could only be resolved by him leaving his job, end of story.

The commander went on to say that, without telling Patrick, he had filed the resignation letter in his in tray and would leave it there for a month, after which it would be passed to higher authority. During this time Patrick would be on gardening leave. I thought this very kind and thanked him.

'I'm in grave danger of losing my best people here,' he finished by saying.

What he did not say, and I only realized it at a later date, was whether he intended to pass on the news verbally.

Despite the leave arrangement, Patrick phoned me to let me know that he was staying on at HQ for a few days as there were other less pressing cases he had been working on that he ought to see staff members about and couldn't just leave them in the lurch, as he put it. The few days stretched to a week. He then contacted me again to tell me that he was going to Hartwood and did I want to meet him there? I almost refused and then realized how bad-mannered that would look to Pamela.

This emotionally worn-out female author who, as was normal in such circumstances, couldn't write a bloody word, climbed into her trusty Range Rover and drove to Sussex. I felt as though I was living in a bad dream.

'You've both been overworking,' said Lady Rowallen when we arrived, raking us both with severe gaze. I had picked up Patrick at the station.

She had a point. I had expected him, with the prospect of a month off before he started to hunt for another job, to look as though he had left all his worries behind him. This was not the case but I hadn't wanted to have an in-depth discussion about it in the car, nor right now, and was hoping he wouldn't give her the news. If she thought he was withdrawing his support . . .

'You could have brought one of the children,' Pamela was saying to me. 'Justin, perhaps. He must have grown a lot since I last saw him.'

I thought of all the priceless antiques, the swords and daggers on the walls of the armory and practically shuddered. 'He's just like his father at that age,' I told her. 'A pocket Vlad the Impaler.'

'He's not that bad,' Patrick protested.

'OK, Ivan the Terrible,' I amended.

We were next in Pamela's company, with Terry, for drinks

before dinner as she had had an engagement during the afternoon. She told us that in order to get over any difficulties of arriving to preside over various, somewhat staid meetings in the company of a young man – she could hardly tell everybody that he was armed – she had hit upon the idea of explaining that Christopher was driving her everywhere as she had hurt her wrist. The slightly sprained wrist was a fact so she didn't feel that she was telling lies. Christopher, we gathered, was learning a lot about rescuing sick horses and donkeys in the Middle East and orphaned children in Aids-stricken parts of Africa.

The lady clearly expected some kind of report from Patrick.

'There has been more progress,' he began. 'As I said last time, the Americans are criminals and the one pretending to be Baumgarten is under arrest, the charges so far being travelling under a false passport and intent to commit fraud. We might not be able to hang being an accessory to murder on him. The business of impersonating another American citizen is a rather grey area which will entail consulting with the FBI. This character worked at the nursing home where Mr Zettinger was being cared for and Clancy Elferdink persuaded him to pose as the old man's illegitimate son, who exists, by the way, and is a priest in Wyoming.'

'Does he know about any of this?' Pamela interposed. 'That his real father's dead, for instance?'

'No idea,' Patrick replied and then went on, 'Elferdink's still at large and we're fairly sure it was he, together with a London mobster calling himself Dimitri Lemotov, who killed your husband and Jordon. Lemotov was under arrest but was sprung from the van taking him to Horsham for further questioning, undoubtedly by the same outfit. They killed him. It looks as though Nicholas Haldane cooked up this whole scheme with Elferdink, who, as I think I've previously mentioned, is a bent lawyer. He then hired hitmen to help carry it out.'

'That's real progress, but dreadful. But how did the gang know that man was being taken to Horsham?'

'DI Barton has a theory that it was an intelligent guess on someone's part. All my money's on Haldane.'

'I had a horrible dream about him last night.'

'Please try not to worry. There's a bit more to tell you. We've discovered, or rather Terry and Barton have, that Haldane and a woman by the name of Bronwen Thomas are passing themselves off as a Mr and Mrs Danton-Hall and live near Newbury. Haldane might have had plastic surgery. They own a racehorse that they've called Hartwood Castle and that arrogant stupidity led us to them.'

'The beasts!'

'For which I suggest Terry gets the Order of the Plastic Gong from your good self a little later,' Patrick went on, I was sure, to introduce a lighter tone.

'I don't think I actually have one of those,' Pamela said, having pretended to give it thought.

'A plastic dustbin lid will do.'

'Oh, yes!'

Terry rose from his seat and bowed.

Pamela laughed and then became serious again. 'But I'm still under siege here for most of the time.'

'Regrettably, yes,' Patrick said. 'But I shall stay here until Haldane's under arrest and if I leave it'll be to go where he can be arrested.'

'Patrick, I'm old enough to be able to tell that you're putting a brave face on that decision.'

He must have felt my gaze on him as well, for he turned to me and said, 'I'm all right with it. Really.'

I wanted to believe him but didn't. It wasn't his fault as someone was holding a metaphorical gun to his head.

Patrick added, 'The earl had friends in high places.'

'Oh, yes,' said Pamela. 'But he never really spoke of it – he was never a man to brag. And sometimes it involved state secrets so he couldn't even tell me. I want your assurance that you're not under some kind of duress.'

'I'm not.'

I didn't add any reservations of mine but suddenly felt very depressed. Someone must have put him under pressure to finish what he had started. The head of MI5? It seemed likely. Or a titled crony of Daws? Was it the same person who had wanted him to investigate in the first place? Who? *Who?*

'What on earth happened about that woman?' Pamela asked all at once. 'The one who came here who you said had disappeared.'

'Her one-time police boss shot her,' I answered before Patrick could say anything. 'He went off his head.'

'Oh, dear, poor man. Having met her I can only feel sorry for him.'

Luckily, at that point it was announced that dinner was ready.

'You can go home if you want to,' Patrick said to me that same evening when we were alone for a few minutes.

I shook my head. 'I'd rather stay here. Besides, I can accompany Pamela on some of her outings to give Christopher a break.'

'Remember how you once promised to love, honour and obey?' This with a quirky smile.

'Yes, for better or worse,' I agreed evenly, having a good idea what was coming.

'It might well be worse. No.'

I must have looked mulish.

'No, Ingrid.'

Despite the fact that we had absolutely no idea what Haldane intended to do, this year, next year, sometime, never, the castle was put on a war footing. With one of the guardians present possessing a military background and two others of similar ilk, that was the only way it could be. There were patrols, we took it in turns to keep watch including during the night, and Christopher was given a little training in evasive driving techniques. With regard to the latter Lady Rowallen could hardly be completely confined to her home – she was finding the situation stressful enough already. Worse, like me, she was extremely concerned about Patrick's mental state.

'What on *earth* happened to him while you were away last time?' she whispered to me in an aside. 'He's going round like a zombie.'

I told her.

'He can't go on like this.'

'It's something he has to do before he resigns,' was all I could say.

'Richard wouldn't have expected him to – to drain himself like this.'

'That's the trouble – I'm afraid he would,' I observed gently.

Not to mention Patrick's parents.

Even though the castle was closed to the public there were staff we had to consider: Helga, the cook, the cleaners and the two gardeners, most of whom lived fairly locally. All of these, bar two, arrived by car and it was unreasonable to expect them to park somewhere in the village and walk the rest of the way. This meant that someone had to monitor arrivals and departures during the day, the registrations of the vehicles involved having been listed. Not to mention keeping watch for the postman and any other delivery vehicles.

It was a stupid situation as this routine had been going on for the best part of a week and everyone was starting to resemble zombies.

'May I make a suggestion?' I said late one afternoon, having hunted around and found Patrick and Terry talking together in the armoury.

'Anything would be welcome,' Terry said.

'Can't we lure Haldane here somehow? For all we know he's just loafing around somewhere with a superior smile on his face hoping Lady Rowallen's worrying herself into an early grave while he decides what to do next.'

'Bait?' Patrick questioned. He still looked and was behaving like a man on some kind of autopilot.

Pamela came hurrying. 'Please advise me as something rather peculiar's happened.'

Terry whipped out a nearby chair from under an oak table for her.

'No, it's all right, thank you. It's just that I was in the sitting room and wondering whether were going to have a thunderstorm as its gone so dark when I noticed a little point of light on the wall. It was red and moved towards me. I was a bit scared and . . . Sorry, you don't think it's important?'

Patrick and Terry had hurried off when she was only halfway through this.

'It might be a laser-guided sniper rifle,' I said as calmly as I could, promised to find out what was happening and followed the men.

They were standing well away from both the large windows of the room and I was just in time to see the tiny red dot of light on an opposite wall before it vanished.

'This could be one of two things,' Patrick said as I entered. 'It's either an ordinary laser torch, the kind that morons shine at aircraft and which are very easy to get hold of, or it's a laser sight on a sniper rifle. If the latter then whoever it is isn't a pro.'

'How's that?' Terry asked.

'The entertainment industry loves them as to heighten tension it can be conveyed that someone's being targeted. But in practice and where distance is involved the light travels in a straight line but bullets don't – there's a curving parabola. Cross-hair sights are far more accurate. It's a very different story for fairly close-up warfare if you have a hand weapon with a laser-guided sight.'

'Thoughts then?' I asked.

'Someone – and we don't need to struggle to guess who's behind it – might be trying to frighten Lady Rowallen just with a laser torch. Or intimidate everybody here. There might really be some idiot out there with a sniper rifle. But whichever it is, I think we ought to find him and the thing to do first is track where it's coming from.'

'Vantage points,' Terry said.

'Yes. There's the tower on the village church but it's probably too far round to the right. Any number of fairly tall trees.'

'I seem to recollect a ruined barn down in the fields some-where,' I said, trying to remember. 'I have an idea that only part of it's visible from here.'

'Even if they were on the roof, or what's left of it, that wouldn't be high enough off the ground.'

Terry said, 'Would chain-mail stop a bullet?'

'If you're thinking of offering yourself as a target we don't have time to do the maths,' Patrick said. 'And I prefer to say no, it wouldn't. In case you were considering getting into a suit of armour, that's not the answer either.'

The little red dot re-appeared on the wall, travelled across a painting of some ancestor or other and came to rest roughly where the heart would be if it was a real person. There was then a crash of breaking glass and the picture fell off the wall, hit an antique bureau and toppled to the floor, scattering some small Chinese vases which fell to the carpet, some broken.

Without a word being exchanged, Patrick and Terry closed the curtains, with difficulty on account of having to avoid the pieces of shattered glass and keep themselves out of sight of anyone outside. I heard Pamela approaching and went to stop her from rushing into the room. Heavy rain started to batter on the windows.

'Is everyone all right?' Christopher's voice shouted from somewhere below as I was endeavouring to reassure her that no one was hurt.

We all left the room, met him coming up the stairs and told him that we were unhurt.

'I shall go and find this joker before he either kills someone here or starts on local people,' Patrick then said.

'If they know you're here it might have been done for no other reason than to lure you outside, sir,' Christopher said urgently.

'I was thinking of asking if you wanted to come with me to watch my back.'

The only member of staff on the premises was Helga, the cook. The cleaners came during the mornings and the two gardeners only worked three days a week and this wasn't one of them. In Patrick's opinion Helga was safest where she was. She was consulted and with typical Germanic stoicism decided likewise. The explanation given to her was that someone was messing around outside with an air rifle and it was being dealt with.

'Please make absolutely sure that the whole place is secured when we go,' Patrick then said to Terry. And to the rest of us, '*Don't* answer any knocks or rings at the doors. Stay up here, set the alarms and don't go anywhere near the windows. When we want to come back in I'll phone you, Ingrid. I'll use a keyword so we both know if there's a problem, in which case phone Barton.'

'Surely you're not just going to walk out of the front door!' Pamela protested.

'No, we're not,' was all Patrick said.

After a short period of time had elapsed while they changed into more suitable clothing, Patrick and Christopher left by the rear door – the one that led into the courtyard, the inner area of the keep. I went with Terry to let them out and the noise as the massive bolts slid home was one of the most horrible sounds I had heard in my life.

'I'd much rather they hadn't gone and we'd phoned the police,' Terry said as we turned to go back. 'I can't explain it but Patrick seems to be coping with this by playing it . . . Sorry, I can't explain it at all.'

'As though he's not Patrick Gillard but someone else,' I said, this having just occurred to me. An alternative persona.

'Is that possible? It's how he's coping?'

'I'm sure a psychiatrist would know,' I replied dully. All I could see in my mind's eye was Patrick sobbing after he had had no choice but to shoot Martin Grindley.

Everything was done as he had asked but for setting the alarms, which was deferred to allow Terry to undertake a one-man patrol, check the entrances and exits, watch the screens for the newly installed security cameras, double-check his security systems, check, check.

We waited, remaining in the same room having carefully rearranged the chairs to safer positions. Pamela had worried about the rain coming in through the hole in the window so I had gone to find a bath towel and, even more carefully, leaned around the closed curtain and put it on the ledge. It was still lashing with rain.

I made no comment but noted that the shot had hit the gilded frame of the painting and the fixings behind it and that was what had caused it to fall, the difference perhaps merely between being shot in the head instead of the heart, whatever Patrick had said about the lack of efficiency of laser-guided weapons.

We carried on waiting, all of us, I'm sure, alert to every sound. An hour and a quarter went by.

'You know, I can now sympathize with the use of boiling oil,' Pamela said at one point, looking up from a book she hadn't really been reading.

'Has that falconet ever been fired?' Terry, who had just entered, asked her. 'To your certain knowledge, I mean.'

'Well, Richard never fired it. He wasn't all that interested in the cannon, and I imagine just thought of all the weapons in there as part of the history of the place and, if times became hard, as an investment. It's probably too valuable to risk firing it – the barrel might burst or something.' She gazed at the speaker searchingly over her reading glasses.

'Just interested,' said Terry. 'During times of unrest the nobility used them to protect their homes. I belong to an exactment society and we recreate battles fought during the English Civil War.'

'Surely not with real cannon balls.'

He shook his head. 'No, just powder.'

The single table lamp we had switched on in the room went out.

'Nothing to worry about,' Terry said, getting to his feet. 'The alarm system has batteries that will last for quite a while. I'll check the power supply to see if it's tripped.'

Desperate to do something, I went to the bedroom Patrick and I were using and despite what he had said cautiously looked out of the window into the courtyard below. The sky was heavily overcast, the rain sluicing across the old setts as though someone was turning a fire hose on them. But there was no one there; nothing moved, not even the jackdaws that nested in some of the chimneys.

Had someone cut off the electricity supply or was the power cut a result of a lightning strike? The latter seemed much more likely. Whatever the reason my cat's whiskers were on red alert and every instinct was telling me to phone DI Barton immediately.

I had another look and could still see no one in the courtyard. Risking all, I opened the window as silently as possible and leaned out, hanging on to the frame to look directly below.

Still no one, just the vehicles that I had expected to see parked there.

Something wasn't right.

The DI had given me his mobile number as well as the one on his desk. The former was engaged. I tried the other and that was engaged as well.

'How can a man be on two phones at once?' I raged out loud.

Calm down, I told myself. Barton was like that.

EIGHTEEN

I had an unsettling thought. Had anyone checked that whoever had made the new hatchway door down in the cellars had actually fitted the bolts on the inside?

Terry was in a walk-in cupboard where the electricity meters were located, possibly once a larder, that was off Pamela's kitchen. 'Nothing wrong in here,' he reported.

I aired my worry.

'Bloody hell, not really my brief, that one. I'll have a look.'

'You go down the stone steps in the old kitchen at the back, through where the wine racks are and along a passageway with doors on each side.'

'I'll find it.'

He went off and I tried the DI again. Still engaged. I left messages on both numbers this time. Then I returned to be with Pamela, not wanting to leave her on her own any longer. The moment I walked through the door another shot crashed through the window, through the curtain and lodged in the wall in a cloud of plaster.

'Patrick and Christopher haven't found him yet then,' Pamela said, her voice only a little shaky. 'Do you think we should dial nine-nine-nine?'

I told her that I'd already phoned DI Barton and that Terry was checking the cellars. Then we lapsed into silence.

After another five minutes had gone by and Terry hadn't come back I left the room again and grabbed the Smith and Wesson from my bag in the bedroom. Not liking at all what my ears were now telling me I then dashed into the kitchen where Helga was beginning to prepare the dinner and unceremoniously escorted her into the meter cupboard, begging her in a whisper to stay there. I prayed that she would do so even if she thought me raving mad.

There was no time to hide Pamela.

'What's this, the original acted thing from beyond the

tomb or the normal hairier version?' I enquired of Nicholas Haldane as he came up the final step of the main staircase. There were four men to his rear, including Ricketts, and the woman we now knew to be Bronwen Thomas, without her blonde wig. She appeared to be the only one openly carrying a weapon, a handgun of some kind, and was glassy-eyed and swaying on her feet.

Seeing the Smith and Wesson they stopped, Mr and Mrs Danton-Hall as they really weren't, plus helpers.

'Your friend, whom I seem to remember was here before, is downstairs with someone holding a gun to his head,' said Haldane. 'Put that weapon down. I'm sure you have no idea how to fire it.'

'I prefer proof to lies,' I told him.

'What on earth's going on?' Pamela said from somewhere behind me.

'I've waited years for this moment, you old bitch!' Haldane shouted at her. 'I'm going to burn this place to the ground!'

'That woman's drunk!' I shouted back, pointing to Thomas. 'She's stoned out of her skull and likely to shoot you in the back as she can't even see straight!'

Haldane uttered a high-pitched titter. It was a disgusting sound to come from a man.

Sniggering, God help me, Thomas raised the gun and aimed it over to my left where Pamela must be, although I dared not turn around to check.

I had no choice, shocked to find that suddenly I too had another persona, and fired. Thomas screamed, pitched over backwards and fell down the stairs, taking one of the men with her. Another shot was fired, but somewhere else – a dull subterranean sound – and then another.

'Go on, she can't shoot you all!' Haldane bawled.

The whole lot rushed at me and I was too close to them. I got one in the shoulder, I think, but was then overwhelmed, knocked over and reduced to clubbing one oaf on the head with the weapon before it was torn from my grasp. They appeared to squabble over who should have it and I succeeded in squirming out from underneath them all, aiming a few strategic kicks as I found myself free. Then a surprisingly strong arm hauled me to my feet and Pamela and I tore down the main corridor.

'Down the stairs into the old kitchen,' she panted over her shoulder, the sounds of pursuit behind us. 'And for heaven's sake, watch your feet!'

The steps were horribly worn and narrow but we reached the door which, as we knew, was locked on our side. It was the work of seconds to unlock it, wrench out the key, go through and slam and lock it behind us.

'Well, I do declare,' said Clancy Elferdink in a phoney Wild West accent. 'It is the emergency exit after all.'

He was sitting, smirking, on the edge of one of the trestle-type tables that were arrayed with a display of copper and brass pots, pans and other old kitchen utensils, and was toying with a Glock in his hand. The one that had killed Richard Daws?

He was looking at me and did not see Pamela grab a sizable copper saucepan and forcefully send it, two-handed, flying in his direction. It caught him on the side of the head and he toppled over backwards on to the table. We grabbed a leg each and hauled him on to the floor where, having clouted him on the arm with a ladle to make him drop the gun, I stood back just in time for Pamela to flail the man senseless with an iron skillet.

'Oh, God, I haven't killed him, have I?' she cried.

I found a pulse on a fat wrist. 'No.'

They were trying to batter down the door we had just come through.

I registered that a strong draught was blowing through the door that led to the cellars and headed in that direction, aware that Pamela was right behind me. How else could they have got in? These stairs were equally worn and narrow and I dared not hurry even though I was desperate to know what had happened to Terry.

We reached the bottom. Light, such as it was, came through what appeared to be narrow ventilation shafts set in the walls and revealed rows and rows of dust-covered wine racks, mostly empty. The rest of the space was filled with neat stacks of wooden crates and cases together with piles of the usual kind of items that people simply cannot bear to throw away. A fair way ahead of us it was brighter but I still proceeded carefully, fully expecting now to come across Terry's body. Open doors into black spaces were on either side but no one jumped out at us.

We reached the light which was flooding through the open hatchway that had been their entry point, together with a lot of rain. The space we had entered was some sixteen feet square with a wooden well cover in the floor. That looked rotten and I kept away from it. A quick inspection of the new hatch revealed that the interior bolts had not been fitted although I knew a steel bar across the outside of it had. They had cut off the padlocks. The hatch was the castle's weak point, Patrick had said. And where the hell was he?

'We'll have to jump,' I said, having looked through the opening as well as I was able to thanks to the water beating into my face, and seen nobody.

'No, there's a ladder,' Terry said, coming into view from where he had been standing below me by the ivy-covered wall. His left arm was a mass of blood that was dripping from his fingers.

'Please catch this first,' I said, and dropped the Glock into his waiting hand. When it was safely in his pocket I sat on the edge of the hatch and manoeuvred myself on to the ladder which was leaning on the wall a couple of feet below me. As I descended Terry steadied me with his good arm.

'Where's whoever shot you?' I gabbled, panicking a bit.

'Dunno. He exited and ran off.'

There was a distant but loud crash from where we had just come from – the door at the bottom of the stairs giving way? – and Pamela squeaked with alarm and came down the ladder far too fast, missing her footing halfway down. I don't know how but we caught her, all of us slipping and finishing up in a heap on the soaking wet grass. Terry took a few moments to recover from the renewed agony in his arm.

As we were still scrambling up Ricketts appeared in the opening above, shouted joyfully over his shoulder to the others that he had found us, grabbed a handgun of some kind and opened fire. By a miracle and in his excitement he fired high

and missed us. Terry had already shoved Elferdink's Glock into
my hand and, with so large a target, I didn't.

We ran and I knew when Terry stumbled and almost fell that
he had lost far too much blood to be able to carry on for much
longer.

'They do have a sub-machine gun,' I said to him when we
paused for Pamela's sake, still in the moat, in the lee of a huge
buttress in the curtain wall. Her Ladyship, gasping for breath,
then insisted on pulling off her knee-high tights and fashioned
them into a tourniquet for Terry's arm.

'Thanks for reminding me,' he muttered.

'No, I mean we must be prepared for someone to have it.'

But he was beyond caring, sliding down the wall to slump
on the ground.

I felt we had no choice but to leave him and go on. We went
uphill now, climbing out of the moat as it had been filled in
from this point. Pamela had wanted to stay with Terry but I
wasn't letting her out of my sight, and we edged our way along
the wall until we approached another buttress. From here, I
remembered, we were near a corner from which we would be
able to see the front entrance of the castle.

Someone was on the other side of the buttress. Fleetingly,
I caught sight of the tip of something that might have been
the sub-machine gun in question. This time I did motion to
Pamela to stay back and, heart pounding, walked slowly
forwards, starkly aware that my feet were making a sound
as they brushed through the long grass. Dominating my
mind was the thought that the others couldn't be far behind,
Haldane with them, or not, although the injured Ricketts, or
his dead body, might be blocking the hatchway.

Whoever it was heard me coming and quickly peered around
the buttress. He looked again and then the rest of him appeared,
together with a sniper rifle. 'What the hell's going on? I heard
shots.'

'They're inside. The bolts hadn't been put on the hatch and
they'd cut the padlocks off the bar. I have Pamela but Terry's
been shot and injured.'

Patrick swore. 'Have you called Barton?'

'Left a message on both lines as he was busy.'

'We'll have to bypass him if he's dealing with another emergency.'

'Where's Christopher?'

'We got the sniper out of the tree after I'd threatened to shoot him, then he tried to make a run for it. Christopher went after him, they grappled and both fell and he's either broken or badly sprained his ankle. I've left him guarding this bloke with Daws' handgun.'

I beckoned Pamela forward and the three of us stood there like drowned rats.

'What are they *doing* in there?' Pamela despaired, gazing in vain up at her home.

A dishevelled figure appeared behind us, or rather staggered into view. 'Sorry, Chief,' Terry gasped faintly when he arrived. 'Can't do any more.'

Patrick sat him down, leaning on the wall by the buttress, and Pamela sacrificed her cardigan, wet as it was, to put behind his head. He urgently needed medical attention. He was given Patrick's Glock as we might have to leave him again.

Three left standing, I thought, one of whom was elderly, in danger of getting hypothermia, and for whom we had responsibility. I kept glancing back the way we had come. A man appeared as I looked and, as Ricketts had done, he shouted over his shoulder. At the same time Patrick swung round and fired the rifle in the opposite direction. I heard the shot ricochet off something.

Where were the police when you really want them?

'Are we surrounded, or is that a stupid question?' Pamela said.

It wasn't, but nobody answered it.

'Where did you get that?' Patrick asked me, suddenly seeing the gun in my hand.

'It's Elferdink's,' I replied.

'I was always very good at netball,' Pamela observed distantly.

He deferred asking for further explanations and fired again at something I couldn't see from where I was standing. There was the crash of breaking glass.

'They've somehow brought a car through the main entrance,' Patrick reported tersely. 'That was the windscreen. Get down!'

Being driven at speed on the grass, the vehicle came into view and a sub-machine gun chattered, the shots banging on to the wall just above our heads as we lay on the ground. I had vaguely seen a man firing through the front passenger window, but he could only swing the weapon around so far and when it had gone by for a short distance I took out one of the rear tyres. The car slewed round and to a halt, teetering on the rim of the moat.

'Bastard,' I heard Patrick say through his teeth and then risked all by standing to fire three shots into it. Whatever the consequences inside the result was that it rolled down the slope and smashed into the castle wall. 'You didn't know I had that, did you?' he then yelled.

There was then silence but for our own heavy breathing. A couple of minutes earlier I had thought I'd heard sirens but nothing had come of it.

'No, it's nothing,' Pamela said when I saw with a shock that her forehead had been cut by a flying stone splinter. 'You do realize that this is the first time this castle has ever been at war.' She uttered a little sound that was a cross between a laugh and a sob and ineffectively dabbed at the wound with a lacy handkerchief.

Those to the rear of us had reached the car but because of its position and the fact that they appeared to be using it as cover it was impossible for me to tell how many of them there were. No one was visible in the opposite direction.

'Change places,' Patrick said, having sized up the situation. 'If anyone shows shoot them.' When we had done so he fired another couple of shots into the car.

'Who the hell needs laser sights?' Terry mumbled and then actually chuckled.

'Haldane!' I snapped on seeing a familiar figure cautiously come into view around the corner of the wall some fifty yards from us. He was waving something like a white handkerchief.

Patrick turned to look.

'They're about to start a few fires as there are far, far too many books,' the man called, gesturing vaguely in the direction of the front of the castle. 'But not if you hand over the old woman. I presume she's with you, eh?'

'You're under arrest,' Patrick told him.

'Shall we talk about this?'

'Come and talk to me here.'

'We did find the lady cook. So I sincerely hope nothing unfortunate happens to me.'

'Don't go!' I exclaimed when Patrick moved to leave.

'I'm the one with the rifle. Please stay right here,' he replied roughly and walked in Haldane's direction.

'You go,' Terry mumbled. 'I'll look after Her Ladyship.' With a huge effort he stood up, sliding his back up the wall. 'Go! I can see if anyone comes round that car. And Ingrid . . .' He fumbled in his jeans pocket and held out what looked like a small television remote control.

'What is it?'

'In an emergency just point it in the direction of the old archway and make sure nobody on the side of the righteous is anywhere near it.'

He was delirious, I thought sadly as he closed his eyes and collapsed again, seemingly on the point of passing out. He had given me the wireless mouse I had seen him using with his laptop. Or was it the tally for unlocking his car?

I did not want to distract Patrick so hung back. He reached the end of what cover he had and then paused, still some thirty yards from Haldane who suddenly hurried from sight back the way he had come. Then Patrick disappeared around the corner.

'It's a trap!' I shouted but the rain and wind hurled my words back into my face. I ran to the corner and looked around it. There were two other vehicles parked inside the heavy wooden entrance gates, which had been forced and were wide open. A couple of men loafed around by them, smoking. Over to my right, some fifty yards from the gates was the archway. I couldn't see Haldane but Patrick was lying on his stomach on the grass, holding the rifle in the firing position. Then, two men came into view through the archway hauling Helga along between them by the arms. She was yelling at them in German.

Haldane emerged from under the archway too and went to walk behind the three. 'What do you say, eh?' he shouted to where he thought Patrick might be, not actually where he was.

'I'm warning you,' Patrick yelled. 'I'm armed. Tell your men to lay down their weapons.'

I seethed. Kill them, I inwardly urged Patrick. Kill all three of those bloody cowards.

Helga freed herself, wrenching a hand away from the man gripping it, clouted him on the ear and then lashed out a kick at the other man who doubled up.

'Over here, Helga!' Patrick yelled.

She ran and someone by one of the cars levelled a gun at her and fired. He missed.

I didn't even think, just ran forward several yards, pointed Terry's gizmo towards the archway and clicked it.

Both cannon on each side of the archway fired in unison with a tremendous roar, and in a few utterly ghastly but at the same time glorious moments everything in front of them had been smashed to pieces, one ball ending up demolishing one of the entrance gate's pillars. A cloud of dust and smoke billowed towards me and in a kind of daze I saw Patrick stand up in this fog just as Helga reached him. He put his arms around her and brought her back to a safer position. I then realized that two people were standing behind me, Pamela finding the strength to support Terry.

'God,' he gasped. 'Oh, God. It worked. Chris and I messed around with it . . . it was only done in case . . . I hope no one legal was hurt.' Then he fainted.

Sussex Police then arrived, in strength, on foot, Barton, a large bandage around his throat, as grim as any cop who has had the tyres of his every vehicle punctured by tacks deliberately strewn across the road.

This detail emerged later, of course, and it wasn't lost on the DI that had his entourage arrived a little earlier, the lapse obviously not their fault, less death and destruction would have occurred. He was characteristically bloody-minded about this as someone on his team who had contacts with informers had already reported to him that Brighton's underworld had been rocking with the news that a mad mobster from London was going round recruiting everyone with a criminal record he could lay his hands on. The handfuls of tacks the extended gang had scattered on the road had been by way of their suicide note. And as Pamela had said, it had been a war.

'Your last war,' she said to Patrick much later that same day, handing him a generous measure of whisky.

Patrick thanked her, smiling a little wanly, but had lost the look of a man under some kind of spell. He had just returned from checking on Terry in Worthing Hospital and told us that he had a quite serious flesh wound that had entailed an operation. He had been sleeping off the anaesthetic and was having blood transfusions but it was thought he would make a complete recovery, though the full use of the arm would take time.

People were still tramping around the premises, incident tape everywhere inside and out, and we had taken refuge in Pamela's kitchen. Helga, having given her statement and not batted an eyebrow, had gone home, promising to return as normal the following morning.

'Haldane's dead,' Patrick said, not adding that he had been as good as obliterated. 'And I blame myself entirely for not having checked that the bolts on the hatch had been fitted.'

'You mustn't,' Pamela said. 'The man turned up a few days ago to do it and broke his drill. It was I who should have remembered to mention it to you.' After a short, reflective silence she added, 'At least Richard can rest in peace now.'

Elferdink was alive, though, and would go to prison for a very long time.

NINETEEN

Someone in the media decided to call the incident The
Battle of Hartwood and the title stuck. The repercussions: debriefings, reports writing, interviews and so
forth would continue for months. The Independent Police
Complaints Commission would become involved and I was
half-expecting to be arrested for causing explosions and
endangering the public.

Christopher had still been at his post and later, after X-rays,
was diagnosed as having a badly sprained ankle. The man he
had been guarding was taken into custody. I hoped that individual
was counting himself lucky as casualties among the gang had
been heavy. Haldane and the two who had been dragging
out Helga were dead; another two who had been standing by
the cars were injured by flying debris. Bronwen Thomas, who
I had shot in the shoulder, was in hospital under guard and
apparently screaming abuse in Welsh at everyone who came
near her.

I gathered that a large part of the nation was captivated by
pictures of the car that had rolled into the moat to ram up
against the outer wall of the castle. Two men had been found
dead inside it, including the one with the sub-machine gun and
another seriously wounded. Those accompanying Ricketts, who
I had glimpsed taking cover behind the car, and who were the
remainder of those on the main staircase with Haldane, had
been located hiding in the grounds by police dogs. They were
probably responsible for Ricketts' death as they had tipped him
out of the hatchway as he had been blocking it and the fall had
broken his neck. The bullet wound he had suffered was not
particularly serious and a couple of pathologists would argue
about that for months too.

It took two days to sort out the immediate aftermath, during
which time Lady Rowallen's daughter, Judy, and her husband
arrived. Her first task while her mother rested was, with police

permission, to restore the apartment to as near normality as possible. I helped her. As Haldane had said, he had intended to start fires and all the books and papers in Daws' study had been pulled from the shelves and out of the filing cabinets on to the floor. It took us rather a long time to put everything back.

Another two days later DI Barton, who was pleased to inform us that charges against Tracy Finch had been dropped, questioned Terry in hospital about the business of the cannon. Christopher's name wasn't mentioned but Patrick knew, as Terry had already told him, that they had dreamed it up between them, Christopher being particularly interested in ballistics. There were quite a few cannon balls and other bits and pieces, as Terry put it, in the armoury, and he had bought the modern equivalent of black powder, Pyrodex, on the Internet. The electrical fuses were also a modern innovation and were used in the film industry in connection with special effects. Apparently the DI had gone away saying that he reckoned that to be self-defence.

Oddly, the power cut had been caused by a lightning strike on an electricity substation a couple of miles away.

Michael Greenway politely accepted the somewhat weighty report I handed to him – he had already received, and I hoped had read, the electronic version – and placed it in his in tray. He didn't seem to know quite what to say.

'My last war,' Patrick said.

'Thank the good Lord for that,' his boss commented. 'You do realize that higher authority is asking me if you're completely out of my control.'

'Then no doubt they've happily accepted my resignation.'

'They haven't, for the simple reason that I didn't forward it to them.'

'I see,' Patrick responded coolly.

'You don't. They want you to go away and bury yourself in deepest Avon and Somerset by being that force's NCA officer in their Regional Organised Crime Unit.'

'Someone else got that job.'

Greenway breathed out hard. 'I was told that enough strings

have been pulled to tow the *SS Great Britain* from Bristol to London and all the paperwork will be forwarded to your address.'

Then he smiled broadly and held out his hand. 'Congratulations.'

'It's none of my business but I really would like to know who you have to report back to with regard to your actions,' Pamela had said to Patrick on the evening before we left Sussex. 'It was patently obvious to me that you'd had more than enough of warfare and carrying guns. Although I shall be eternally grateful to you I feel responsible and a bit angry that you were put under such pressure.'

'I don't have to report back to anyone,' he had told her. 'She'll see it on TV and read about it in the papers.'

'Oh. *She?*'

'I was asked to meet a fine lady upon a white horse.'

'At Banbury Cross?' I had enquired, thinking him evading the issue because he didn't want to talk about it.

'No, in Windsor Great Park.'

Lightning Source UK Ltd.
Milton Keynes UK
UKOW01f1424020317
295719UK00001B/35/P